Marjory Madge

M. M. Madge
Whittington House
Cainscross Road
Stroud
Gloucestershire GL5 4EX
Tel: 01453 757601

D1808397

THE VOICE OF CECIL HARWOOD

A.C.Hamord

THE VOICE
of
CECIL HARWOOD

A Miscellany

Edited by
OWEN BARFIELD

RUDOLF STEINER PRESS
LONDON

First Edition Rudolf Steiner Press, London 1979

© Rudolf Steiner Press, London 1979

ISBN 0 85440 329 9

Printed and bound in Great Britain at
The Camelot Press Ltd, Southampton

CONTENTS

Introduction 7

I Early Poems and a Short Story
Poems 21
Mr. Bowlby and the Silver Stater 39

II Later Poems 51

III Drama, Legend and Fantasy
A Rope Their Pulley, a Melodrama 85
King's Forest *or* The Shepherd of New Gifts 123
Coronation Masque 161
The Masque of Midas *or* Asses' Ears 175
Tobias, An Easter Mystery 205
Fantasia on Three Voices 225
Drama at Bockley Manor, a Hallowe'en Story 237
What the Gas Men Found, a Hallowe'en Story ·251

IV Essays and Recollections
The Book of Tobit 263
The Appreciation of Poetry 271
W. O. Field 283
C. S. Lewis, A Toast 291

V Songs and Verses Composed for Special Occasions 299

Poems, Songs and Verses (Index of first lines) 318

Introduction

I had better begin by mentioning some of the things the ensuing volume is not. It is not a plenary collection of Cecil Harwood's 'literary remains', neither is it the end-product of a careful winnowing of those remains by an editor concerned solely with literary values. It is certainly not presented as an embodiment of his contribution as a thinker to the growing body of anthroposophical literature which is coming into existence alongside the immense legacy from Rudolf Steiner himself. That, it is hoped, is something which will follow at a later date in the shape of a companion volume, to consist of a selection from the numerous essays and articles he wrote during his life, mainly for anthroposophical periodicals or for the journal of Michael Hall School, where he taught for so many years.

The circumstances of Harwood's life, and particularly the firm decision he made at a relatively early age to dedicate all his energy and devote all his abilities to furthering the aims of Spiritual Science, brought it about that his total literary endeavour, if the expression may be allowed, was distributed among an unusually large number of disparate genres. Having abandoned, or perhaps sacrificed, at an early age all literary ambition as such, he wrote thereafter things that were needed in different places rather than things he chose, unprompted, from his own place. In an age when much – even more perhaps today – was being written and orated about art for art's sake and poetry, if not all literature, if not all language, being an end in itself, he unhesitatingly treated his own writing, including in a large measure his own poetry, as means to ends beyond themselves. For the same reason no doubt he was all too careless about preserving copies, once they had served their purpose – a habit which has not made any easier the task of editing some of them for posterity.

In spite of all this many have felt, as I do, that we do hear the same individual voice speaking through all those diverse modes; a summoned voice rather than a vociferous one egotistically determined to make itself heard at all costs; but recognisably the same voice speaking, whether in a poem, a school play, a substantial essay, a brief memorial address or a fireside Hallowe'en story. Academic critics might prefer to say the same 'literary personality'. Whatever it is called, it is something that made itself felt already in the course of his life, and many anthroposophists in particular became familiar with that voice from reading as well as from hearing it now in this place and now in that. Moved, I suspect, hardly less by affection than by admiration, they sometimes expressed even during his life a strong desire to have its scattered utterances gathered in one place, so that they could be enjoyed and considered together. Now that he is no longer with us in the flesh, the generosity of one of them has made that possible.

Quantitatively speaking Cecil Harwood gave out far more in the form of spoken lectures than he did in the written word. Apart from his paramount contribution to its administration, he is remembered in the Anthroposophical Society in Great Britain, and indeed in a much wider circle both here and abroad, above all as a lecturer of surpassing ability and charm. Remembered as a lecturer in general, whereas he is perhaps remembered as a writer only of this or that. Here the intention has been to recall and present him as a writer in general.

The author of two books on Education and one on Shakespeare certainly was a writer as well as a lecturer. Any attempt at a critical appreciation or evaluation of what follows would be beside the purpose of this Introduction, and in any case would be better done by someone less close to him personally than I had the good fortune to be. Nevertheless a few random observations may not be out of place. Harwood had begun writing long before he began lecturing, and (which is saying much the same thing) before he ever heard of Rudolf Steiner. Indeed he probably had some notion of making a career of it. The contents of Section I all belong to that period. *Mr Bowlby and the Silver Stater,* for instance, was written in 1923 or the early part of 1924 and published some months later in the Christmas number of a now long defunct weekly periodical, *Truth.* I have long felt that it deserved resurrecting for its own sake. The double surprise at the end betrays a touch of craftsmanship which many short story writers might envy, and which I fancy served him in good stead much later on when he came to be telling at Michael Hall School those Hallowe'en stories, a couple of which are included here. And as to the 'voice', am I not right in feeling that the special Harwoodian brand of (what is the right description? tranquilly mischievous?) humour, familiar to all who often heard him speak, is already audible, for example in the following passage, which I have ventured to italicise:

> . . . the Secretary cleared his throat to command silence, and, glancing hastily round the room, remarked tentatively: "I think we are all here now."
>
> "All but Mr. Bowlby," replied a member, and a general smile went round, in which the Lecturer, who had never heard of Mr. Bowlby, *discovered too late that he had joined.*

Prose fiction is one thing, poetry is another altogether. Let me now confess that in the early 'twenties of this century the ruling, if normally unspoken, thought in the minds of Harwood, C. S. Lewis and myself was whether any one of us, and if so which, was going to turn out a great poet! There is a reverberation from those far-off days in what was to be one of Harwood's very last public utterances, the *Toast to the Memory of C. S. Lewis,* which will be found near the end of the book. In quantity his output was rather less than mine and much less than Lewis's, but it was by no means negligible, and Section I represents rather than reproduces it. The decision to divide all the poems included here into three sections, *Early, Later* and *Composed for Special Occasions,* was made after some hesitation and is, I hope, a wise one. Here I will only mention that, although the boundary between *Early* and *Later* looks chronologically arbitrary (the earliest of the *Later* was written only a month or two after the latest of the *Earlier*), there was never any doubt in my mind where it must come. Memory – and he showed me both soon after they were written – merely confirms what internal evidence would have established without its help, namely that *Heart and Head** was written before, and *The Recall of the Stars* after, he first heard and met Rudolf Steiner in Torquay in August 1924. Read now together they reveal, they positively proclaim, that in the month or so that elapsed between them the soul from which they sprang had reached and passed the nadir of its spiritual adventure in this life; while the second of the *Later* poems (*At Ille Labitur*) evinces already a prophetic awareness of its being such a turning point.

Otherwise they are not arranged in chronological order. With one or two exceptions the haphazard collection of manuscripts, or more often carbon typescripts, which are all I had to go on, made that impossible. The date (March 1944) of *Second Front* is subjoined to the title; otherwise I fear the period covered by Section II must be taken to extend from 1924 to the end of the author's life, and I have mainly pleased myself as to the order in which they appear. The reader should, I feel, be left alone with them, but I am reluctant to let them go without one of those random observations which I have said I would permit myself. Looked at as a whole, they seem to me to reveal a definable poetic impulse. The frequent macrocosmic references or allusions, whether direct or through the incarnate Word, suggest an insistent endeavour to develop in verse that 'objective', as distinct from personal,

* The title is mine. I have ventured to supply with titles this and some other poems which lack them in manuscript, for the convenience of readers who might wish to refer to them. Also I feel a sort of obligation to record that, quite soon after it was written, he himself expressed dissatisfaction with it, mainly because the opening line 'They were the nobler days, those days of war', was insincere. His real feeling about the days of war (World War I of course) is better reflected in the last two stanzas of *The Soldier's Coat*. Ed.

feeling on which I believe Harwood felt the continued life of lyric poetry will in the long run depend. An overriding impulse, not a self-imposed limitation or a rigid rule. For the sprinkling of personally directed lyrics, from which I have selected *Faces*, *Running* and *Laura*, show clearly enough that, like Spenser's Colin Clout, he could still, on occasion, 'pipe to please himself'.

The third Section, which I have entitled *Drama, Legend and Fantasy* is perhaps the one that is most *distinctively* characteristic of Harwood as writer. I decided to include in it the long narrative poem *Tobias*, though that could equally well have gone with the *Poems*, mainly because a good many readers will probably have heard – and seen – it in the shortened form in which it has several times been presented on the stage in Eurythmy. It is nevertheless, to my mind, an outstanding instance of that overriding impulse to which I have just referred. The fact that it *is* a narrative, and not (as they used to say) an 'effusion', makes of itself of course for objectivity. Yet one feels so strongly after reading it, or I do: No one but Harwood could possibly have written just so! Here is something of a paradox, to which I will return a little later.

If one were to persist nevertheless in seeking something else in English literature to compare it with, I fancy a good choice would be Wordsworth's blank verse poem *Michael*, where we find the same unhurried narrative pace, the same grave manner, and a vocabulary well able to accommodate, without declining into baldness, the idioms of common and even colloquial speech – as thus (from *Tobias*):

> And now he sadly thinks,
> Groping to find the tally in some drawer,
> 'The boy must go, Tobias, my dear son.
> Our only hope. I say he must. No matter
> What Anna thinks. I feel it as much myself.'
> But dares not for a time speak out his mind . . .

and even the same close attention to little details of everyday life, including domestic life –

> That night the lamp burns late, while Anna sews,
> And even old Tobit plies polish and brush . . .

details that never grow tedious because, as each one falls on the ear, to become at once absorbed into the total cadence of the verse, it is felt as a single meticulous drop leaked from a whole cistern of contemplative wisdom somewhere in the poet's own being.

The difference is that Wordsworth's poem applies a style of this description to the telling of a story that is *all* rural domesticity; whereas one half of *Tobias* is, outwardly at least, a fantastic oriental tale about a giant fish, witchcraft, white magic, a demon and an archangel. And what is distinctive to it is the successful preservation of that one style, of one and the same calm and familial approach to the matter in hand, throughout both contrasted elements of the drama:

> The boy obeyed, much wondering why,
> But dared not ask, so changed was Raphael's voice
> Like music moving to a harsher key;
> And with the Angel's help, and his new knife,
> Opened the fish, and from its belly drew
> Heart, liver and gall, and put them in his bag.

Not even at the point where supernatural peril has just horrifyingly revealed itself and the central mystery is plunging deepest, are we allowed to forget Tobias's schoolboy pride in his new knife, bought (as we find ourselves guessing) especially for the journey.

It is a wild story; and there are good Christians who dislike it for that reason, feeling it more suited to the *Arabian Nights* than to their Bible. Harwood, as it were, tames and transforms it for a modern English reader, having shown, as well in his earlier Essay as in the solemn speeches of the *Easter*

Spirit that frame the sections of his narrative, why it was so well worth that labour of love. But when a writer has clearly found his appointed subject and, in the very shaping and handling of it, seems also to have found himself, one is really minded to abjure any critical comment and simply exclaim: here is literature; here is poetry; enjoy it!

The play *A Rope Their Pulley* was written during the Second War, and before *Tobias*; the *Fantasia on Three Voices* a good deal later. It appeared in the *Golden Blade* for 1953. I feel that in both of them he was to some extent experimenting with what might become a new form, especially so perhaps with the play. They are the only two items in the collection which may be felt to be 'difficult'. I at least felt that about the play, when I first read it. But I also suspected that, as a good play should be, it was written to be performed rather than read, and that the difficulties might well vanish from, or even enhance, a good production on the stage. I wish very much that I could have been there when, some years later, it was given an amateur performance – and I am told a successful one – on the stage in Sheffield. I should add that, even without that advantage, most of my difficulties were cleared up by a second and third reading, though I also wondered whether this would have been the case if I had not been acquainted in advance with the figures of Lucifer and Ahriman as they are presented in the Spiritual Science of Rudolf Steiner. Firefly and Cinders – and this is what the reader or spectator must somehow manage never to let himself forget – are *deceivers*; and they remain so even while they are endowing the two human characters with genuine self-knowledge. It is difficult – but for the very same reason that life itself is difficult.

All these three, the play, the *Fantasia* and *Tobias*, were, as far as I know, written without any prompting from circumstance, simply because he was moved to write them. With the remainder of Section III we are in that region I referred to at the outset, where so much of Harwood's literary life was spent, so much, that is, of the little of his life he spared to literature at all. They came in response to a demand, and were composed primarily as means to an end rather than as ends in themselves. Or perhaps that is not quite true of the two Hallowe'en stories, where the only 'end' was entertainment. It was Harwood's custom to tell these stories (which by tradition had to have a 'spooky' touch) at the annual Hallowe'en party for the Upper School at Michael Hall. He always did it extempore, or from a few scrappy notes, and I feel sure that the examples included here – both from the 1950s – were not written in advance of the telling but were elaborated later by request. I was both surprised and delighted to find any in writing at all; and now the reader should try to imagine himself not reading, but listening; hearing him tell them in the relaxed atmosphere of a warm, firelit hall in Kidbrooke Park with a great deal of Hallowe'en gear about, such as candles in pumpkin-heads and apples floating in tubs, and a throng of young and old folk, some of them in fantastic costumes, gathered open-eared about him in chairs and on the floor.

King's Forest and the two *Masques* were also written for Michael Hall, in one case at least with particular pupils in mind for the leading characters. They were performed in the open air at the school's annual Midsummer Festival, the first at Streatham in 1931 and 1932 and the last two at Kidbrooke Park, Forest Row, in 1952 and 1956 respectively. They were not the only dramatic pieces he wrote for performance by school children but are, I believe, the only three that have survived. For me one of their most noticeable features is their persistent echoing of older poetic modes and manners. This is something quite different from the imitative inheritance audible in some of the early poems, as indeed it is in most men's juvenilia. A discerning reader for instance might guess from such a poem as *The Strain Upraise* or *The Soldier's Coat* that the youthful Harwood had been strongly attracted by the verse of Thomas Hardy, and he would be guessing correctly. But the deliberate echoes of older, and particularly of Shakespearian diction and even mannerisms in the school plays are another matter. If one felt bound to find a literary label for them, it would presumably be *pastiche* rather than derivativeness or Wardour Street. But I do not feel them that way, and I have come to the conclusion that the reason for it lies in the circumstance that they were in truth conceived and executed as means rather than ends. We remain at least half aware, while we are reading or watching them, that they are addressed to children, and of the poet's eagerness to familiarise those children with their lawful inheritance, with the cultural habitus, so to speak, of their mother country and their mother tongue. "Children must first walk on the broad highways of literature", he writes at the end of his essay on *The Appreciation of Poetry*, "before they explore the byways . . . so that they are ready to enter upon their mighty heritage."

But neither is that the whole story. An affection for the old, and even for the merely old-fashioned, simply because it *is* old and out of date, was an element deeply ingrained in Harwood's earthly personality. If he had been born in the eighteenth century he might even have become an antiquary. Consequently, if he had, in writing the school plays, that ulterior object of introducing the children to the traditional diction and cadences of English verse, he also very specially and affectionately *enjoyed* doing it. One could perhaps say: by that part of him, what was intended as a means was also being enacted as an end in itself. And that was why he did it so well. That is why the old is there so charmingly integrated with the new, the echo with the voice; so that we feel confronted with something really novel in the whole genre of plays for children. If there is anything to be compared with it, I would say it is Lewis's invention of that 'high language' which the children find themselves speaking at certain junctures in his *Chronicles of Narnia*.

One might, if the occasion were appropriate, dilate somewhat here on the relation between subjective and objective experience, between personal and superpersonal, even between microcosm and macrocosm; and on ways of bridging the sorry gulf between them. There is what is, broadly speaking, the oriental goal of eliminating the

personal, whether by sitting cross-legged for hours at a time
on the floor of a secluded ashram or whether by some other
means. But there is also the way of the consciousness soul,
which was for Rudolf Steiner the truly occidental way; the
way which entails acknowledging personal bias and bent,
using them open-eyed less and less for their gratification and
more and more in the loving service of humanity, and thus
enhancing and developing rather than eliminating them; the
way by which the personal itself is in the end to grow
superpersonal. But this is an introduction and not a sermon.

In Section IV the two essays on *The Book of Tobit* and *The
Appreciation of Poetry* really belong by class to the later volume,
which it is hoped will follow in due course, and to which
reference has already been made. But I felt that the former
belongs properly with *Tobias*, the one being a critical and the
other a creative treatment of the same subject matter. It was,
I think, written some years before the poem, which, however,
I have not succeeded in dating, and was printed in the former
quarterly magazine *Anthroposophy* in 1932. Again, the essay on
The Appreciation of Poetry, which appeared in 1948 in the
Michael Hall School journal *Child and Man*, seemed to fit well
into a volume containing so much of his own poetry. And
then there was the further reflection that the two pieces offer
to the reader a tempting foretaste of that later volume, which
will consist entirely of such essays.

Walter Ogilvie Field appeared in 1958 in the journal *Mosaic*
produced by the Old Scholars of Michael Hall School, which
reproduced at the same time a fascinating sketch by A. A.
Milne of Field's startling battle exploit during World
War I, when he captured an enemy machine-gun post
without firing a shot. I had in mind, in including it, that this
Miscellany is likely to reach a good many alumni of the school
where Harwood taught for so many years of his life, and that
the older ones among them probably find it difficult to think
of Michael Hall without at the same time remembering 'Wof'.
Like the Hallowe'en stories, the *Toast to the Memory of C. S. Lewis*
was in fact delivered orally and afterwards 'written up' by

Harwood at the request of some of those who heard it. It was printed by the New York C. S. Lewis Society in their monthly Bulletin, *CSL*, for September 1975, and was, I think, the last thing to be published before Harwood's death, at the age of 77, in December of that year.

I have labelled the brief concluding Section *Songs and Verses Composed for Special Occasions* though I have not always been able to identify the occasion. I know, however, that the *Prologue* was spoken when the open-air stage for theatrical performances at Kidbrooke Park was used for the first time; and that *For a New House* was composed for the opening of a new hostel (Little Odell) while the school was at Minehead during the war; and I assume that *Sleeping Beauty* was written for a performance by young children of that well-known fairy story. The *Kindling Song for a St. John's Fire* was (again for the first time at Minehead) certainly written to accompany the ritual event which always concludes those Midsummer Festivals that also called forth the three children's plays. *Alleluia for All Things* was written to be sung by the children to the music of Vaughan Williams's spirited setting of the hymn; 'For all the Saints'.

Brief as the Section is, I fancy there are things in it which readers here and there will value more highly than anything else in the book, precisely because they will already be so familiar with the sound of them. One wonders for instance how many thousands of times one at least of the *Graces before Meat* ('Sun, earth and air . . .') has been listened to at one meal or another in buildings throughout the English-speaking world. The fact remains that it is a scrappy Section. Perhaps 'Appendix' would have been a better label. Whatever it is called, there is this also to be said for it: it may give the reader some idea of the editor's own experience on first encountering Harwood's 'literary remains' – those few dilapidated folders, and within them, in any sort of order or disorder, those still more dilapidated MSS, or copies (for fortunately some of them *had* been printed here and there before), which he had taken such little trouble to preserve. It may also evoke from that reader some of the mental agility which the editor found it required, to be whisked to and fro between contrasting responses called for by, let us say, on the one hand the avowed, though useful, triviality of the *Three Poems for Practice in Eurythmy*, and on the other the truly Parnassian clangour of the *Alleluia for All Things*, with which the whole volume fittingly concludes.

It would have been a completer whole if it could have included those other well-known productions of Harwood's pen, his renderings in English of the *Oberufer* mystery plays, and of Rudolf Steiner's 'Calendar of the Soul' (*The Meditative Year*). But these are already available in book form and it was felt to be impracticable. It will have achieved therefore its modest aim if it finds a welcome place on many shelves alongside these, and alongside the three books already referred to, *The Way of a Child*, *The Recovery of Man in Childhood* and *Shakespeare's Prophetic Mind*.

In conclusion let me recall that the early poem *Nous n'irons Plus* was addressed to myself at the close of a happy period of two years, during much of which we had been residing together. I have tried to treat my task of collecting, arranging and introducing this Miscellany as that of an objectively moved editor rather than a close and lifelong friend. The fact nevertheless that Cecil was indeed such a friend turned what looked in prospect like an arduous and even formidable undertaking into a deeply moving personal experience and a seemingly effortless labour of love.

Owen Barfield
South Darenth, Kent
January, 1978

I

*Early Poems
and
A Short Story*

THE HOUSE

These are the blocks I trod on,
  The paving cracks I missed,
When we went on the spaces
  To school or school-boy tryst,
And walked the broken kerbstone's
  Perilous twist.

And down this street came bowling
  My merry hoop and I,
Firm on the ringing steel would
  The curling skimmer lie,
And the sure helmsman drive it
  The people by.

Behind that gate in sunshine
  Have long adventures lain,
Those windows framed me, counting
  The sliding drops of rain,
And from her dear room echoes
  My mother's pain.

"O Brick and Slate, be joyful!
  See, it is I your son,
That in a hundred gardens,
  Since yours, have safely run,
Though far the dim road stretches
  To find the one."

"And I have been a soldier
  And heard the bullets sing,
Where many straight young bodies
  Were broken for their King,
But still, by my good angel,
  I keep my Spring."

'I keep my Spring' – back echoed
  The blank upstanding wall.
The door stood open. Clamour
  And riot in the hall . . .
O Children! hides that laughter
  No care at all?

A THANKSGIVING

Darling, do you remember,
   With twelve tall months between,
Below was black December,
   Above an April green,
When in the young Spring weather,
   Like some four-footed thing,
We walked the wood together
   And made the thrushes sing?

Those leaves lie heaped and blackened
   That tossed above the glade,
Their windy strings are slackened,
   Their music all is played;
But still in these high places,
   Under the fresh green sound,
We lift light-hearted faces,
   And only touch the ground.

A MODERN JOURNEY

Here in the daytime, open-eyed,
We'd follow back the countryside,
Travelling in less lonely dream
To see the ploughman hold his team,
And children leaning in a line
Answer our white and fluttered sign,
While at their backs the cattle feed
Indifferent to our dragon speed.
And here, on nights as pitch as now,
Have shone the Pleiads and the Plough,
And when the ditty of the wheel
Drowned on the bridge's drum of steel
How bright beneath us grew the shiver
That rippled down the rich black river! . . .
But windows, where the landscape wheeled
Or stars returned, a film has sealed,
And one unchanged Interior stains
The triptych of the sightless panes,
The vault, the wicked winking light,
Faces returning dimly white
The vague unpointed gaze that delves
Among our dark reflected selves.
Till, nodding with the gentle roar
From the quiet earth beneath the floor,
Our watchful chin-propped heads pretend
A sleep, and to the journey's end
Rapt, mute, discordant, flank to side,
In a bright ghost-walled gloom we ride.

A VERY FINE CAT

Of Dr. Johnson's affection for his cat Hodge Boswell writes "I recollect him, . . . when I observed he was a fine cat, saying *Why, Yes, Sir, but I have had cats whom I liked better than this* and then as if perceiving Hodge to be out of countenance, adding *but he is a very fine cat, a very fine cat indeed!*"

> Why yes, but though a Hodge, Sir,
>   The present fancy feed,
> I must to other mousers
>   Affection's palm concede,
> To kinder cats and wiser
>   And cats of purer breed –
> But Hodge is a very fine cat, Sir,
>   A very fine cat indeed.
>
> And while the glorious members
>   Of the great feline seed
> For tail or coat or whisker
>   Win each a several meed,
> For Hodge's general virtues
>   A general voice shall plead,
> For Hodge is a very fine cat, Sir,
>   A very fine cat indeed.
>
> What though the social column
>   Be broken like a reed?
> Though nought survive the ruin
>   But Whiggish lust and greed?
> 'Mid total labefaction
>   Shall stand the vital creed
> That Hodge is a very fine cat, Sir,
>   A very fine cat indeed!

THE EMPTY ROOM

Midnight, and O the deeper gloom
That sprang to welcome in that room
   The lamp's unshaded glare!
The ghosts of pictures on the wall,
The shelves with spaces short and tall
   For books no longer there!

"Now let returning darkness fill
This desolate place and hide – " But still
   The light continued shining,
And when I pulled the cupboard door
The vacant shelves inside it wore
   No printed paper lining.

But crannied by a curious fall
Between the book-case and the wall
   Behold a sacrifice!
A book entangled like the ram
That God prepared for Abraham
   When Isaac almost dies.

What can the slippery volume be
So tightly clasped by Destiny
   That grudges I should touch it?
A pocket Horace, by all that's evil!
Printed, bound, lodged there by the Devil
   For drowning me to clutch it!

A century back, and I might draw
Some consolations through this straw,
   Imbibing truth genteelly,
And flavouring a gnomic line
Declare the turn immensely fine,
   And sentiment perfect – really.

What wretched stuff! With purple lips
Divine Augustus nectar sips
   In Tyrian purple vesture;
Here's Chloe, amorous as a dove,
Melting with artificial love,
   The patriot's dying gesture. –

So far Contempt would have its look,
But Apprehension snapped the book
   And thrust it on the shelf,
Lest, taken with the fall and flow
Of syllables, I might forgo
   My sorrow and my self.

THE STRAIN UPRAISE

What elfin thought possessed
The Unknowing to divest
(As he clattered down the stairs' dark maze)
Me of the twelve year mask
Of present time and task,
Humming "The Strain Upraise
Of Joy and Praise"?

I soared on high toe-tips,
Great eyes and bursting lips,
As children will whose souls are hence.
The Quiring Multitude
Loomed round me, snugly pewed,
Here vacant and here dense,
Like sheep in pens.

Like sheep? Can older thought
As water thus distort?
Those glossy men and ladies trim
Guess not, as they sing their psalm,
How it comes dropping balm
From lips of Cherubim
And Seraphim!

THE SOLDIER'S COAT

Along the narrow corridor,
   And up the felted stair,
That half forgotten soldier bore
The brief life's common dress and pall
    And left it hanging there,
With limp sleeves lack-a-daisical
   And a great stitched tear.

Well, entered I; the loose form swelled,
   Assumed heroic mould,
And seemed the Spirit once it held –
As wind returns to make alive
   The sail's dead sunken fold –
Was breathing in it to revive
   The soldier bold.

Ay, he who bore this house of cloth
   Like snail upon his back,
How went he forth? With snail-like sloth?
Or soldierly? Of dreams enticed,
   And poets in his pack?
A doubting soul? Or one whose Christ
   Made straight the track?

Or ponder more his present pride
   Who, by past fire annealed,
Commands the great Wheel backward glide –
Here stand the lines, the bugles blow,
   God and the right our shield!
O rapture to revisit so
   The proud red field!

Nay, Soldier, hang not on a spell,
    Dream not in dream a dream,
Those rotting acres and the smell,
The old sick tune, the palsied knees,
    The Terror's iron scream –
Not these the breath of God! Not these
    The summoned theme!

And swaddled in the long grey dress,
    Or stark and plain to see,
Death's every shape and shapelessness,
One cleft face smiling with its half –
    O Blindman Memory!
Put up that masking, mocking scarf,
    Thou hast caught me!

NOUS N'IRONS PLUS . . .

Nous n'irons plus au bois, no more O friend! O friend!
Our laurels are cut down, our glory sets behind;
And is it hard, when Heaven blows, for the reeds to bend?
O we were oaks, and laughed alike at reeds and wind!

We shouted, and the Morning Stars together sang,
For we were sons of God and could there be an end?
O Eden! and the Gate that murders with its clang!
And shuts us from the wood for evermore O friend!

A MEETING WITH R.M.

Pyramids, lady, stood and stand
By common stone on common sand,
The Syracusan's table spread
Lacked all things, lacking common bread,
And speeches tuned to common-sense
Have sounded chords of eloquence.
Nor would I (to begin) forget
Those other meetings where we met,
Unlooked for spirits whom their kind
Ran to embrace – but call to mind
The painted walls, pervading glare,
Acres of polished maple where
My feet, unfriended through the press,
Threaded the maze of friendliness,
Or halted, while my wheeling eye
Embraced the boundless company,
But found no answering beam at all
Within the great electric hall.
Seemed equal now to stand or move,
When from the gallery above
Clattered the mad and solemn din
Of cymbal, drum and violin;
At which (a triple fate designed)
Jump with the chord our eyes aligned,
And while their archery left the string
Of either bowman quivering,
Fitting my footsteps to the band
I crossed the room to shake your hand.
Warm fingers and a laughing word!
No sweeter sound Admetus heard
When first Alcestis spoke, and he
No longer doubted this could be;

So looked, so well and little said
Leontes and Hermione dead . . .
O then how finely came to bloom
All the confusion of that room!
Those grating tongues, like fiddles racked
But in the tuning for the act,
Fell to a murmur, hushed, and soared
In the first drawn ecstatic chord;
While still, their busy flights above,
Like a rare singer rose our love,
Content upon his part to tower
By pureness though he might by power.
Thus stood we gazing, till at last
Our souls advanced, and met, and passed,
And in each others' eyes we lay –
Was it a minute, or a day?

THE MOTH

Listen, unquiet moth, and know what's said of you
    By students of your kind who have a notion
That Nature in the crusted pin-point head of you
Has packed a senseless bundle of machinery,
    Whose pulse and motion
Is fed and governed only by the scenery.

Tonight, they would relate, some sensitive cell,
    Dulled by the darkness, stretched a tiny tendon
That set your musky wings vibrating well,
And bore you swiftly on your flowery vagrance,
    Condemned to spend on
Each bloom the time dictated by its fragrance.

So it befell unwittingly you dived
    Where flowed towards my lamp a stream of bright air,
That washed you up against the gauze contrived
To keep you troublers of my inky labours
    Out in the night air –
Thin party-wall for such persistent neighbours!

There, as you dabbed against the net hung slack,
    The air, disturbed by forces scientific,
Parted the folds, and presto! through the crack
The light-waves whisked you rudderless, until
    You dashed terrific
Against the light-house, and, for once, lay still.

Too late you stirred, and now attacks incessant
    On the transparency that since has crowned you,
An upturned glass, proclaim you convalescent,
Listen, unquiet moth, to my confession
    For in that round you
Must yet prolong this lonely midnight session.

Now whether their psychology be fiction,
　　Who'd call you a machine, I have my notion,
But won't affirm for fear of contradiction
By wiser heads – not here I take my stand,
　　But on emotion,
To all concerned proclaiming by this hand,

My faith that with a microscopic rapture
　　You floated where my beaming lantern beckoned,
A siren of the eye, the way to capture,
At which, I swear, or else I'm much in error,
　　For a brief second
You trembled with a nearly human terror.

And for the hand that gave night to your blindness,
　　As you again enjoy the flowers' caresses,
I own I think you feel a minute kindness,
A warmth, though not amounting quite to gratitude,
　　That still expresses
A not unreal emotional beatitude.

AN EPITAPH ON A SUDDEN DEATH

I waited, when my childhood perished,
    For all my life to die,
But lived, and saw the love I cherished
    Stolen, and still was I.

When friends were faithless and oppressed me
    My blood ran cool and red,
And breath was hot, though doubt possessed me
    That all that breathed was dead.

These are the woes men ease with weeping,
    My being bore their strain;
But not the drop that in my sleeping
    Hardened within my brain.

HEART AND HEAD

They were the nobler days, those days of war,
There was a stirring in the mind, a tread
Of thousand hopes where now these ruins are.
Love was new love to dream on, Death to dread,
Ah! Death not dreadful now! Ah! happy dead!
You do not know, who are become a star,
This darkened earthly motion, heart and head
Creeping on parted pilgrimages far.
    God! for a faith to grapple them! But whence?
    Blurred echoes in the mind's unending cells
    Dart mocking tongues and snatches, ghosts of sense
    Dissolving so to darkness. Nothing else?
    No whispered prophecy? O listen again!
    There comes no other answer from the brain.

Mr. Bowlby and the Silver Stater

Fortune had again smiled on the activities of the West Marches Historical and Antiquarian Society. The weather had shown from the first that it had no intention of proving false to the splendid consistency of the whole previous week, and even the oldest member – who remembered them all – had to admit that the programme arranged for the forty-seventh annual excursion was equal, if not superior, to any of the forty-six which had preceded it.

The place of meeting was the historic old town of Southborne, and the morning had been occupied by a leisurely visit to the castle – a remarkably well-preserved specimen of Norman brickwork – and the more hasty inspection of a Roman villa, which had recently been unearthed at a mile's distance from the town. The arrangements for the afternoon were of an entirely different order, the honorary Keeper of the town museum, a past president of the Royal Numismatic Society, having undertaken to deliver an informal lecture on the fine collection of coins and medals recently bequeathed to his native town by the generosity of a distinguished inhabitant. It had even been provided that, in the event of the day beginning with rain, the lecture should be delivered in the morning; so perfect were the foresight of the Secretary and the condescension of the Lecturer.

Lunch was served at the Lamb and Flag, almost opposite the Museum, after which the party strolled across the road in groups of two or three, and were ushered by the attendant into a large room darkened by sunblinds and furnished with a round mahogany table and padded leather chairs. The Secretary stood at the far end of the room with the Lecturer, and introduced the groups one by one as they arrived. Compliments were exchanged, and several successive members alluded, with a bright smile, to the hospitality of the Round Table.

After ten minutes of fresh introductions and murmured conversation among earlier members, who had been swept to the windows by the waves of later arrivals, the Secretary cleared his throat to command silence and, glancing hastily round the room, remarked tentatively: "I think we are all here now."

"All but Mr. Bowlby," replied a member, and a general smile went round, in which the Lecturer, who had never heard of Mr. Bowlby, discovered too late that he had joined.

It was generally assumed that nothing could be done until the missing member had arrived; conversation was resumed, and the Secretary whispered to the Lecturer that Mr. Bowlby was regarded as the eccentric member of the club and always did what was least expected of him. "But he is quite an authority on Numismatics," he added, "and has a small collection himself. And I know he is looking forward immensely to your lecture, Mr. Hewitt."

Mr. Hewitt replied that he only hoped he would be able to satisfy Mr. Bowlby's expectations.

The numismatist arrived at last, through the door which communicated with the Keeper's private room, into which he had somehow found his way. He was introduced to Mr. Hewitt and the faces of the Society, which had begun to show signs of anxiety, cleared at once. Not that they had been concerned for Mr. Bowlby's personal safety; but the Secretary, in stating that he was quite an authority on numismatics, might have added that he was the only member of the Society who knew more of that subject than the encyclopaedia had told him the night before. He was relied upon to take the lead in the discussion which would follow the lecture, and show that the Society could pilot itself through even the least charted of the waters of antiquity.

The chairs were suitably disposed round the table, a glass of water was fetched for the Lecturer, the President made a short introductory speech, and the lecture began.

The room was both hot and dark, and the party had lunched well. The Secretary had already been compelled to nudge his neighbour on the left, and was showing an almost too noticeable anxiety at the drooping appearance of a member opposite him, when the Lecturer drew towards him a large brass-bound box which reposed alone near the centre of the table.

The lid proved to be stiff, and, when it finally started, the bottom of the box descended with a bang on the table. The drooping member at once sat upright and remarked: "Really," in an impressive voice. The Secretary plainly showed his relief; and the whole Society watched with enthusiasm, when the Lecturer drew out, as though by a conjuring trick, tray after tray of glittering coins. One by one he described their origin, drew the attention of his hearers to their peculiar beauties or defects, and circulated them for inspection round the table. The members turned them over gingerly, like small and disagreeable animals, between the thumb and forefinger, and after a brief inspection handed them on to their eager neighbours with exclamations of: "Superb workmanship", "remarkable vigour", or "obviously decadent", in accordance with the opinion already expressed by the Lecturer.

There were Babylonian and Phoenician shekels, Attic drachmas, Roman sesterces, soldi from Byzantium, German thalers, deniers bearing the heads of mediaeval popes, Venetian sequins, and, the gem of the collection, a unique silver stater from Syracuse, struck to commemorate the defeat of the famous Athenian expedition, showing a sinking trireme on the obverse and, on the reverse, Artemis covering her face with her hair. Each in its turn was lifted carefully from its place, passed with elaborate precautions round the table, and at the end of its journey fitted again gently in its division of the tray. It was inconceivable that those very coins had been once jingled cheerfully in purses, flung hurriedly into tills, and tossed high in the air, to fall as heavily on the rough ground, by soldiers gambling round their camp fires. But the continual passing of the coins was sufficient to keep every member's attention actively concentrated on the lecture.

There was loud applause when the Lecturer concluded, which was repeated when the President described his discourse as the most lucid exposition of an intricate subject to which it had ever been his pleasure to listen. The Lecturer replied in becoming terms, and the President was about to declare the meeting open for discussion when Mr. Hewitt looked up from the box, in which he was replacing the trays, and remarked:

"I think some one still has the Silver Stater."

Arms and elbows were at once removed from the table, but they revealed nothing. The Lecturer again lifted the trays from the box, but without success. The coin was certainly not on the table. "It must have fallen on the floor," some one suggested. But it was not on the floor. "Or on the chairs." But it was not on the chairs, though hands were thrust to the very bottom of the furrows which crossed and recrossed the padded leather.

"Will members kindly loosen their coats and feel in their pockets?" asked the Secretary. Members displayed the linings of their pockets to each other, opened their coats and waistcoats, and even shook their trousers; but nothing fell to the ground except a tin trouser-button, to which no one ventured to lay claim.

"No doubt it would roll some way," remarked Mr. Hewitt, anxious to show that he had no suspicions. Three or four members immediately started to examine each side of the room, and the sunblinds were drawn up to give more light. They crawled under side-tables, and ran their fingers under the edge of the carpet and along the cracks between the linoleum and the wall. But they found nothing and one by one wandered back to their places at the table. Meanwhile, the Lecturer had again examined his trays, and the other members had turned the chairs upside down and inspected the under-side of the table with the aid of matches. The half-dozen or so who had received them last had been confused by the fact that the Lecturer had described the coins more rapidly than they circulated. They could not be quite sure whether they had actually seen the famous Silver Stater. On the whole they inclined to think not.

The President rose to the occasion.

"Gentlemen," he said, "the plain fact is that a coin – and a coin of value – which was passed round this table within the last half hour, is now missing. The least we can do, both for the honour of the Society and out of gratitude to Mr. Hewitt, is to submit ourselves to be searched by the police before we leave this room."

The honorary Keeper protested that this was quite unnecessary, but the suggestion was enthusiastically applauded. Mr. Hewitt finally submitted, though only in order that the Society might satisfy itself as to its own honour, and the attendant was despatched with a note to the town police-station. There was nothing to do while they were waiting; but in the general silence the majority of the members imagined themselves already stripped of their clothing and sitting round the table in a state of nature.

The silence was broken in an unexpected manner; Mr. Bowlby, who had been remarkably quiet ever since the loss of the coin, suddenly declaring in an emphatic voice:

"I decline to be searched."

Everyone was too astonished to speak, and the objector was left to repeat his declaration: "I decline to be searched."

The Secretary was the first to recover his tongue.

"But, my dear Bowlby," he said, "we are all going to be searched. And no doubt it will be done with every possible regard for decency," he added.

But it was not that which had troubled Mr. Bowlby, who merely reiterated: "I decline to be searched."

"Perhaps Mr. Bowlby will oblige us with his reasons," suggested the President in the voice of authority.

"I will give no reasons," was the reply, "but I decline to be searched."

It was generally felt that Mr. Bowlby had carried his

eccentricity rather too far this time. The Secretary whispered to Mr. Hewitt that they often had trouble with their friend, but he always came round in the end. The honorary Keeper smiled, and whispered back that he quite understood. A member rose to his feet:

"I think, gentlemen," he said, "that we need not disturb ourselves unduly at the attitude Mr. Bowlby has seen fit to adopt. The rest of us can submit ourselves for examination first, and if the coin should be found on any of us Mr. Bowlby will be spared the necessity of the search. If not, no doubt the police will be able to draw their own conclusions."

There was a general expression of approval, and the two members who sat next to Mr. Bowlby started conversations with their neighbours on the other side. It was best to show these truculent people at once that their behaviour was not of the least interest to anyone.

The attendant returned with a sergeant and a constable. They made notes on the furniture of the room and the position of the members, and conducted a second thorough search of the floor and chairs. The honorary Keeper then placed his private room, through which Mr. Bowlby had entered, at their disposal, and they withdrew to make their arrangements.

The President made another appeal to Mr. Bowlby in the name of the honour of the Society, but in vain. The sergeant reappeared and announced: "I will take the gentlemen two at a time, please."

The President and the member who had determined the attitude of the club to Mr. Bowlby were the first to offer themselves. At the end of five minutes they emerged, adjusting their ties, with a look of conscious innocence on their faces. Two other members immediately stepped forward, and the door of the private room closed behind them. The sergeant had asked that gentlemen who had been examined should keep themselves separate at one end of the room, and across that forbidding no-man's-land nobody cared to put those intimate questions they would have liked to ask at closer quarters. But the President was heard to whisper to the most advanced of the unproven: "Not *quite* everything."

Altogether there were twenty-four persons present, including the Lecturer, who had submitted himself in the third couple amid general applause. The Secretary, who had been busy supplying the sergeant with names, was the last to go. When his turn finally came he walked up to the one remaining member and laid his hand on his shoulder.

"Come, Bowlby," he said. "A mere formality."

But he was shaken off, and passed through the door to his ordeal alone.

When he reappeared with the sergeant and constable everybody in the room felt his heart beat faster.

"So you have not found the missing coin?" inquired the President.

"We have made a thorough examination," replied the sergeant, "and we have found nothing – so far. But there is still one gentleman to be searched." He walked up to the table where Bowlby was now sitting alone.

"Come, sir! We don't want to have to take you along with us."

Bowlby sprang to his feet.

"You will be pleased not to touch me, officer! You have no right to search me without a warrant. And I will not go with you."

The sergeant drew a pair of handcuffs from his pocket and placed them on the table.

"We will give the gentleman three minutes to be reasonable," he remarked to the room in general. Then, as something still seemed needed to complete the effect, he addressed himself to the constable. "Lock the door, Collins," he said.

The tongue of the lock grated into its socket. The sergeant stood with his watch in his hand facing Bowlby. The strain was intense. The sunblinds, also, had not been lowered since they had been pulled up to throw more light on the search, and the room was hot to the point of suffocation. One of the members turned white, reached forward for a chair, missed it, and fell heavily to the ground.

He was at once surrounded and stretched on his back. His collar was unfastened, his waistcoat unbuttoned, and his shoes unloosed. One member relieved the constable of the doorkey and thrust it down the patient's back; another seized the half-drunk glass of water from the table and emptied it in the neighbourhood of his mouth. The sergeant, with admirable devotion to duty, remained facing Bowlby; while the constable, having no further orders, continued to guard the firmly locked door.

Before the three minutes were up by the sergeant's watch, the patient had moaned, breathed, lifted his head, declared himself better, and been helped into an arm-chair in the corner. He was at once forgotten, and everyone's eyes fixed themselves once more on the actors in the principal drama.

"Time!" said the sergeant, returning his watch to his pocket. "Come Mr. Bowlby!"

For answer, Mr. Bowlby smiled and pointed to the table. Close to the edge, by the Lecturer's chair, lay a shining, round, silver object. It was the missing Stater.

Mr. Hewitt was profuse in his apologies, and no one could imagine how they had neglected to look in so simple a place as under the glass of water. The sergeant ordered the constable to unlock the door, and, with a little trouble, the key was recovered from down the back of the convalescent member. Shortly afterwards both men left the room richer, in proportion to their rank, than when they entered it.

As soon as the door closed behind them, the President again rose to his feet. He wished to remind the society that its constitution left very full powers in the hands of the President in the matter of the suspension, and even the expulsion, of any member whose conduct he considered to have brought its good name into disrepute. Reluctant as he would be to use those powers, he felt that the behaviour of one of the members that afternoon constituted an insult to the society, and to its host and Lecturer, such as could not be overlooked. But it was not his wish to punish any one unheard, and he therefore gave Mr. Bowlby this last chance of offering his explanation, or his apology, to the society.

Mr. Bowlby again achieved the unexpected.

"Certainly, Mr. President," he replied, springing cheerfully to his feet. "But first, I fancy it would be of interest to the Lecturer, and perhaps to the whole society, if I were to correct him in one unimportant detail of his admirable and learned discourse. He stated that the Syracusan Stater, which his museum is fortunate enough to possess, was a unique specimen. It is not generally known, as yet, that another of these coins, in an equally fine state of preservation, was recently brought to light in the neighbouring town of Catana. I think you will all agree with me," he added, drawing a small shining object from his pocket, "as to the difficulty of distinguishing the two."

II

Later Poems

THE RECALL OF THE STARS

Return, O stars. Countless as you, they wait
Your coming on the cliffs of earth, and stare
Unresting, in part hope and part despair.
Return. The wind sets homeward. He that late
Fixed with his sovereign eye your bounds of state,
Pale princes in the empty courts of air,
Has hailed the watcher who sets free his care,
Whose master-key unlocks at last heaven's gate.
    O my sweet lost ones! O my soft, my own!
Heard you the trumpet, dreaming in your towers,
And with the dew-drops fallen, come you down
To dwell among us in the homely flowers?
Even to those levels that no thought may span
Thus eloquently streams the breath of man?

AT ILLE LABITUR

My soul, there is a river
That makes no haste for ever,
As through the wide heart of the world it rolls
　　To a sea that no man knoweth,
　　Nor from what place it floweth,
Bare mountain slopes or dreadful rock-bound holes.

　　More secret than old Nile
　　Whose cunning did beguile
The ancients to discern its desert spring,
　　Vaster to perish on
　　Than the great Amazon
That swells an ocean with its outrolling.

　　There comes no spasm or shiver
　　On the smooth skin of that river,
But the watchers on its banks do clearly scan,
　　Brushed by the weeds' long laces,
　　Their hands and pallid faces –
It is called the river of the sorrow of man.

　　And the beam of joy distils
　　An essence there that fills
The shining valleys with a quivering sadness,
　　Though a God gave his blood
　　To purge that bitter flood,
Thenceforth to flow serene with light and gladness.

　　Not from the springs of pain,
　　Nor from the dismal plain
Where, thronged with ranks of Pluto's restless legions,
　　Styx, Lethe, Phlegethon,
　　Cocytus, Acheron,
With sheer Avernus drain the ghostly regions.

But where man's breath and force
   Conceal their troubled source
That river gushes in one common laver,
   The blood within his veins
   And current of his reins
Draw from its potency their pulse and savour,

   That do his small soul teach
   The parent flood to reach,
And dare on the immense his cockle-shell . . .
   Thou too make quickly tight
   Thy tender craft, my sprite:
Is now the time? Dear hearts and friends, Farewell!

DAY AND NIGHT

When I straighten my body into my bed at night,
And the smooth sheet flows like white surf to my chin,
I creep back into the womb of the world mother:
I shut consciously the lids of my eyes,
I spiritually close the gates of the sense of hearing,
I forget all touch and taste and the intake of breath and I wait.

And suddenly I swim through the waters of the flood;
There is no rainbow, and I stand in another light in Eden;
The souls of the animals fawn about me,
Nor am I afraid of their vast shapes and great variety.
I eat of the plant before it has become root or stem or flower,
I play with light like fine sand and let it drift through my
    fingers,
I do not hear but I am music,
And I know that if it ceased I would not be.

It is hard that when I wake I must forgo all these experiences,
To see light only reflected and be imprisoned in a day,
To hear so seldom the faint earthly echo of that music,
To live among voices that speak not of that light.
I am lost among sounds and words that do not know me –
Come, music, thou alone art real substance;
Come, poetry, make me to know myself.

SOVEREIGN LOVE

I hold that Love is king and lord
    With sway on earth and sky and sea,
No sword so mighty as his sword,
    No mercy like his charity.

I do believe it is his care
    That makes the blessed sun to shine,
That what is foul he turns to fair,
    And what is fair creates divine.

I know he changed my heart to gold,
    I know he gave me eyes to see,
And heart and sight I freely sold
    To serve him without fear or fee.

Then if his bounty throw me still
    A look, or scatter me a sigh,
I am most richly paid, and will
    Proclaim Love's goodness till I die.

THREE WORLDS

I dreamed I suddenly was one
   In some great host of birds that sing
And drink the air into their bone;
   The wind was firm beneath my wing,
We rose, and the bright vale along
I wheeled and panted in their song.

It was most glorious to be borne
   Incorporate in that rushing soul,
No more to sink, a fragment torn,
   A self without the living whole:
Of song or flight we had no heed
Who were God's singing and his speed.

A long, long age we wheeled, our flight
   His shade upon the azure sky.
Not we who floated shadow-light,
   It was the Earth swung low or high.
And while to its own night it spun
We drank with golden throats the Sun.

At last like wind on summer days
   Dappling the silver-seeded grass,
Or fall of softest snow, or haze
   Of breath warm-breathed upon a glass,
With such light stir we touched the ground
It gave no answering shock or sound.

But from that touch there leaped a sword
   Of pain, that pierced from heel to head.
I cried; swift wings bore up my word
   And grew into a cloud that spread
And thickened into night. I fell:
Earth broke; I knew the fear of Hell.

I was the life of that new land,
    I was the Earth, the Heavens were I;
All creatures stood within my hand,
    I was and knew them utterly.
I strove to love them, but in vain,
My heart was pain and only pain.

I knew them to the very bone,
    Yet loved them not for all I knew.
In them I loved myself alone,
    And still a voice within me grew:
Ah, keep alive that pain, it cried,
In that alone thou hast not died.

Live then, I answered, Fear and Strife;
    And Earth and Death be mine again,
But give me not alone my life,
    Nor only feed my heart with pain.
Upright I stood, even as I spoke.
My feet were on firm earth. I woke.

I woke and knew that neither death,
    Nor sleep, nor wayward dream could show
Who gave me Life more dear than breath,
    And Love to take away my woe,
Ensouling, lest our soul be blind,
This earth that feeds the waking mind.

It was the twilight hour of morn
    When twittering birds have stirred and drowsed,
And silently the light is born,
    And only the fresh breeze is roused;
But now, though yet the hills were grey,
Rang out the first clear song of day.

THE MARKET-PLACE

How can I pipe my dances
　　When London will not leap,
Or mourn now London river
　　Has grown too old to weep?

All day I stroke my whistle,
　　But past me as I play
Ahriman rides his chariot
　　And roars the notes away.

FACES

All day I sought from street to street
   A face to bring me back your face,
And some had gracious looks and sweet,
   But not your sweetness and your grace.

And some were kind and viewed me fair,
   As though they partly guessed my smart
And would have wished me luck, but their,
   Their pity could not heal my heart.

On some I saw a shadow dwell
   That brooded in a way I knew –
These mirrored back myself too well,
   But none could hold the glass to you.

Yea, Love himself might not awake
   The very gaze on which he fed,
Since nothing out of heaven could take
   The graving of so dear a head.

But when a spirit in my heart
   Whispered how true you were, how good,
Your face in every look and part
   Flashed like a lightning through my blood.

SECOND FRONT
(March 1944)

When has there been a waiting as now we wait?
  Not when invincible arms, in France or Spain
  Embarking, fired the hill-top beacon chain;
Nor when three hundred bivouact at Hot Gate,
The world's knife-edge; or Jahveh's mountain State
  Watched for the Assyrian by his Angel slain;
  Or Colum's monks signalled the sea-borne Dane,
Then died amid their cloister desecrate.

These marched to spoil, those stood to save a land:
  But now the spoiler stays, and those who go
With terrible lightnings in their eye and hand
  March sail swim fly to unmake a world of woe.
The moon brings Easter. Christ into this flood
Of slaughter, pour one drop of merciful blood!

THE REPENTANT CITY

(Our blessed Saviour is nowhere noted to have laughed. Dr. Donne.)

The preacher paused, the people shook;
A terror loosed their limbs and took
    Their inmost juices;
When seeing their frames too strongly fraught
He raised a different voice that taught
    A prayer's mild uses.
                    Blest Lord, unsmiling Jesus,
                    Tollatur mundo risus;
                    Mother of Jesus, Mary,
                    Fac tecum nos maerere.

Sudden – though some their voices cracked,
And some had none, and some were racked
    With mirthless laughter –
Shattered a shout from roof to floor,
And thousands thronging at the door
    Repeated after.
                    Blest Lord, unsmiling Jesus,
                    Tollatur mundo risus;
                    Mother of Jesus, Mary,
                    Fac tecum nos maerere.

Soon as the woeful sound began
Up every street the newsboys ran,
    Down every alley;
And through the suburbs round about
From every hill they raised the shout,
    In each wide valley.
                    Blest Lord, unsmiling Jesus,
                    Tollatur mundo risus;
                    Mother of Jesus, Mary,
                    Fac tecum nos maerere.

Then to the windows high and low
The heads, as to a common show,
  Came thickly stealing;
But by the drops that from them fell
Like dew in star-light, you could tell
  That they were kneeling.
                Blest Lord, unsmiling Jesus,
                Tollatur mundo risus;
                Mother of Jesus, Mary,
                Fac tecum nos maerere.

The bellman, balancing his trade,
Forgot to cry it freshly made,
  All light and airy,
But while above the church-bells clang
He to his smaller clapper sang
  A miserere.
                Blest Lord, unsmiling Jesus,
                Tollatur mundo risus;
                Mother of Jesus, Mary,
                Fac tecum nos maerere.

The milkmaid dropped her foaming pail
And watched it gushing in the stale,
  Nor wept the ruin,
But cranks and kisses in the bar,
And giggling fits and gauds that are
  The soul's undoing.
                Kind Lord, unsmiling Jesus,
                Tollatur mundo risus;
                Mother of Jesus, Mary,
                Fac tecum nos maerere.

And ladies walking for the air
Plucked out the riband from their hair,
    The hat's bright feather;
Which steeply stamping in the ground
They sank, but not upon a swound,
    And prayed together.

> Sweet Lord, unsmiling Jesus,
> *Tollatur mundo risus*;
> Mother of Jesus, Mary,
> *Fac tecum nos maerere.*

The children heard, and caught their hoops,
And turned in inward-facing groups,
    Wondering greatly;
Till, practised by a passer-by,
They pressed their tender palms on high
    And cried sedately.

> Dear Lord, unsmiling Jesus,
> *Tollatur mundo risus*;
> Mother of Jesus, Mary,
> *Fac tecum nos maerere.*

The soldier at the palace door
Let slide his musket to the floor,
    Himself down sliding,
And all that entered there besought
To spend their spirits (which were short)
    In tears and chiding.

> Great Lord, unsmiling Jesus,
> *Tollatur mundo risus*;
> Mother of Jesus, Mary,
> *Fac tecum nos maerere.*

Which theme he did so well maintain
That even the courtiers were fain,
   And would believe it;
But what from God they deem divine
They must their temporal lord incline
   So to receive it.

        Blest Lord, unsmiling Jesus,
        Tollatur mundo risus;
        Mother of Jesus, Mary,
        Fac tecum nos maerere.

But he unwound his dear's caress,
And called his printing men to press
   A proclamation:
That with the evening steel and stone
Were clamorous that the word was flown
   To all the nation.

        Dread Lord, unsmiling Jesus,
        Tollatur mundo risus;
        Mother of Jesus, Mary,
        Fac tecum nos maerere.

But even the penitent in fine
To Morpheus must their eyes resign,
   Though swelled with weeping;
So when their lids were fast and dried
The river loosed his murmurous tide
   And kept their sleeping.

        Blest Lord, unsmiling Jesus,
        Tollatur mundo risus;
        Mother of Jesus, Mary,
        Fac tecum nos maerere.

And on his banks the nightingale
No more sat brooding on her tale,
   Poor soul, of losses,
But mourned all night her greater loss
Whose babe hung bleeding on the cross
   Between two crosses.

> Blest Lord, unsmiling Jesus,
> *Tollatur mundo risus*;
> Mother of Jesus, Mary,
> *Fac tecum nos maerere.*

ONLY BETWEEN
(from the play, *A Rope Their Pulley*)

Only between the rock and sky,
  No life above, below,
The thin-spread film of mantling soil
  Where rose and lily blow.
And there to music of the sun,
  On hoof and pad and wing,
The morris of the months and days,
  Proud life goes rioting.

Only between two silences,
  Mute high and dumb profound,
Flows on between those viewless shores
  The river of sweet sound;
And there all lovely voices float
  Of brook and tree and bird,
The miracle of breath and string,
  The marvel of man's word.

Only between the light and dark,
  Blind dark and light unseen,
The rainbow glory of the world,
  Sky-blue, sun-red, earth-green;
And there the tender hues of Spring
  Meet Autumn's aureole,
And wall and wood and canvas take
  The colours of Mansoul.

Only between two monstrous deeps
  A foothold of good land,
That never shows a step ahead
  And fails me if I stand,
Yet, would I keep my manhood whole,
  In man I must not stay,
But faring on, I, more than I,
  Shall know and be the Way.

EASTER

This is the day that dearth has died.
   From swelling sap and surging stream,
The young year trumpets forth his pride,
   Earth opens to her summer dream.
This is the day that dearth has died.

This is the day that God has died.
   Weep, Angels, and all Ranks of Light,
Your Strength's foredone, your Love denied,
   Your Dayspring whelmed in utter night.
This is the day that God has died.

This is the day my heart has died.
   I see them pierce his palms and soles.
How high they lift the crucified!
   Earth rocks; again that thunder rolls.
This is the day my heart has died.

This is the day that death has died.
   See, Spirits, Light from darkness born
With what rich hues 'tis glorified!
   How teems the living heart this morn!
This is the day that death has died.

NOW LIGHT IS LORD

Now Light is Lord; the high hour of the sun
  Swells with clear notes of birds and insect hum:
The earth, one radiant flower with petals blown,
  Yields up her golden sweetness and her dream.

From what pent darkness of the sunken year
  This many-petalled flower to heaven is flung,
From what long midnight leaps this noonday fire,
  From what cold silence bursts this heat of song.

Earth joys in the familiar, the loved scene.
  How old that just unfolded delicate wing!
The rose reviving is the rose again,
  Those notes to wood or hedge or heath belong.

But man revives not so, his way is bare
  For winter or for dream, for mute, for song.
Earth's sounds are hushed his latest voice to hear,
  All Nature waits what offering he will bring.

COLD CHRISTMAS

Earth and Water, Air and Fire,
You my senses most desire,
Have all your summer passions died?
What are you at Christmastide?

Earth, Air, Water, you are one,
Earth is stone and Water stone,
Air that is the living breath
Freezing breathing things to death –
Where is Fire to get you Soul,
Make you separate and whole?

Earth is stone and Water stone,
Life is bone and love is bone,
The milk is frozen in the pail,
The mind is frozen in the skull,
Who shall melt them together
In the bitter weather?

The milk is frozen at the door,
The heart is frozen at the core,
Who shall fetch the living coal?
Where is Fire to get them Soul?

Yet in one small plot of earth
Cold clay is warmed to birth,
Iron in burning blood is smelted,
Waters of the womb are melted,
And the frozen air is shaken
With the gasp of breath intaken,
And the milk for him is warm,
And another child is born.

On a morn at Christmastide,
Down a lane with plough beside,
With a musing-quickened ear,
I heard the turning of the year,
Like the dawn-sense, or the knack
To know the tide is past the slack.
February brought in frost,
But that music was not lost,
March came in with deeper snow,
Still the sap would sing and flow,
And open senses caught the sound
In the mid-March crocus ground.

Shepherds round the glowing coals
In their simple dreaming souls
Heard the song and saw the light
And knew what child was born that night,
Hearkening across the silent snow
His first warm cry of human woe.
The song ended, the light faded,
They woke hungry, they woke jaded,
Back the old life came again,
The misery of snow and rain
And the longing for the morn –
But another world is born.
Earth is red with human blood,
Christ is come from Jordan flood,
Cities shattered, nations beggared,
He is on the Mount transfigured,
Men deny the human name,
He is risen as a flame
Leaps to spiritual form –
And another Man is born.

Fire and Water, Air and Earth,
You that gave my Body birth,
You that are my Spirit's grave,
Grant my soul the thing I crave,
Warm my heart and steel my feet
To meet what I on earth must meet,
Steel my feet and wing my mind
To find what I on earth must find,
Life that rises from the stone,
Blood that pulses in the bone,
Why without the lurking death
Love itself can draw no breath,
And the heart of man is born
On the freezing Christmas morn.

THE WORD

The sun sees not the light it throws
    But through the dark of heaven peers,
Nor knows its shining Self, but knows
    The earth, the moon, the wanderers.

The flowers feel not their wafted smell,
    But quicken with the quivering bee;
And eyes see not themselves, but well,
    How well the world's brave show they see.

Only the Word, divinely wrought,
    Knows what it is and what it wills,
At once the thinking and the thought,
    The Soma and the thirst it fills, –

And does with double power reveal
    The art engraced in human soul
The wounding of the world to heal
    And make the broken vision whole.

EVENING VERSES

Now, when the wheeling stars
    From the great sun receive
The measure of those hours,
    Its light must ever leave,

Turn back the wheel of time
    In strength of heart and mind
Some joy or wonderment
    In those past hours to find.

Even to the dawn that gave
    This ageing day its birth
Seek out some new-won thought,
    Some print of sorrow or mirth –

From mirth a kindling grace,
    From sorrow strength to gain,
From hope a spring of life,
    Wisdom itself from pain:

So shall those vanished rays
    Suffer an alchemy,
And the new rising sun
    Find them as light in thee.

. . . AND MARBLE TO RETAIN

Whenever the monks went into the Chapter
The shafts of the porch were matter for laughter;
For Purbeck pillars were then the rage,
And the Abbot had had them brought by barge,
Jet-black, smooth as a trollop's face,
And spotted and specked like a sad disease.
It went in a twitter of whisperings
That the blackness stood for the Abbot's sins,
While the little white shapes with twist and curl
That shone through the dark skin of the whole
Were devils waiting to take him to Hell.
They would wink as they passed and then forget them
(A pretty fancy of God's to spot them)
And in ordered octagon, niched together
Under the stone-ribbed stretched umbrella,
Ponder the power of the chaptered rule
To purge the passions that damn the soul.

To-day an unprepossessing lady
Came to look round the monks' old abbey.
With the help of her guide she noticed from the nave
The lack of alignment in an arcade:
Three capitals also were not set square
On their clustered stems. The Chapter-house door
Was badly centred – but there she halted
And all her hedgehog hardness melted,
Seeing and stroking, with eyes new lighted,
The velvety, jet-black, ammonite-spotted
Purbeck pillars, a seine of shells,
Palaeozoic funerals,
Univalves, bivalves, conches, spires,
Whose lips once breathed, through delicate hairs,

Rhythms of waves, of tides, of moon,
Mouthing their meals to the planets' tune,
The surging, resurging prodigal pouring
Life of the waters devoured and devouring,
Calcinisation of ocean and aeon,
All in the head of a lonely woman
Scanning the columns the monks had reared,
That told her of things they never heard.

A glance at the roof and she turned to leave
With thoughts that gave her room to breathe:
When a monk came in with delicate face
But a look of the sun in his downcast eyes
And hands pressed like fine leaves together.
They passed but neither saw the other.

ALMOST THIS

No hedge on the road,
No birds in the hedge,
No chorus in the dawn,
No cuckoo in the spring,
No flowers in the field,
No butterfly in the flowers,
No violet in the bank,
No fish in the stream,
No hens round the farm,
No cock among the hens,
No worm in the plough,
No stooks in the glebe,
No stacks in the yard,
No thatch on the barn,
No swallows under eaves,
No cottager in the cottage,
No wood on the fire,
No water from the well,
No sea without oil,
No beach without stain,
No air without smog,
No rain without grime,
No quiet in the sky,
No road without fumes,
No lane without trash,
No seed without poison,
No fruit without spray,
No spray without death,
No joy in the world,
No love for the earth.

RUNNING

You passed me, running through the night;
   I had no will to call your name,
And blunt that moment's keen delight,
   Make embers of that leaping flame.

But as across a starry sky,
   Awed by Orion or the Plough,
We see a meteor flame and die,
   And that alone is lovely now,

Your passing so, like some fierce spark,
   Made shadowy all familiar things:
That footstep died into the dark,
   But in my heart it lives and sings.

LAURA

I took a plank of close-set grain,
  I made it smooth and good,
Foamed over from my gliding plane
  The crisp sweet curls of wood;
All day I worked them, pair by pair,
  Each plank its fellow sound,
A fence for my ribbed boat to wear
  And sail the seasons round.

With jointed posts I shaped the keel,
  I bored and pegged and strained,
Her helm was very light to feel,
  Her sail was russet-stained,
And on the taper mast I nailed
  A rood of ivory, –
But Laura begged my boat and sailed,
  And did not sail with me.

I gathered herbs from moor and field,
  Both root and leaf and bloom,
The rainbow colours they distilled
  I stretched upon my loom;
And there I made them breathe again,
  I dewed their starry eyes,
And planted on that shining plain
  The tree of Paradise.

The tree that stood when Adam's breath
  Was life and love alone,
And Eva's had no taint of death,
  Upon my web had grown, –
But Laura came and looked and sighed
  And begged it for her shawl,
And left me, lovely in her pride,
  To scan an empty wall.

One other precious thing I had,
  Too dear to spurn or sell,
I groomed my little mare and bade
  Her carry Laura well,
Then turned my face from all I knew
  And vowed it good to part,
But ever as the long miles grew
  Her name was in my heart.

And O it sang so sweetly there,
  As though a rose should sing,
That words like bees made thick the air
  To sip that honeyed thing,
Till from my mouth it drew the breath,
  The song her name had made,
And riding homeward through the heath
  She heard and stopped and stayed.

'O take me with you in your boat,
  Or set me on your mare,
Or on your woven web to float
  Poised in the dream-filled air.
Your song, like lightning from on high,
  Did shine my spirit through,
You gave me to myself – and I,
  Shall I give less to you?'

THE WATERFALL

The waterfall is clamouring to the stars;
Those jars and frets, the language from its throat,
Pulse with the repetition of high sense
Too tense for music, bare of thought and word.

The stars look down and answer with a sign
In line and curve, the splendid script of heaven;
Bear on his back, the Dragon's far-tossed tail,
The Whale with flukes in air, Orion prone.

There is a hurrying between sign and sound,
The ground is swelling to that pictured fate,
The parent stars are smiling on that birth
With mirth and tenderness and fear and love.

I am the stranger between earth and star:
I mar their confluence with my muttering,
I am the rift that holds their spheres apart,
My heart alone unites them. I am Man.

WORDS FOR A CHORALE

O Sun of Worlds!
Thou hast to earth descended.
Our sickness with thy bitter birth is mended;
And with thy death this darkened star grows splendid. –
O Son of Mary!

III

Drama, Legend
and
Fantasy

A ROPE THEIR PULLEY

A Melodrama in Three Acts

*

CHARACTERS

FIREFLY, alias Sir Ralph Cole
CINDERS, alias Dr. Burns
PETER ARNOS
LEWTI ROSS
MICHAEL ROSS, her brother

SCENE

Outside and Inside a Cottage in Wales

The essence of melodrama is that it appeals to the moral sense in a highly simplified state. . . . Melodrama creates people so morally simple as to kill their enemies in Oxford Street, and repent on seeing their mother's photographs.

G. K. Chesterton

ACT I

[Enter in front of the curtain together CINDERS *and* FIREFLY. CINDERS *wears a black beret, a dark wind jacket with zip fastening and close-fitting trousers.* FIREFLY *wears a soft country hat, a loose jacket, blue corduroy trousers, and suede walking shoes. He carries a transparent oilskin mackintosh.]*

CINDERS. I rather thought I should find you here, my dear Firefly. Gosh, what a spot! But I fancy it must be the place the Bogey meant. *[reading from a paper]* Climbers' or Artists' Cottage, stone built with slate roof. Aspect S.W. Snowdon five miles, forty degrees W., Tryfan eight miles, three degrees W. I'll just check up on it. *[taking out a pocket compass]* It's lucky the mist doesn't trouble people like us – it's come down remarkably thick. Let me see. Magnetic variation twelve degrees thirty west. Right to a minute. The Bogey is no genius, but there's no doubt he has a clear head and a gift for detail.

FIREFLY. He pulls your leg every time, Cinders. Map references and compass bearings! You're one of those people who can never enjoy the view because you're always taking out a map to see where you are.

CINDERS. I admit I enjoy exercising my intelligence. I suppose the Bogey thought the ordinary postal address good enough for you?

FIREFLY. When will you learn not to underrate the Bogey? He has imagination. You could learn a lot from him.

CINDERS. I hardly need to go to him when I can learn from you, my dear sir. But you haven't answered my question. Educate me, educate me.

FIREFLY. Well, if you really want to know, the Bogey told me to find the cottage in Wales where De Quincey would most have enjoyed teaching Wordsworth to smoke opium. What an idea now for a competition in one of our literary weeklies! Describe in not more than forty lines and in the manner of the *Excursion* – But I fear the idea is a little beyond you. Did you ever hear of De Quincey or Wordsworth?

CINDERS. DE QUINCEY? No. Wordsworth? Oh, yes. He was a bit of a revolutionary in his salad days, one of your kind. But he became quite respectable in his old age, a real constitutionalist. As a matter of fact my grandfather had the job, that's how I know. But talking of jobs, what's on to-day, do you know?

FIREFLY. Not the first thing. Something quite small I should say, in this out of the way spot. One of those lonely artistic souls, probably. They rather affect this kind of place, since your crew made the towns so intolerable.

CINDERS. I grant you our modern towns still leave much to be desired. But they're improving, definitely improving. I shall soon have one or two entirely underground. What do you say to universal air-conditioning, a constant temperature, artificial sunlight all the year round – and of course complete immunisation against every known disease?

FIREFLY. I honestly doubt if you'll gain much that way, my dear Cinders. You'll sterilise the men as well as the milk. What's a little dirt as long as we keep the passions, the grand unchanging human passions? I remember when we worked with the seven deadly sins and family feuds and religious ecstasies, yes, and men who signed their souls away with their blood. We made some progress in those days.

CINDERS. But how slow, how slow in all those thousands of years! So my firm had to be called in to finish the job. And just look at the difference our new inventions have made. Do you know the great mistake your boss made, Firefly? He advertised himself too much. Plays written about him, pictures made of him, sermons preached on him – he even got himself into Holy Scriptures. Now we advertise a lot too – I'm a great believer in advertising – but we don't advertise *ourselves*. We get much more done by working anonymously behind the scenes. Look at us. Hardly anybody knows that we even exist. Who has ever written a play about us, or painted – I say, *Cave!* here's the Bogey [*They turn to some Presence visible only to them, before which they speak with forced self-confidence.*] O Good evening, Highness. Firefly and I received your messages, and we both got leave for the day.

FIREFLY. We understand it is to be for a day only; we are to have from sunrise to sunset, quite in the old style. But it isn't clear to us yet what it's all about.

CINDERS. Your Highness has no doubt come to enlighten us. We are all ears. . . . I say, don't go away without telling us, when we've come all this distance just to, – Good Lord, He's gone!

FIREFLY. All ears and no hearing, Cinders. You are terribly insensitive to atmosphere. It's useless to pipe ditties of no tone to a spirit like yours. When will you learn that words are not necessary for the communication of thoughts? Now I understand the situation perfectly already – and not a word said the whole time.

CINDERS. You generally manage to miss the point, Firefly. Of course I understand the Bogey as well as you. But we ought to train him to express himself publicly, we ought to get him on the air. We've got nothing to take hold of at present. We need a rope to pull him down with.

FIREFLY. O give him a rope and he'll hang himself. You can't pull him down. But look over there. What a superb sight the rising sun can be. Sunrise to sunset. A day that will die and never be born again, a stone falling into the ocean of time and sending its ripples to eternity. What will it –

CINDERS. Don't talk so loud. The woman's heard you. Get over there; we don't want to be seen yet. [*They retreat to the corners of the cottage.* LEWTI ROSS *comes out from the cottage, i.e. through the middle of the curtain.*]

LEWTI. Is that you, Michael? You're not back already? My God, I could swear I heard a voice. Careful, my girl. You're hearing things now, you'll be seeing them next. You've got to keep sane till Michael comes back. Do you hear? He can't be back for hours yet. He's only just gone. And he wouldn't come in by this door anyway. But you've got to keep sane till he comes back, you've got to keep sane till Michael – [*She re-enters the cottage.*]

FIREFLY. Quite a helpful appearance. I understand things even better now. But I don't like that name. It's a bad omen. Playing into the hands of the Bogey I call it.

CINDERS. Omens and auguries and prodigies, why will you go on living in the past? They're all dead and buried years ago. It's a mere coincidence, the chances of which are mathematically ascertainable. I look on it as a fortunate occurrence. It broke the tension at one of those absurdly theatrical moments you will indulge in.

FIREFLY. Names mean more than you think, Cinders. They aren't the same as registration numbers.

CINDERS. I think you'd better turn yourself into a clairvoyant when this job is over. You can advertise in the theatre programmes – theatre-goers like that sort of thing. But do let's get to business. Of course the man is the main objective.

FIREFLY. I agree; but there might be a little diversion with the girl as well. Happily she is in such a distraught state that we needn't be too careful. It will all seem a dream to her afterwards.

CINDERS. The whole thing can plainly be done by suggestion. But the man must be kept alive. None of your tricks, Firefly.

FIREFLY. O you needn't worry – though I suppose you noticed that awkward moment when the Bogey came?

CINDERS. Yes, so I thought I had better warn you. The injuries are nothing. But there isn't much will to live. However, I fancy we can supply that.

FIREFLY. We must put on some sort of show for the girl to start with. Have you any special choice?

CINDERS. I'm pretty much at home in the medical profession myself. How does this strike you now? [*He places horn-rimmed glasses professionally on his nose.*]

FIREFLY. I fancy belles-lettres or the fine arts. Dr. Burns, your friend, the eminent critic, Ralph Cole – no, I believe a title would not be out of place, Sir Ralph Cole, if you please.

CINDERS. Very well, Sir Ralph, I take it we have lost our way in the mist, like this Michael fellow is doing, and providence has guided our steps to the only cottage within six miles. It is also a trifle early, but I think no questions will be asked in view of the general state of affairs.

FIREFLY. I agree. So, if you're ready, we'll ring up the curtain on the little drama.

CINDERS. I suggest we knock and walk straight in. It's the back door but our entry is unconventional anyway.

FIREFLY. Don't forget I'm senior partner and have the first helping. O, I'll leave something for you.

[*He knocks three times in the manner of the French theatre. The curtain rises and discloses a cottage living room. There is a fireplace with pots and pans, an old sofa, an iron bedstead, a rather solid table with some rather rickety chairs, and among other junk in the corner some empty beer bottles and a climbers' rope. There is a door in the centre back of the stage with a window beside it on the left, and a door to another room in the right wall.* LEWTI ROSS *is bending over the bed on which a man is lying.*]

CINDERS. Please forgive our intrusion but –

FIREFLY. We really had no idea, believe me –

LEWTI. O, Who are you? Did my brother send you?

FIREFLY. I must confess we brought ourselves. We lost our way in the mist, and thinking the cottage was probably empty at this time of the year, we just walked in. A charming place for a climbing holiday, when the sun shines. And painting too, I see.

LEWTI. Then you're not the doctor from Portmadoc? Of course you couldn't be so soon, but –

FIREFLY. No, I'm afraid not. But if it's a doctor you're wanting, my friend here, Dr. Burns, will no doubt do his best for you.

LEWTI. O, do have a look at him, doctor. We had an accident, climbing you know. I don't think anything's broken, but we stitched up a pretty ghastly cut on his head, and he's been unconscious ever since.

CINDERS. Let me have a look. Breathing pretty good. Pulse steady. I'll just go over him.

FIREFLY. Not your husband, I think.

LEWTI. No, a friend of my brother who lives here. Michael and

I only arrived yesterday, and we went out at once for a bit of practice – just a rock face quite near – and this happened. It took ages getting him home on a hurdle.

FIREFLY. And your brother's gone for help, I suppose?

LEWTI. Yes, he went just now. But the mist's dreadfully thick, and there isn't even a cart track here since the landslide last spring. Did you come over the pass?

FIREFLY. I hardly know how we came, – there was so much mist about. And I leave all the map-reading to my friend the doctor.

CINDERS. No bones broken, happily. I think he should be all right. Any hot-water bottles?

LEWTI. I'm afraid not.

CINDERS. A few of those beer bottles might help. They've got screw tops.

FIREFLY [who has moved towards some canvases stacked in a corner]. May I look at the paintings?

CINDERS. We must fill them in a basin or they'll crack. Not too hot, that'll do.

LEWTI. I'll wrap them in these old towels.

FIREFLY. Do you know this is very remarkable work?

CINDERS. Give me the bottles, and I'll put them in the bed. By the way, my friend's opinion is worth having. He's a real connoisseur in these matters.

FIREFLY. I am really quite staggered. Wonderful. Wonderful. May I ask the name of the painter?

LEWTI. Peter Arnos is his name. I think his stuff is wonderful too. Doctor, do you think he'll – do you really think he'll – come alive again?

CINDERS. I see no reason why he shouldn't be perfectly all right. But what a strange thing to say.

LEWTI. You're not joking – being kind to me, Doctor. You see it was all my fault. He will come alive again?

FIREFLY. My dear young lady, you are rather overwrought. How can you ask such a question?

LEWTI. Because, just before you came he stopped breathing. And I looked at his face, and I knew he wasn't there. Doctor, I never knew before that you could see when someone – could see when someone . . . [in an excited voice and almost shouting]. Why don't you give him that rope? That one there. Can't you see he needs it? He wants to tie himself on to the figtree. The whirlpool's sucking him down. Hold on, Peter. I'm bringing it as fast as I – [*She has taken the rope from the corner and carried it towards the bed, where she collapses and is caught by* FIREFLY. *The rope falls on the bed.*]

FIREFLY. Another patient for you, Doctor. I suggest you attend to her in the next room, and leave me alone for a bit with this one. Come, I'll help to carry her in.

CINDERS. I shall be only too happy to take her on. Meanwhile the man shows some signs of coming round. You'll have plenty of time, though, while I'm fixing the girl. But remember to be careful. I'm not attending any funerals to-day. I've got a professional reputation to keep up.

FIREFLY. What a disgusting weight these women are! [*They carry* LEWTI *into the next room.* PETER ARNOS *slightly raises himself on the bed.*]

PETER. Thank you, Lewti. I think I'll be all right now, if only I can hold on. It was awfully good of you to bring it. They can't reach me here, you know. I say they can't reach me. . . . [*He falls back and drops the rope on the floor.* FIREFLY *re-enters and stands behind the bed.*]

FIREFLY [*In his original voice*]. Well, now that we have no other company, Mr. Arnos, I think we can drop appearances and raise ourselves to the world of realities. My time is rather short, so please come and sit over here, and we'll have a little conversation together. O, you can work your body from outside just as well as from inside, if you try. Splendid. You'd better put this jacket on. Let me give you a hand. This way please.

PETER [*speaking in a clear but somewhat mechanical voice*]. You look terribly familiar.

FIREFLY. O, yes, I'm a very old friend. And I've come on a most painful errand – old friends often do. I've come to tell you the truth about yourself.

PETER. Really? Well, why don't you begin?

FIREFLY. I scarcely know how to. But perhaps I should start with a question or two. About this accident. Would you be so kind as to tell me precisely how it happened?

PETER. I'm afraid I'm really too confused about it still. Ask Lewti or Michael. They saw it happen.

FIREFLY. Well, as a matter of fact, one of them has been so good as to tell me. You were just doing a little practice climb, and you fell. An accident, of course?

PETER. Of course.

FIREFLY. You are a very good climber, I think, Mr. Arnos?

PETER. I'm generally considered so.

FIREFLY. Rather extraordinary, wasn't it – a good climber – one of the best in the country, if I may say so – and you fell in a little after-tea exercise with two novices. Can't you be a little more explicit?

PETER. I told you I really can't remember.

FIREFLY. Come, Mr. Arnos, you're not being honest with me. I suggest it wasn't an accident at all.

PETER. Not an accident? You're not going to tell me – to tell me *that*.

FIREFLY. I wasn't present myself, so I can't vouch for it personally, of course. But all the evidence seems to point that way.

PETER. You mean I really –

FIREFLY. Yes, Mr. Arnos, I think there is no doubt that in a court of law they would use the crude word – suicide.

PETER. My God, I believe you're right. Yes, you must be right. I must have killed myself.

FIREFLY. I told you it wasn't an accident.

PETER. So I'm dead am I? And you're the first person I have met in the Spirit World. How do you do? It's all horribly like one of those modern plays.

FIREFLY. Now do be serious, Mr. Arnos. Things are much worse than that. You're not dead at all, not in the least. And you're coming back to life pretty quickly. I think you know what that means – after an accident like this.

PETER. So I tried to kill myself and failed?

FIREFLY. Yes, you failed.

PETER. And Lewti and Michael told you all about it?

FIREFLY. Not a word. There's no doubt they will try to hush it up. With luck you will get out of an official enquiry, though of course people will say things.

PETER. But Michael knows and Lewti. And I'm coming back to them. My God!

FIREFLY. I told you the truth was painful. But we haven't got down to the motives yet, and I feel sure you will feel better when you've made a clean breast of the whole thing.

PETER. Can't you leave the sordid story alone?

FIREFLY. For your sake, no. We must know all the facts before we can plan for the future. So a few more questions please. First about this girl Lewti. You've always liked her, haven't you?

PETER. Yes.

FIREFLY. And half of you – the better half – wanted to marry her – we needn't say anything about the other half. And then she began to be successful. Critics took notice of her, she sold her pictures, while yours hung fire. And you knew you work wasn't good; you hadn't found yourself; and there might be no self to find. You might be the onion in *Peer Gynt*. Am I right?

PETER. Yes, go on.

FIREFLY. And you thought it would be intolerable to be the husband of a successful woman. Didn't you say 'Damn women, I've got painting', or something like that? So you shut yourself up here, and gave yourself three years to produce something, and, as you put it – to find yourself.

PETER. Where did you learn all this?

FIREFLY. O, I'm an old friend, remember. Then her brother brought her here, and they looked at your canvases. Of course they praised them – but not for the things you thought needed praising. And the more they praised them, the more you felt they were no good. Or else the world would never see what you were after. So you went climbing – and this happened.

PETER. Hell and damnation. Why do I fail in everything I do? I can't even make a decent job of killing myself.

FIREFLY. Now don't start damning yourself – it's a silly trick. You've got a lot to your credit, young man. We'll pass over the painting for the moment, but I think we may say that you got on pretty well with the other half of the programme, that your three years' solitude were not in vain, that you – found yourself?

PETER. Yes, alone here with the mists and the mountains, I found myself. No, that's rot. There were no mists, there were no mountains. There was only me, me, me. I was above creation. I was outside the world. I looked down on it from a great height; and I saw it had no sense, no meaning, no core. And then I knew for the first time what painting means – to do for the world what God could not do. Yes, I could take this chaos of hostile substances, this riot of incompatible forces, this coil of jarring colours, and give it form, harmony, significance. And because I could do this, I was greater than God.

FIREFLY. You found your immortal, imperishable self. You became a god, you discovered that the Spirit does not need the body. Then the girl came, and you knew that you still loved her, and that it would be hell on earth to marry her – hell for her as well as for you – O yes, you saw her point of view as well. And the wind spoke to you on the rock face.

> 'Now, Now. It must be Now. Now is the moment to lose the self in order to find it. Now, or it will be too late.'

So you jumped.

PETER. And failed again. Because you're right. I'm not dead. I can feel myself coming back to life. Sometimes I hardly see you. O God, I shall have to face her again after this, and –

FIREFLY. Now stop. It's not necessary for you ever to see her again. Listen to me. Living here alone, you have learnt that no one can really find himself, his true self, until he faces the mystery of death. You tried to face it, but you faced it through fear and not through courage. Now you are given a second chance. You can jump again.

PETER. No!

FIREFLY. Why not?

PETER. Because I have painted nothing yet. And I will paint something before I die. I will, I will, I will.

FIREFLY. My dear young friend, you are suffering from a momentary depression. Before your friends came you knew very well what wonderful work you had done. Have you really changed your mind, just because they did not at once see in your pictures quite what you see in them? Do you completely distrust your own judgement?

PETER. What do you think? Are they good or not?

FIREFLY. I had not meant to tell you. But since you ask me, I must. They are masterpieces. You will never surpass them. If you were to die tomorrow you would leave an imperishable name behind you. Future generations would weep for you as they weep for Keats and Chatterton.

PETER. Are you quite sure?

FIREFLY. I am quite sure. But can *you* be sure that you will be able to keep your inspiration? Can you always live at the intensity of the last three years?

PETER. I don't know. And perhaps I don't care – if I have achieved something already. You really think I shall live?

FIREFLY. What a magnificent meaning you give to the word! Yes, you will live, and perhaps all the more if your paintings are few. Leonardo, Giorgione, can you not count their pictures on the fingers of your hands? What company you would have, my friend. Now once again let me tell you that you are given a second chance.

PETER. But I must come back to life first, and Lewti is waiting for me . . . and I can't bear it.

FIREFLY. No. In the world where you and I are now there is no need of gross material action. You need only think and imagine. But some simple stage properties are a wonderful help to the imagination. Look; this is not a table; it is a precipice. You can see the smoke rising from its waterfalls and the threadlike glitter of the river tumbling from its foot. Here, quickly, the last traverse. [*He places a chair by the table*] Now you are at the summit. Now the four winds of heaven blow freely round your brow. This is the hour, if ever, for the godlike deed. Now say again the words that sang to you like trumpets when you failed. This time you will not fail.

PETER. 'Give me my robe; put on my crown; I have Immortal longings in me.'

FIREFLY. Immortal longings! What have they to do with mortal flesh? Immortal longings! Let them breed immortality! Jump.

PETER. Out of my way then.

[*Curtain*]

ACT II

[CINDERS *is standing at the foot of the table supporting* PETER ARNOS *whom he has caught as he fell.* FIREFLY *is looking on.*]

CINDERS [*helping* PETER *to the sofa*]. You damned scoundrel. So you did try to get the whole meal for yourself. Do you know, Firefly, if you weren't so useful to me, I'd clip your wings tomorrow. Now, while you have been trying to steal a march on me, I have been making a little discovery in your interest. Listen to this now. There are two principals in this case – not one as you so innocently imagined, and it happens that the girl is more in your line than mine – women generally are. She's all for casting herself down from the pinnacle of the temple. So you can get on with her in the next room while I have my turn with the man. Come on, out with you.

FIREFLY. All right, all right, I admit my enthusiasm carried me a little far, but you needn't lose your temper about it. It was a beautiful scene, don't you think?

CINDERS. Thoroughly decadent, I should say. Shut the door please, and mind you have the girl ready when I want her. She may be useful to me.

[*Exit* FIREFLY]

Now, Mr. Arnos, you have had a very narrow escape. These suggestions are frightfully dangerous things. Look at St. Francis and the stigmata and all that. In fact, if I hadn't come in time to catch you, it would have been all over. So you can count yourself a very, very lucky man. Just sit quiet and you'll soon feel better.

PETER. You're the second person who's come here to-day, and whom I'm sure I've seen before. Didn't I meet you once in America?

CINDERS. Maybe. I'm often over there. But I spend a lot of time in the old country too.

PETER. Yes, I certainly know you. I can't understand it. Where's the other one gone to?

CINDERS. O he's finished with you for the present. He wanted to make a little business deal with you, but he didn't quite get what he wanted. And then he's rather apt to turn nasty. What are you thinking about?

PETER. I'm hardly thinking at all. But scraps of poetry keep running through my head to-day. Now where does this come from? –

'Ere Babylon was dust
The Magus Zoroaster, my dead child,
Met his own image walking in the garden.
That apparition, sole of men, he saw.'

I say, you're not my image are you, my double?

CINDERS. Now that's a very interesting thought. I suppose we men are all doubles of each other in one sense. You see God said, Be fruitful and multiply. Now doubling is the first kind of multiplying. That's what the germ cell does, and what you did first at school – twice one is two, you know. Yes, I suppose we are all doubles of each other – cells in the same social organism.

PETER. You're just playing with words. What do you want with me, anyway?

CINDERS. I want to put two alternatives before you – and perhaps assist you in the choice between them. I saved you from – suicide, and have some claim on your gratitude.

PETER. What are they?

CINDERS. You have to choose between going forward with me, or going back with him.

PETER. Didn't I tell you scraps of poetry kept floating through my mind to-day? Though it isn't words this time but a scene – a scene that words once painted for me. There are two monsters, one high on a cliff over there, and one at the bottom of a great whirlpool, screaming to suck you down, like the bath water when you were a child. Yes, I was a child when I first saw it. And there was a man clinging to a fig-tree that grew from the rock above. And the whirlpool filled and grew calm, and the man dived and swam between the monsters and was safe.

CINDERS. Now if you will keep going back to the past, I'll have no more to do with you. I want to talk to you about the future. Because you're coming back to life, you know, and there's a difficult question waiting you.

PETER. You mean Lewti?

CINDERS. Well, no, not exactly. That's a minor problem, and I think we can find a way to settle it satisfactorily. I mean – your painting.

PETER. There's no problem there, I shall never paint again after this.

CINDERS. Now you are pretending to be superficial as though painting were a minor relaxation you can drop if you choose, like a cigar after dinner. Come, my friend, do be serious with me. Do you tell me you can see the whole world one great bubble of colour, and not paint? You know very well that living and painting mean one and the same thing to you.

PETER. Yes, it was a silly thing to say. I know I shall go on painting. But perhaps the mere fact that I said it, proves that I shall never paint anything worthwhile.

CINDERS. Allow me to speak to you as an older man. I know a little about painting, myself, though I don't pretend to be so eminent a critic as your other friend. In fact I have only recently become interested in it, but my opinion is none the worse for that. You are young, and you have great ability, genius I would even call it. But I think you have not yet quite found either your subject or your manner. That's all, and there's nothing new in it. In all arts the young are copyists and experimenters. Milton couldn't find a subject when he was young, and it took an accident – a suicide if I remember rightly – to start Dickens on the right lines. Perhaps your – accident may have the same happy result.

PETER. What amazes me is how often you say the very thing I was thinking. Do you know I feel as if there were some tremendous new force in me at this moment, something titanic waiting to be born, waiting to take hold of the earth and heavens and reshape them to a new pattern? – Something completely beyond any revolution or renaissance or reformation the world has ever seen; something you could only compare to the creation of man himself.

CINDERS. Now you are yourself again. What did you call them? Immortal longings. Your job is to bring them to earth.

PETER. That's easy to say.

CINDERS. But not so easy to do. Perhaps I have some ideas that might help Mr. Peter Arnos, the Leonardo of the modern age.

PETER. You can't paint on theory.

CINDERS. You are quite right. How easily one slips into the conventional phrase. I am not referring to theory but to experience.

PETER. That's better. Go on.

CINDERS. Let me put it this way. Only a very, very few people – I think you are one of them – realise that an entirely new experience of life has come to mankind in the present century. *Homo sapiens* was the old definition of man; people thought they lived by and for knowledge. But that has all altered. I don't want to discard knowledge – it is quite necessary to have it – but knowledge has become subservient to something else, something far higher and more worthwhile than mere knowledge.

PETER. What is that?

CINDERS. Power. *Homo potens* is the new definition, *homo omnipotens* the new goal of man. Do you think that all the mathematical knowledge that goes into the making of a machine is worth one ounce of the pleasure in power that comes to the man who drives it – the pilot chasing through the clouds, the man at the wheel of the speed launch scarcely touching the water, the humble motor-cyclist stepping on the juice in the country lanes? They are the people who enjoy what is new in life – the mystery of power. But, alas, they are ignorant and scarcely know what they enjoy; while you artists, who ought to feel, to rejoice in, to express all this, you still paint the surface of things as though the hidden wells of power had never been tapped. Your ancestors painted still life – you must learn to paint dynamic power. Then you will reveal to men their own experience of life; then you will be great artists, then you will move worlds.

PETER. It was for something like that I came here. I felt that all pictures were too still, just as Van Gogh felt that all the Northern Masters were gravy when he saw the rich colours of the South. So I came among the eternally moving clouds and mists, these driving rains and tumbling streams, and I lived with movement till sometimes this cottage seemed to sway and scud in the heavens like a lost piece of cloud fallen from its natural height on a windy day.

CINDERS. Your aim was right; but your approach was wrong – lamentably wrong. You can't learn from the elements to-day; wind and rain and frost and thunder have nothing to teach modern man. They are merely the passions of the earth, and the passions have been outmoded by the new vitality. You must go deeper than that, my friend. You are not living in the Renaissance now.

PETER. Where must I go to, then?

CINDERS. You must go into the secret places. *You* can visualise the titanic forces of the earth itself, *you* can interpret a new God to man, you can enter into the machine and paint the very staff by which it lives, the throb and ecstasy of illimitable power.

PETER. You don't mean painting machines? If so, you may as well stop talking, there's nothing to be got that way.

CINDERS. No, I don't mean that. It isn't a question of what you paint but of the vision from which you do it. Once that is right you can paint a sunflower or a sewing-machine, it doesn't matter which.

PETER. And where is the vision to come from?

CINDERS. I told you before, not from theory but from experience. I said that the elements are the passions of the earth. The first machines lived on these elements, wind and water and steam, just as men used to live on their passions. But now the machines have gone deeper; they live on the secret forces of the underworld, coal and oil, electricity, magnetism – perhaps soon on the atom itself. And men have gone deeper too, into the hidden world of the unconscious where the energy is stored by which they live and move, and think and act. You must give yourself up to that unconscious power in yourself.

You must become it, it must become you. Then you will truly interpret the modern experience of life. Then your paintings will have the dynamism of the machine.

PETER. And be as dead as the machine too, in all probability.

CINDERS. Now that is just where you make your mistake, my friend. You think machines are dead; but they are not; they act and evolve, they mould men and control nations. Have they not stamped a new face on mankind, a face which *you* must idealise, as the Greek and Renaissance faces were idealised − the face of *homo potens* − the face that reveals the mastery of illimitable power? And what is the real secret of the machines? They live and are strong because they accept the sacrifice of life. Think of those giant forests of monstrous marestails crashing in ruin upon ruin, a whole world turned to coal that they may chiefly live! Think of those innumerable creatures, winged, scaled, finned night-mares, laying corpse on corpse that they may exult! Who shall say by what sacrifice of what god magnetism and electricity entered the earth, that they might be lifted up? Power is to accept the sacrifice of life. All religions have known this. The machines practise it.

PETER. But they do not know it.

CINDERS. Do not be too sure of that. But there at least you can be more than their equal. You can accept consciously the sacrifice that is offered to you.

PETER. You mean my daily bread?

CINDERS. I am talking to a painter, not to a ploughman. If French rolls made painters, we should all be Picassos.

PETER. What are you thinking of, then?

CINDERS. I am thinking of a sacrifice which is being offered you to enable you to become the great painter you should be.

PETER. Who is offering me this sacrifice?

CINDERS. Now this is where your two problems come together − like negative and positive electricity − to end (we hope) in a flash of light.

PETER. The frightful thing is that I know what you are going to say, and yet I have got to hear you say it.

CINDERS. Don't forget that I am really yourself asking

questions for yourself to answer. Now here is an interesting one. Do you know that this girl Lewti only came here because you asked her?

PETER. Yes.

CINDERS. And she had sworn never to see you again unless you asked for her?

PETER. Yes.

CINDERS. And you know why, too. You knew – and she knew as well as you – that she had a kind of fatal influence on you, a fascination that destroyed you – shall we say like Fanny Brawne had for Keats? You would not break with her, but for your sake she broke with you. You know what that cost her?

PETER. I know she has not painted since.

CINDERS. And painting is not a less thing to her than to you. But there is something else she would do for you if she were certain you wanted it.

PETER. Go on.

CINDERS. I intend to go on – to the end. You cannot live with this girl – and you cannot live without her; a situation which presents us (as I think I said before) with a choice of two alternatives. Either you cease to exist – or she does. The first has been tried and failed. There still remains the second.

PETER. You're not suggesting I should – murder Lewti?

CINDERS. My dear sir, why will you talk in such unpleasant terms? We are not living in the sixteenth century. And I am not suggesting you should take any active steps in the matter at all, because I have reason to believe that she is perfectly prepared to take the initiative herself.

PETER. What do you mean?

CINDERS. I mean that if she thought that by liquidating herself she could help you to fulfil your destiny, she would take that rope and hang herself tomorrow. Perhaps even to-day.

PETER. I don't believe it.

CINDERS. I hardly expected you would. It is highly to your credit that you do not believe it. But as I am most anxious to convince you of the truth of my supposition, with the help of your other friend I will produce some evidence that I think even you will find acceptable. [*Calling through the door*] Will Miss Ross come this way please.

PETER. What are you going to do?

CINDERS. I propose to make a formal interrogation – I am a great believer in forms. You shall hear the whole proceedings, but you must not interrupt the witness. Indeed it would be no good your doing so, because Miss Ross will be on another level, on a different floor as it were, and nothing you say will be heard there. I know it will be annoying not to be able to butt in, but the wireless has no doubt accustomed you to that by now. So let me help you to make yourself comfortable while you listen.

FIREFLY [*entering with* LEWTI *who appears like a sleep-walker*]. This way please Miss Ross. Let me place a chair for you. My friend and I only wish to ask you a few questions.

CINDERS. It will be to your interest to be entirely frank with us. And we shall not keep you long.

[CINDERS *and* FIREFLY *seat themselves at the table facing* LEWTI.]

LEWTI. Who are you, and what do you want?

FIREFLY. We did introduce ourselves before you collapsed. I think it is hardly necessary for us to do so a second time just because we are meeting on another plane.

CINDERS. I think it is only fair that Miss Ross should know we are friends of a very dear friend of hers, and the questions we shall ask her will all be in his interest.

LEWTI. Who do you mean?

CINDERS. Mr. Peter Arnos.

LEWTI. You call him my friend, do you?

FIREFLY. How quickly you come to the point. It was certainly an unfortunate way of putting it. Love and friendship are, of course, very different things. But we are right in thinking that you love Peter Arnos?

LEWTI. I think I do.

CINDERS. Do you think he loves you?

LEWTI. I think he hates me.

FIREFLY. Hates you! Why should he hate you?

LEWTI. Because before he met me he was single-minded.

Painting was all his life. I spoiled that for him. That is why he came here – to shut me out of his life, and get on with his painting.

FIREFLY. And just as he was getting on well with his painting – you know how well – your brother got a card with a scribbled postscript. Let me see, what did it say?

LEWTI. Let Lewti come too.

CINDERS. Quite right. The postcard happens to be stuck in this very book. Here it is. What an impression that would make on a jury, now.

FIREFLY. So you took the risk and came. And you know what you have done?

LEWTI. Yes, I have spoiled it all for him again. He was on the threshold of great work – work which can only be attained by absolute concentration. Then I came; and I heard that concentration snap like a rope in a squall. And I felt as though I had murdered him. So we went climbing, and – and he fell. You know that if he dies it will be because of me? Yes, I will have murdered him by my folly. O God.

CINDERS. Thank you. I think that is enough about the past. Let us consider the future for a moment.

LEWTI. There is no future for me.

CINDERS. What do you mean?

LEWTI. There is no future for me.

CINDERS. What do you mean?

LEWTI. I had rather not say.

FIREFLY. My dear young lady, how can you think of your own feelings at a moment like this?

LEWTI. Why should I tell you?

FIREFLY. Because it is the only way you can help Peter Arnos.

CINDERS. Because you must be honest with yourself.

FIREFLY. Because you are strong and independent and do not believe in conventions.

CINDERS. And are not ashamed to do the right thing in the teeth of the world.

LEWTI. No, I am not ashamed. I shall be proud to do it – for him.

CINDERS. To do what?

FIREFLY. You can tell us. We are his friends, and yours.

LEWTI. To kill myself – so as to make the path free for him to the light of the sun. He lives for the light as no man before him has ever lived. The cloud must go. Well, what have you to say now?

FIREFLY. I can only applaud your self-sacrifice, dear lady. A genius like your friend appears only once in a thousand years, and for spirits like his the way must be prepared and the path made straight. Of course your action will be misinterpreted, but not, I think, by him. And history will no doubt discover the truth and vindicate your character.

CINDERS. You can go now, and please accept our thanks for the straight-forward way you have given your evidence. My friend here will assist you back to your bed, where you will no doubt soon return to what your favourite poet – I see your name in his works here – has aptly called 'single vision and Newton's sleep.'

FIREFLY. There is only one more thing. It is not strictly our province to advise you as to method, but I did notice a very convenient beam in the next room. And a climber's cottage should hardly be without a rope. This way, please.

[FIREFLY *leads* LEWTI *off, and* CINDERS *goes over to* PETER ARNOS.]

CINDERS. Now my friend, we will come down a storey to your level again. What do you think of things now? You see the girl is perfectly prepared to disembarrass you of her existence.

PETER. You bloody villain!

CINDERS. Really, my dear Sir, you have no right to use such terms to me. I have done nothing but elicit from the girl some information which may be highly useful to you. The responsibility for the situation is much more yours than mine.

PETER. But you want me to exploit it.

CINDERS. I want you to accept it. You see the thing has gone rather further than I thought when I left her. It is plain that she intends to sacrifice herself in your interest. The question then is not, Will you accept the sacrifice, but,

Will you exert yourself actively to prevent it? I confess, I don't myself see why you should.

PETER. I have no will to prevent it. I have no will either to do or not to do anything. I doubt if I even have the will to jump again.

CINDERS. You can put that out of your mind. It would do the girl no good – she would certainly kill herself then – and would do you no good either.

PETER. I think you are right. I am damned both ways. And it is easier to do nothing.

CINDERS. Now listen. I want you to get outside this narrow personal view of the situation. I know it is all extremely unfortunate for you, but the private life of an artist is not the important thing about him. It's what his art does for the world that counts. You know as well as I do that humanity in this machine age is going into an artless world and that means a world without faith or vision. O, I don't count the decorative stuff they put on the walls of canteens. There is nobody who can interpret life to them, nobody who can give them a creed to live by. The cult of the individual is dead. You can show them something beyond the individual, the eternal impersonal force they all serve. You can fill the world with a new vision. Will you do so?

PETER. I tell you I don't know. I can't act. I can't even choose.

CINDERS. Let me put it in an old picture. Zeus is once more hanging the golden scales in the heavens. In the one pan is the hope of humanity, in the other the life of a single poor girl without even the desire to live. You are the Fate which is above Zeus, my friend. Which shall it be?

PETER. If I had faith enough in my own powers, I might be able to choose. But I haven't. In some ways Lewti is a better painter than me.

CINDERS. She has talent only – you have genius. Let me tell you one last thing. Did you never hear that one person by dying can give his powers to another, that the mantle of Elijah can fall upon Elisha? There is something you are still groping for in your technique. In her subconscious mind the girl knows she can give you this, by dying for you. You must look behind appearances and see the realities. She has willed to do this, for you and for the world. Will you accept it?

PETER. I might do, if I really believed –

CINDERS. You fool, you have all this offered you and you still do not know your own mind. I tell you there can be no Mights and no Ifs. You must answer a plain Yes or No. Come. The time is short.

PETER. Do you know what you are asking?

CINDERS. Do you know what to answer?

PETER. You are asking a suicide to become a murderer.

CINDERS. I am asking a man to make up his mind. For the last time is it Yes or No?

PETER. On the word of a suicide then, Yes.

CINDERS. You have chosen like a man, and an artist. Now go into the world and paint. In your pictures people will see the new revelation of power, the new type of humanity towards which evolution is struggling. By accepting this sacrifice, you have begun to kill the personal in yourself. You can now create with all the force of the impersonal, with all the dynamism of the unconscious. And – let us not be hypocritical – your pictures will sell. Now you are no doubt somewhat exhausted. These times of great spiritual crisis do take it out of a man. So I will say good-bye for the present. Let me help you to lie down. Don't be alarmed if you don't see me very clearly. You are rapidly regaining what they call consciousness. Gently now, don't hurry. Ah, quite gone now, quite gone.

[*While he has been talking,* FIREFLY *has re-entered and stands behind the bed.*]

CINDERS [*taking off his professional glasses*]. Well, we can dispense with these now. Not a very significant person, but he might found a useful little coterie. If you ask me, we have made a very creditable job of it, and I congratulate you on your work with the girl. She fell like a ripe plum – perhaps I should say apple to you. With a proper division of labour, Firefly, we should get on capitally together.

FIREFLY. So we're friends again, are we? Well, how about a

little celebrating together? I think we can safely leave things to take their course now.

CINDERS. Hadn't you better go and look after that brother of the girl's – what was his name? O, yes, Michael – he might be troublesome. Keep him wandering about. Mists are your line, I think, not mine.

FIREFLY. Thanks, I'd rather not. I don't see why you need have mentioned him. The Bogey always plays fair in this sort of thing, and I've no doubt he will give us a full day.

CINDERS. O very well. Anything to get away from this God-forsaken spot.

FIREFLY. You choose your epithets with uncanny felicity, my dear Cinders. Come on. O, I may as well leave this rope in a handy spot, where the girl will see it. [*He places it over the end of the bed.*] Don't you think that was a very pretty idea of mine – a real touch of poetic justice? I fancy it will take too. This way, if you don't mind.

CINDERS [*speaking American*]. O.K. partner.

With intelligence like mine and a sense of humour like yours, I reckon we'll conquer this God-damn world yet.

[*They leave through the door at the back of the stage. Curtain rather slowly.*]

ACT III

[PETER ARNOS *is lying on the bed.* LEWTI *enters from the other room and goes towards him. She looks intently at him for several seconds; then, catching sight of the rope, she begins to gather it up.* PETER *stirs, and she drops it again hastily.*]

PETER [*talking in his natural conscious voice*]. Hullo, Lewti, I say what's all this?

LEWTI. Are you better, Peter? I'm afraid I'm not much of a nurse.

PETER. Nurse? What do you mean? O, I remember now. I fell from the Devil's Rock. What a ridiculous thing to do. Yes, I'm better thank you.

LEWTI. You'd better not talk about it. I doubt if you ought to talk at all just yet.

PETER. You don't know me, Lewti. I've been practically alone for three years, and that would be excuse enough for talking and arguing, even if – God, did you hear what I said?

LEWTI. What do you mean?

PETER. Don't you sometimes hear your own words coming back to you like an echo after you've spoken them, the same words but with a different meaning?

LEWTI. Yes, what came back to you then?

PETER. The thing I said first. You don't know me. Do you realise what that means?

LEWTI. I think it means you don't know yourself, Peter.

PETER. No, that's not true. It would have been true yesterday, but now I do. But *you* don't know me, Lewti, and when the words came echoing back to me just now, I suddenly realised that this was the very thing I wanted to say to you. And it's so simple and so true that you won't believe it.

LEWTI. O, yes, I believe it. But didn't you know it before?

PETER. Of course I did. But I never felt it before – that frightful gulf between what one pretends to be and what one really is. Do you know, I believe you can't be really great, or really good until you know how petty and how wicked you can be? And you may have to learn that by experience. You may have to sink to the depths in order to rise to the heights.

LEWTI. Yes, when men believed the seven sins were deadly they were also great saints – and great artists. But have you sunk to the depths, Peter?

PETER. Of course I have. And that's what gives me hope. I might still do something great, if only I could see the way. But there's a mist over everything, the road is blotted out. O damn! Why are things so much more difficult for us than for our fathers?

LEWTI. Don't be too sure of that. They had a struggle too.

PETER. Yes, but their enemies were outside them. They could see what they were fighting. It was so in painting anyway. They were fighting for freedom, the young generation against the old. And they got free – and they painted.

LEWTI. Well, and what about us?

PETER. We? We were born free, and there was nothing left to fight. We had no resistance to overcome. Nothing to believe, and nothing to reject. But little by little we found a new enemy, more terrible and mysterious than any our fathers had faced. We had to fight – ourselves.

LEWTI. You mean we had to discover ourselves.

PETER. No, when you discover yourself, that is the end of the fight. Then you know there is nothing to fight for, and nothing to fight with. I know that – since yesterday. But before that, when it still seemed worth struggling, there wasn't a decent clean battle. God and the Devil kept changing places. I never could be certain which was which.

LEWTI. Have you found that, too? When I was young there was always the shining St. George, and the scaly Dragon. And I thought life would always be like that, right or wrong, crooked or straight. But it's not so simple as that, not like that at all. It's more like walking in a forest with dragons on each hand, and only a distant glimmer of light to show the way.

PETER. And you struggle on and the light goes, and you know there is no way forward. You must go to left or to right, where they are waiting for you; and you cling to the

moment's safety with fingers and toes, but time hurries
you on, and you have only the frightful choice between
them; and the grinning jaws are leering under your face,
and the taloned hands are clutching your hair, and I'm
sorry, Lewti. I had a nightmare you see – one I used to
have when I was a child. I thought I was Odysseus
hanging between Scylla and Charybdis. It's funny how
these things come back again. Only then I used to wake
up to lights and the comfort that it was only a dream.
Now I've woken up to find it's true.

LEWTI. So that's why you wanted the rope – to tie yourself on
to the tree. You did want it, didn't you? That wasn't only
a dream, like . . .

PETER. It *was* a dream. But it's not a dream now.

LEWTI. You've woken up, Peter. Yes, I think you've woken up.

PETER. But *you're* asleep. Wake up, Lewti. Look at me. Can't
you see me hanging from the tree, and the monster
above and the frightful whirlpool below?

LEWTI. Yes, I can see you. But perhaps I can bring you a rope
again.

PETER. No. I wouldn't take it if you did. There's something
holding me back. Nothing but a miracle can save me
now. Go away from me, Lewti and don't ever come back.
I'm not worth coming back to.

LEWTI. I won't come back if I can't help you. But you'll go on
with your painting, won't you? You didn't mean what
you said yesterday, that you had come to the end of that?

PETER. Yes, I shall go on painting, even if I have come to the
end. I suppose you think I came here to paint? But it
wasn't only for that. I'll tell you. I came here to find the
City of God. I couldn't find it in myself – so I came to
look for it in these mists and mountains. But there's a
wall round that city. O I've walked round it night and
day, and there's no way in, no gate, no gap, no chink, in
all that solid masonry. O God, why can't the miracle
happen? Why can't I blow on the trumpet and see the
walls fall down? Let me in. Let me in. Let me in. I say,
I'm sorry – I'm talking nonsense again. I'm still a bit
weak, you know. And I'm muddled. I'm not even quite
sure whether it really happened.

LEWTI. It's I who ought to be sorry, Peter – I know I shouldn't have come at all. And now I've been exciting you too much. You were right, I'd better go. Good-bye, Peter Arnos.

[*She begins to take the rope from the end of the bed.*]

PETER. No. Don't go yet. Read me something first – that is if you can see. It's darker than ever, isn't it?

LEWTI. Yes, the mist's coming down thicker than before. I hope Michael hasn't lost the way. He ought to be back soon.

PETER. Michael? Of course, he was here too. Where's he gone to?

LEWTI. He's gone to telephone for a doctor. I'm terribly afraid he may have lost himself in the mist.

PETER. O, he'll be all right. And I don't want a doctor anyway. He'd only be a nuisance. Sit down. What are going to read me?

LEWTI. There's a note-book here of Michael's and a postcard – your postcard – stuck in at a poem he's been writing.

PETER. O he's still writing is he? Let's hear it. What's it called?

LEWTI. There isn't a title.

PETER. Good. We'll make the title afterwards. Begin. [*Lewti reads*]:

> Only between the rock and sky,
>> No life above, below,
> The thin-spread film of mantling soil
>> Where rose and lily blow.
> And there to music of the sun,
>> On hoof and pad and wing,
> The morris of the months and days,
>> Proud life goes rioting.

PETER. Rather stiff sort of stuff. Go on.

LEWTI. Only between two silences,
>> Mute high and dumb profound,
> Flows on between those viewless shores
>> The river of sweet sound;
> And there all lovely voices float
>> Of brook and tree and bird,
> The miracle of breath and string,
>> The marvel of man's word.

PETER. More like tapestry than painting. Next verse.

LEWTI. Only between the light and dark,
   Blind dark and light unseen.
The rainbow glory of the world,
   Sky-blue, sun-red, earth-green;
And there the tender hues of Spring
   Meet Autumn's aureole,
And wall and wood and canvas take
   The colours of Mansoul.

PETER. Well?

LEWTI. Only between two monstrous deeps
   A foothold of good land,
That never shows a step ahead
   And fails me if I stand,
Yet, would I keep my manhood whole,
   In man I must not stay,
But, faring on, I, more than I,
   Shall know and be the Way.

That's all. He showed it me before we came, but I think I
understand it better now.

PETER. What do you want to call it?

LEWTI. I would like to call it *The Pulley*, Peter.

PETER. No – that's plagiarism. And it's not true either. Call it
The Rope, and put a footnote to say that the rope broke.

LEWTI. The rope broke. And no one could mend it afterwards
– not even his best friends. You must write that, Peter,
not me. Here you are.

PETER. No, it's only a crazy symbol that keeps running
through my head to-day. It would spoil Michael's page.

LEWTI. You can tell him then. He'll be back any time now. I'm
going.

PETER. Lewti, could you do one thing for me?

LEWTI. What is it?

PETER. Stop Michael coming back.

LEWTI. Stop Michael coming back – why?

PETER. I don't want him to come back. O Lewti, can't you
meet him and take him away again? You see it was all
wrong your coming here – I ought never to have asked
you. I just want to go on painting here alone. I've made
up my mind, and if he comes it will all be spoiled again.

LEWTI. I know I must go out of your life. Do you really want Michael to go as well?

PETER. Yes, I'm not strong enough. I can't free him. He knows things I don't because I'm not ready to know them. I only want to paint.

LEWTI. What sort of things?

PETER. Things that only he knows. Things that you can't tell anyone, because they are beyond words. Things that you can't even paint. Things that would make me stop painting, because they are beyond art, beyond life, beyond everything.

LEWTI. Is that why you hate Michael?

PETER. I don't hate him. I love him. But I love him differently from everyone else. Yes, I love Michael just because he's a man.

LEWTI. Isn't that the only real love, Peter?

PETER. No. There are all kinds of love. There are men in general, going out at dawn into the fields, streaming up the road to factories, standing like sheep in queues and sitting huddled in trains and buses – you can love them in a kind of way in general. Of course at first you hate them for their apathy and mediocrity, but then you grow sorry for them, and out of that sorrow a kind of love is born. Then there are your friends, whom you love for themselves, even for their limitations and failures. But there is a kind of selfishness in that love. They share the same interests with you, they appreciate you, you feel safe with them, you live with them as in a warm and lighted room in the middle of a dark world. But it's not like that with Michael. You know there must be something in us greater than ourselves, something that makes us all men, that wants to make us all angels. That's what I sometimes see in Michael, and what I think he sees all the time in all men. Yes, I believe he would see it even in the Gestapo man making a jelly of his face or mutilating his children before his eyes. And I can't see it, and I'm afraid of it.

LEWTI. Michael might help you to see it.

PETER. I don't want to be helped. I want to make my own way by myself. You'll see, Lewti, – I shall be different after this. By God, I'll do something yet.

LEWTI. I believe that, Peter. I believe it with every little bit of my mind and body. I see I can't help you – but at least I won't hinder you. I'm going now. Thank you for all you've been to me.

PETER. I've given you nothing but pain and trouble.

LEWTI. No – you've given me pain and trouble and something else as well. You won't see me again Peter. I'm going to kiss you – but not in the way you once kissed me. Good-bye, Peter Arnos.

PETER. Good-bye, Lewti. Tell Michael I love you both but the devil came between us.

LEWTI. I may not meet him. There's a mist, you know, and anything might happen.

PETER. Yes, anything might happen. So you'd better go now. Stop. Where are you taking that rope? Bring it back, I want it.

LEWTI. But suppose I want it, too?

PETER. You've got no business with it. It's not yours. Bring it back at once.

LEWTI. What do you want it for?

PETER. I don't know. I just feel I must have it. It may be that dream. I don't know.

LEWTI. Here you are, then. I daresay I can find something else.

[*She goes into the inner room.*]

PETER. And he bound himself to the tree by the rope, and waited till the whirlpool filled, and then he plunged and swam between the monsters and was safe. Of course that's wrong. There wasn't a rope really – he just clung on with his hands. I suppose I got it mixed up with climbing. Or perhaps there's a deeper reason. I'm not strong enough to hold on by myself. I need a rope. But the rope won't hold me. I see the frightful whirlpool below, vast, bottomless, screaming to suck down the sun and the moon and the stars and the earth and all men and Peter Arnos and Lewti Ross; and the rope is slipping, slipping, slipping through my hands; and when I go Lewti goes and all men and the earth and the stars and the moon and the sun; and the rope is slipping,

slipping, slipping, and the rope is slipping, slipping – my God, what's this? Lewti, Lewti, Lewti, come here at once. Come at once, at once, at once.

LEWTI. Whatever's the matter.

PETER. Why's this rope frayed?

LEWTI. It's the rope that broke, of course. What are you asking that for?

PETER. The rope that broke – when did it break? There's something coming back to me. Tell me where it broke.

LEWTI. Don't you really remember?

PETER. There's a kind of blank. Perhaps it was the shock. Tell me at once, Lewti.

LEWTI. I lost my nerve on the Devil's Rock. And you belayed and swung down to me. And just as you'd jockeyed me to safety the rope gave and you fell.

PETER. Is that how I fell? You swear to me that is how I fell?

LEWTI. I swear. What did you think? Didn't you realise you saved my life?

PETER. No, I didn't. I thought I had thrown myself down.

LEWTI. My God, whatever made you think that?

PETER. Because I was going to, Lewti. I was saying something to myself, and when it ended I was going to jump. And then I remember I looked down and saw you white and stiff below me.

LEWTI. And you came and saved me.

PETER. No, it was you who saved me – from death and worse than death. I was at the end of things, Lewti. Can you still love me after that?

LEWTI. I was at the end of things, too, Peter. Why do you think I wanted the rope?

PETER. I know now why you wanted it. I believe I knew all the time. You were going to – hang yourself with it.

LEWTI. Yes.

PETER. And I know the reason too. You thought your life stood in the way of the great painter Peter Arnos. So you were going to remove it. Am I right?

LEWTI. Yes.

PETER. And the great painter and abject little worm Peter Arnos was perfectly prepared to allow it to happen.

LEWTI. But actually he stopped it.

PETER. By accident.

LEWTI. Do you think it was an accident?

PETER. No, I don't. It means too much. Lewti, you just gave me the last kiss, the kiss of death. Will you give me the first kiss now, the kiss of life?

LEWTI. Will you promise to go on painting?

PETER. No, I won't. But if God gives me you to make me a better man, He won't make me a worse painter. Will you promise yourself?

LEWTI. Promise what?

PETER. To go on painting.

LEWTI. I can't promise either. I don't know.

PETER. Then we're quits. So kiss and be –

LEWTI. Friends, Peter?

PETER. Yes, friends and lovers too. [*They kiss.*] And painters by the grace of God.

LEWTI. Look, the sun has broken through the mist. Come to the window and show him the shining of our hearts.

PETER [*opening the window*]. The eddies of mist have been touched with gold, darkness is turned to light, the great evil has become the great good.

LEWTI. Look, there's someone coming up the track. Over there by the bridge.

PETER. It's Michael. He is walking among the mountains and they are dancing round him for joy.

LEWTI. He is like the Archangel, and the dragon mists are melting into light under his tread.

PETER. He is going round the landslide. We shan't see him from here. Come and look through the window in the other room.

LEWTI [*at the door*]. O Peter, just now I went in here to find darkness and death; and I never knew that all the music of Heaven and all the light of the world were sounding and shining for me in one little room.

[*Exeunt*]

[*The door at the back of the stage opens and* FIREFLY *and* CINDERS *enter.*]

FIREFLY. Well, it's something to come in by the front door, even into a hovel like this. I never could understand your passion for backstairs work, Cinders.

CINDERS. What matters in life, my dear Firefly, is not the door you come in by, but the door you go out of. We look like going out the back way this time.

FIREFLY. Yes, thanks to your trying to kill two birds with one stone.

CINDERS. Nonsense: it would all have gone perfectly well but for your theatrical emphasis on the rope, an idea in itself perfectly sound, if not made too much of. You always were for ornamentation rather than sound structural principles. Look how you're trying to spoil my new functional architecture already with your Egyptian reliefs and –

FIREFLY. We'll have that out later. The Bogey will be here any moment, and in defeat, my boy, the great thing is to keep up appearances. Never let the enemy know that *you* know you have been beaten. Oh, good evening, Highness. We just came to say, now the sun has set and the curtain is about to fall, how pleased we have been to take a part – however small – in your latest little drama.

CINDERS. I would like to associate myself with my colleague's remarks. I prefer more action myself, and not quite so much talking. But there was hardly a dull moment in the whole piece, and it was most refreshing to see the Unities observed again.

FIREFLY. I would call it a decided success, Highness, and I congratulate you heartily. Of course there have been one or two unusual and even puzzling features. You kept yourself far too much in the background, if I may say so; and, in spite of the rather crude clue you gave them, the happy couple may not even realise to whom to be grateful. But it isn't quite finished yet, and we feel sure you have a first-class ending up your sleeve. As an Artist you have always commanded our sincere admiration.

CINDERS. So with your Highness' permission we will make ourselves inconspicuous and slip out of the back door as soon as it's over. Thank you very much.

Phew! Well, we got over that all right, and you kept your end up very well, Firefly. Come on. It will have to be the back door this time.

[*The curtains are drawn to narrow the stage.* CINDERS *and* FIREFLY *stand on either side of the opening, looking up stage with their backs to the audience.* LEWTI *and* PETER *re-enter.*]

LEWTI. Lie down again, Peter. He'll be here in a minute, and if he sees you walking about – What are you bolting the door for?

PETER. He must knock and enter with ceremony. This is one of the high moments of the world. Don't you know whom we are letting in?

LEWTI. My brother, your friend.

PETER. No. Our child, the man God has helped us to create. Our father, the man God sent to give us new life.

[LEWTI *and* PETER *place themselves on either side of the door facing the audience. Three knocks are heard on the door.*]

LEWTI. Come in, Michael with the love in your heart.

PETER. Come in, Michael, with the glory round your head.

LEWTI. Come in, Michael, with the strength in your hand.

PETER. Come in, Mankind, to the fulness of life.

LEWTI. Come in, Mankind, to the healing of the soul.

PETER. Come in, Mankind, to the vision of God.

[PETER *draws back the bolt. The curtain closes leaving* CINDERS *and* FIREFLY *outside.*]

FIREFLY. Two very emotional people in a most dangerous state of spiritual ecstasy. The curious thing with these mortals is that they always fancy these states will last, and don't bother to go on creating new ones. So the inevitable reaction comes, and then we have another chance.

CINDERS. I think it will be obvious to everyone that the whole thing was only a dream. You heard those three knocks, apparently repeated from earlier on? Well, you know how dreams work. Those knocks projected themselves backwards into someone's sleep, and the whole course of events took place between his hearing them in sleep and hearing them awake. The entire thing probably only lasted a split second.

FIREFLY. If you and I could have the world to ourselves for a split second, Cinders, what would we do with it!

CINDERS. Now don't get melancholic. We're getting on very well. Just a little more forgetfulness, a trifle more narrowing of the mind and the game will be ours. Come along now. It's time we were all going.
[*He takes* FIREFLY *by the arm. To the audience as they go out.*]
But you people had better be careful. There won't always be a rope, you know.

[Exeunt]

(*Curtain*)

KING'S FOREST
or
THE SHEPHERD OF NEW GIFTS

✳

CHARACTERS

MARGARETTA
a country maid
SIMON PRATLEY
a labourer betrothed to Margaretta
ROBERT THE FARMER
THE QUEEN
DAMOCLES
Chancellor to the Queen
RICARDO
a courtier
FAVIL
a courtier
SHEPHERD
EVIL SPIRIT
GOOD SPIRIT
FAIRIES
KING

FRAGMENT OF A LEGEND

A certain Kingdom was accounted the happiest on earth in that it was ruled over by a King whose every action was the perfection of wisdom. The climate of the country was temperate, and crops of all kinds grew abundantly in its fruitful soil; but the pride and jewel of the Kingdom was a certain great forest, which had come to be called King's Forest because it was the practice of the King, at certain seasons of the year, to lay aside all cares of state and wander, alone or with some chosen companion, through its glades, drinking and eating nothing but the water from its springs and the wild fruits which grew on its trees and bushes.

One year a dreadful storm visited the kingdom during Midsummer Night. None dared venture abroad before noon on the next day, when it was found that the whole of King's Forest had been destroyed, by lightning or other agency, during the night. The King, who had been abroad that night, did not return, nor was any trace found of his body, although the most exacting search was made.

His young daughter now ruled over the Kingdom, with the help of the old Chancellor, but from that time the crops grew less abundantly; the people lost their industry and their happiness of spirit; and it was rumoured that the young Queen herself was not safe from the intrigues of her courtiers, from whom she would often endeavour to escape that she might herself search the countryside for any trace of her lost father. So it continued for seven years. . . .

ACT I

SCENE. *The edge of a forest, the trees of which bear no leaves, although it is midsummer.*
[*Enter* SIMON PRATLEY: *he begins to mow. Enter* MARGARETTA.]

MARGARETTA [*softly*]. Simon Pratley. I see you, Simon Pratley. O Margaretta, Midsummer day's to be your wedding day, and that's to-morrow, and there's the man you are to be mortally married to in the morning. How strong he is swinging that great scythe, like a little stick. He's mopping his brow with his handkerchief. On he goes again – 'twill be sweet hay that Simon mows. Why 'tis the handkerchief I gave him last Whitsuntide, with the red spots and the picture of the Queen in the middle. Often have I said to myself: If Simon should be a prince in disguise! Then I would be a princess to-morrow! and what would I not do then? There should be dancing every Saturday; and I would make laws that all men do honest work for their living; and I would wear my jewelled crown and robe when I went among my people. But here comes Farmer Robert. Fare you well, Simon Pratley. I would think shame to be caught spying on a man before I were his wedded wife. I will meet you here to-morrow morning, Simon, 'twill be a sweet Midsummer day for us. The pigs need their swill too, and I must not neglect the poor beasts to go gazing after my husband.

[*Exit*]

[*Enter* ROBERT *bearing a scythe.*]

ROBERT. Ho, Simon, not another stroke I tell you. Sun's down and moon's up, and I'll not have a blade of grass mown but the eye of day sees it fall while this weather's holding.
SIMON. Well, Master, 'tis your meadow not mine; but there's a bucket-like cloud yonder I like not. I saw lightning too an hour ago over King's Forest.
ROBERT. Summer lightning, Simon. Hear it not, fear it not.
SIMON. But 'twas forked lightning, Master, a triple fork, and

speared this line of blasted oaks as I might aim my fork at
a clump of grass, digging my patch.

ROBERT. No harm to the oaks then; they're dead these seven
years.

SIMON. Master, a man that is to be married to-morrow has
many strange and foreboding thoughts.

ROBERT. Well?

SIMON. There are things happening in our time that make a
man wish he might have been his own grandfather.

ROBERT. Well again, Simon?

SIMON. Master, seven years ago there was sap in these yellow
trunks, green leaves on every twig, and birds singing in
the boughs. How came this great forest to wither and
perish in a single night?

ROBERT. Seven years ago this day, and the King to vanish that
same night! It was a fearful thing. You must ask the
Queen's Counsellors that, Simon.

SIMON. The Queen's Counsellors! Much they know about it.
'Tis said they brought it in the Act of God, which is as
good as to say they knew not what did it.

ROBERT. Then ask the young Queen herself, Simon. I hear she
thinks no more highly of her Counsellors than you seem
to.

SIMON. There'd be more sense in that than you think, Master.
She knows the woods and the fields and the creatures
that live in them. Often have I seen her, and hid to let her
pass, wandering at night alone among the thickets or on
the heath under the stars. She'll not lose her way like the
old King her father, and never be heard of more, nor his
body found to this day.

ROBERT [who has been gathering sticks]. This dry stuff makes
good firing. Take a few sticks with you, Simon, and let's
be going.

SIMON. Master, I wouldn't burn a twig in my hearth – not if
the Queen herself commanded it.

ROBERT. Why not? It's dead wood, like all that men burn.

SIMON. Yes, Master, but it died unnatural. 'Twould burn hot,
but 'twould never burn bright. My soul would shiver
even if it warmed my bones. None but our Shepherd
dare burn it, who can do no wrong.

ROBERT. How so?

SIMON. Have you not heard? Our Shepherd of New Gifts? – whose feet have melted the snows that his sheep might pass the mountains in safety? Whose pipe brings shrew and hedgehog and the shy creatures of the wood creeping about him. Who –

ROBERT. Enough – if there be more marvels (for some such I have heard), tell them me as we go home together. But a breath of silence I pray you, before we go. See the evening star in the sky, how mild and clear it shines. What is man to look on such beauty? Ay, what is man? Can'st remember the Shepherd's Song, Simon?

SONG
[spoken from without and performed by Nature Spirits on stage]

O man, what art thou then?
The earth that bears thy tread
Thou think'st it could not will
But be so dumb and still,
The footstool of thy deed.
Yet would it undergo
For thee and thee alone,
Gladly to be a stone,
And suffers woe on woe.
O man, what art thou then!

O man, what art thou then?
The plants that give thee life
Thou think'st they cannot feel
The spurning of thy heel,
Thy sacrificial knife.
Yet they thy strength uphold
With joy that in their death
Thou draw'st thy earthly breath,
And know a bliss untold.
O man, what art thou then!

O man, what art thou then?
The beasts that throng thy hand
Thou think'st could not devise
But be so humbly wise
And rest at thy command.
Yet has their Spirit sought
To be in kind subject,
That thou might'st go erect
And have at will thy thought.
O man, what art thou then!

O man, what art thou then?
The stars that crown thy head
From out the deeps are heard,
The Suns await thy word,
What hast thou answered?
Speak, O thou man, and take
The summons of thine hour;
Awake thy sleeping power,
All things shall then awake.
O man, what art thou then!

SIMON [*who has been gazing intently in one direction during the song*]. Master – Quick – Hide! She is coming. Here behind this bush! [*Pulling* ROBERT *with him*]. She will see us. Lower. Lower.

ROBERT. Who is coming, Simon? What's all this? –

SIMON. O Master, Quiet! She will hear you. It is the Queen, I say. [*Enter the* QUEEN.]

QUEEN. So. All are gone.
    One with a scribble to the Court. Another
    To buy a shoe-string in the village shop.
    How hard I tugged to break the old one! Last,
    And hardest to shake off, old Damocles,
    My medicine, I think I see him now
    Toiling up the steep lane he left me in
    With basket heaped with strawberries from the farm.
    Fools' errands all! And I the greatest fool,
    Still seeking and not finding? Yet this man,
    This Shepherd of New Gifts, the name he bears,

And all they tell of him – I must be sure.
My kingdom hangs upon it. Here I'm safe.
Not one of them dare follow to this wood,
Not even Damocles. They fear it's haunted,
But dare not say so, lest, admitting evil
They must let in good Spirits to their minds,
Against their hearts wished judgement.

        Spirits good,
Who enter here no more in leaf or flower
Or salty root, be yet alive in me;
Wave at my head and feet, breathe in my breathing,
Lift up my spirit to the gracious gods
While here I rest my body. [*Sits*] Shepherd, to-morrow
I'll know you, bring you joy, or bring you sorrow.

           [*She lies down*]

ROBERT. Come, Simon, softly. We must steal away through
 the forest. We might frighten her if she saw us now.

SIMON. Through the forest, Master, I dare not, no more than I
 dare say to the Queen she must not stay here this night.

ROBERT [*pulling him*]. Come, there's no help for it now.

SIMON. Master, we cannot leave the Queen here by this forest.
 And I dare not come – for Margaretta's sake. O will no
 one tell her?

QUEEN [*sitting up*]. Who's whispering behind those bushes?
 Come out, and show yourselves. Come out, I say. Who
 are you?

ROBERT. An honest man, your Majesty, that has mown his
 field this day, and was resting here with his servant when
 you came, and not wishing to disturb you was setting out
 homeward through the forest.

QUEEN. I believe you, good man. Fare you well.

SIMON [*plucking up courage*]. You must not stay here at night,
 Ma'am. You must not indeed. It's an evil place, and
 nothing comes here but comes to evil. Simon Pratley
 says it, and there's not a more truthful subject in all your
 kingdom.

ROBERT. Simon will have it that the wood is haunted, your
 Majesty, and 'tis certain the folk round here will not
 come near it after dark.

QUEEN. A fair warning, Master Simon.

But there is good coming to this forest to-night. See,
here are sticks. Take them and burn them on your
hearth. If they burn bright, good. If not, pray for an
ungracious Queen who would not listen to her loving
subject's warning.

SIMON. I will take them, and did you say burn them, Ma'am?

QUEEN. Yes, and be sure you will have a bright fire to boil
your kettle in the morning. Fare you well.

BOTH. Fare you well, your Majesty.

[Exeunt]

QUEEN. Two honest men; or say one fool, one coward.
One feels a danger, but wills not to know,
And so o'ercome it. The other feels it not,
So sleeps secure, and so is overwhelmed.
I hear another step. No peace even here?
[*Enter* RICARDO]

RICARDO. Madam, your eye looks pleasure and surprise,
At my so quick return. Know then the cause,
I scarce had left you, when I met a post
Speeding to town. To him I gave your letter,
Which I doubt not will be to hand this night;
And now, returned, I wait your royal pleasure.

QUEEN. Pleasure? I have no pleasure. What is yours?
To roam with me this withered wilderness?

RICARDO. Your Majesty, that post so light for you
Was heavy charged for me. My brother's dying,
Would speak with me at once. I have his letter.
I would not for less reason ask to go,
But eagerly attend you.

QUEEN.   Nay, to your brother,
And be his conscience easy as your own.

[Exit RICARDO]

He is afraid. Dying men write no letters,
Nor true men dangle them. Here comes one more,
They are braver than I thought. You have found me, Sir.
[*Enter* FAVIL]

FAVIL. Beauty that shines by night who would not find?
My Queen, I have performed my task. Your lace
I draw from next my heart. Suffer me now
To draw this shoe. As willing to my hand

Sweetly it comes. Would that the heart I serve
Were half as yielding! I'd lace it to my own
Beyond all putting off. See, it is done.
Now grant me my reward.
QUEEN. You have laced my shoe.
FAVIL. Reward indeed! But Madam, let that shoe,
Or my strong arms, carry you from this place.
Here is no bed for Beauty, nor fit couch
For Beauty's humble and adoring slave.
QUEEN. Here is the bed I choose. Choose you your own,
Or stand and be my watch.
FAVIL.   Madam, not I,
I cannot watch for Spirits – and they say
There's nothing else that's living in this wood –
Who know not if such things as Spirits be.
I dare not do it, though you call me coward.
QUEEN. I call you honest rather. Fare you well.
I shall not want my watch. Here's Damocles.
FAVIL. Madam, I go, kissing this hand to you
Which will not soon forget it laced your shoe.

[*Exit* FAVIL]

QUEEN. Another coward, and boasts it, to be told
He much belies his courage; which being said
It so plucks up his soul he half believes
He is most valiant. Welcome, Damocles.

[*Enter* DAMOCLES]

DAMOCLES. God bless your Majesty! I have the strawberries
You did command of me, here in this basket,
With foliage interleaved to keep them fresh,
Which took some care. I trust 'twas worth the doing?
QUEEN. Delicious, Damocles. Sit and share my supper.
Here is a rare one. You have caught me, Sir,
And like a child found out I'll speak my sin.
I did intend to slip you all, and pass
This night in the wild alone; and still I should
But that a rustic fellow I found here
Made fearful speech against it. Should a Queen
Be moved by vulgar fears? I am half inclined –
Dreading I know not what. Advise me, Damocles.

DAMOCLES. Madam, you must think thus. You are a Queen.
The safety of your people roots in yours.
Danger is all men's lot – It is a tree,
So vast it shades the world. But if one leaf
Falls on your path, one rustle of true fear
Flickers its shadow there, your duty's plain.
Forbear, for your most faithful subject's sake, forbear,
Though fearless for yourself.
QUEEN.   True fear, you say.
Sits danger crouching in this withered lair?
DAMOCLES. Madam, there are no wild beasts in this wood.
QUEEN. No wild beasts, no. But what of wilder things?
O Damocles, what mean these withered boughs?
Why has a rot, like poison from a sore,
Run through my kingdom since their withering?
My people listless, loafing in the streets,
As men that wait bad tidings. Never merry,
Unless it be a riot; the songs they sing
Such as make sour the hearing, and their feet
Earthbound even when they dance?
Why do the cottage gardens want their flowers?
Children wear old mens' faces, and grey beards
Speak childishness? The very fruits of earth
Are gross and savourless, and Heaven's bird
Clings to the sod, dropping such leaden notes
As do congeal the earth they fall upon.
DAMOCLES. Madam, thus far my old foot goes with yours,
Though limping where yours leaps. Some superstition,
As strange as pestilent, has late o'erspread
Your kingdom, to whose working I assign
The ills you magnify. This forest now,
Dead since your father's death (for lacking news
We must account him dead), seven years ago
Should have been hewn for timber, and the soil,
Well tilled and tended, had been brought to yield
Crops, I doubt not the richest in your realm.
It may be – mark I do not say 'tis so –
The powers invisible, whose blasting hand
Palsied these oaks, had signified therein
We should make tillage here, which being left

They are wrath against us for it. Yet not one
Of all your foresters will enter here,
No woodman's axe rings out, nor woodman's cart
Creaks in the silent alleys; the poor wife,
Gleaning sparse sticks, will leave this bounteous crop
Unharvested, and see her babies crouch
And shiver at the embers. Remedy
Or means to help I know not, save one thought
I will not even think, lest fancy sail
Too near to danger.
QUEEN.   Think it, Damocles
    And speak it too.
DAMOCLES. Madam I dare not.
QUEEN.   Why?
    Is mine the danger? Then I give you back
    Good as you gave. If my own peril be
    My people's peril, their safety too is mine.
    And I secure in their security.
    Think boldly then. Believe me I half catch
    The thing you fish at.
DAMOCLES.   Then, Madam, be it said,
    I see no help but this. If you this night
    Should sleep within this wood, and witness found
    That morning saw you scatheless, cry would go
    Full-tongued throughout your realm: "The Queen has
        broke
    The forest spell. Up men! Follow the Queen."
    What next? The axe speaks out, the cleansing plough
    Opens the sickly soil, and superstition,
    Like to the blinking owl surprised by day,
    Will look the fool he is.
QUEEN: You cautioned well.
    If morning find me scatheless – as must be
    Where danger's none . . . I'll do it, Damocles.
    Betwixt these oaks, noble in ruin, that seem
    The gate of this dejected house, I'll make
    My quiet pillow. Listen, I hear the clock
    Strike midnight in the village. Seek you a bed
    And happy dreams attend you.
DAMOCLES.   No, good Madam,

Here is my bed; my duty stays with you,
Your watch and witness.
QUEEN.   Not so, Damocles,
You shall not risk old bones on this harsh ground,
You are too dear a Counsellor. Besides
I will do this alone. No matter why,
I will so do it. It is your Queen that speaks,
No more your pupil. Do not provoke me.
DAMOCLES. I see your mind is set, and like the reed
Bow where I may not stand. Yet grant me this:
I have a cloak your royal father gave me,
It is a robe of worth and will protect
Its wearer 'gainst a thousand perils. Make it,
Pray you, your coverlet, that I may sleep,
Thinking it shields you. See, I will spread it. So.

[*As he spreads the cloak, it is seen to be embroidered with snakes,
dragon heads, etc.*]
[*A clap of thunder is heard. Enter the* EVIL SPIRIT. DAMOCLES
stands erect by the QUEEN, *and speaks with his back to the*
SPIRIT.]

DAMOCLES. Master, have I done well? Behold the girl
At your dread word, even as her father, brought.
EVIL SPIRIT. Fool, dilatory fool! you have wrecked all.
The kingdom almost but for your misdeed
Were ours this day, its soul become our chit
To poison with our purposes. Expect
The torment that awaits your treachery.
DAMOCLES. Treachery, Master? Why what have I done?
It is the Queen lies here, the spell is on her.
The Queen I say. I brought her to you.
EVIL SPIRIT.   Abject!
Are you then taught by me and do not know
Our powers have moments and due times, exact
As any God's? Senseless! Could you not feel
The midnight sun that strikes beneath your feet
Had passed the nadir, and his piercing rays,
Falling oblique, boasted the day new-born?
And what a day! The day when Nature sleeps
Her farthest sleep, and earth's delighted soul

Floats to the nearer Heaven, to receive
And utter benediction; the day
You mortals call Saint John's, when no bad thing
(For such the Gods account us) may compound
Witchcraft or villainy, or mutter spell,
Or plot deceit; the day when those small sprites –
Sylphs, salamanders, fays of wood and stream –
Have license free, above the ground, to work
Such harmless tricks as their scant wits devise.
See, yonder are their lights. So soon they come.
We must away. Even on such as me
They have some power, and for you, should they find
Such grossness here, they would rush numberless
As wasps through whose soft nest unwarily
Some ditcher drives his spade, in fury so
Seek out each one a several place of spite,
Twist sinew and stitch flesh, crack every joint
In your old body, and pinch you till your skin
Were spotted as your soul.
DAMOCLES.   Master, I come,
Though not repentant nor afraid. Yet first
I shall take off a jewel from this child
She wears upon her bosom. It is called
Clear Sight. Her father gave it her
That day I brought him hither. 'Tis virtuous
For him that wears it.
EVIL SPIRIT.   Touch it not, lest it scorch
The hand that grasps it. 'Tis through your misdeed
We leave it here. Take up your cloak and come.
I shall instruct you how we yet shall hope.
                                    [*Exeunt*]

[*Enter* FAIRIES]

FAIRIES. Midsummer day! Midsummer day!
What is your fancy? Which is your way?
By one or by two? How will you go?
Over or under? Where do you wander?
Guess! and again! In sun and in rain,
Through foul and through fair, by water, by air,
About and around, now lost, now found –

Can you not stay? Quick then away –
What is your fancy, elfin say?
FIRST. I will ride upon a cloud
And peal a blast of thunder loud.
SECOND. Down a precipice I'll throw
An avalanche of shining snow.
THIRD. I will shake the dusty dyes
From the wings of butterflies
And with them limn a vision –
FOURTH. Where?
THIRD. In the hot and quivering air.
FOURTH. I will lead a swarm of bees
Buzzing into distant trees.
When the bee-man follows, back
And drop them down the chimney-stack.
FIFTH. I will climb into a steeple,
Jangle the bells and wake the people.
SIXTH. Backward I will twist the clock.
SEVENTH. And I will whirl the weathercock.
EIGHTH. I'll make a cruel rider's horse
Throw his master in the gorse,
From the prickles he shall cry
While his beast is grazing by.
NINTH. Moping miser I will meet,
Scatter gold about his feet,
Lead him over ditch and stile
Stuffing pockets thirty mile.
Staggering home at end of day
He shall find his gold is clay.
FAIRY KING. Fairies, well said! We shall see sport this day.
But first your ranks; we'll walk our ancient way
Through this loved forest, once our chief delight,
Now all o'ergrown with ivy, aconite,
Fungus, and every moon-struck parasite.
Your hand, my Queen. Fear not. I shall you bring
Where oft we danced beside the mossy spring.
Follow, my fairies.
FAIRY QUEEN. Stay. I hear a sound,
Some step that breaks the sticks upon the ground,
None of our footing.

FAIRY KING.   Fairies, skip away,
Or seem a bush, or log, or cock of hay.

> [*Exeunt severally, or seem bushes, etc.*]

[*Enter* MARGARETTA]

MARGARETTA. Here is a kingdom come topsy turvy when a
poor girl is knocked out of her sleep at night by
noblemen demanding beds in the Queen's name! I
could have found it in my heart to refuse the gentlemen,
but 'tis my wedding day, and I would have no one
wishing me ill this day. What a dream I was in, too!
Simon was a true Prince and I the Princess Margaretta.
Let me see, I was about choosing my coronet at the
jewellers, when the great shining stones, emeralds,
rubies, termagants and the like, began dropping on the
floor. Drop, drop, drop; knock, knock, knock. For 'twas
not stones dropping, 'twas a knocking at the door. And
so I awoke, and my dream was ended. Well, here I will
sleep till Simon comes in the morning. It may be my
dream will come back to me again. I would not be a
stickler for a coronet either. I would be a Queen and
wear a crown, if need be. Were I a Queen I could at least
sleep safely through the night in my own bed.

> [*She sleeps*]

QUEEN [*awaking*]. I heard a voice. Heaven defend me!   Yet
I thank it that it woke me. I am sure
No wild beast walks the woods, nor robber roves
Desolate moor, nor frightful apparition
Haunts echoing cloister walk, but would appear
After my dream an angel visitant.
Half-strangled by a loathsome snake I lay
That reared its hooded head, yet would not strike
But hissed between my eyes; I felt its breath
Cold on my burning cheeks. How much I envy
The meanest girl that on her bed this night
Sleeps out her dreamless sleep. There is no sound.
Would I were her! Yet as poor Queen best may
I'll seek oblivion until the day.

> [*She sleeps*]

[*Re-enter* FAIRIES]

FIRST. Fairy King, what shall we do
    To these impudences two,
    Trespassers upon our mirth?
    Shall we sink them through the earth?
SECOND. Or in some hollow in the ground
    Shut them with a bramble round
    That no mortal feet may win it?
THIRD. Or split an oak, and pen them in it?
FOURTH. Or freeze their fingers till they wake,
    Then roar like lions in the brake;
    It were sport to see them run,
    Each should fear the other one!
FIFTH. Or squeeze, as once we fairies did,
    A charm on every sleeping lid;
    What she sees when she doth wake
    Each should for her true love take.
FAIRY KING. Back, or your chatter wakes them, little elves.
    Silence! your petty plans keep to yourselves.
    This is no middling mirth. Can you not see
    Here lies a Queen that would a peasant be
    And here a peasant-girl would be a Queen?
    Sure mortals only speak what mortals mean!
    Change me these two, and let the Queen appear
    A peasant-maid to all that find her here,
    The maid like to the Queen. I would not miss
    For half my elfin gold the sport of this.
    Shall it be so, my love?
FAIRY QUEEN. Ay, fairy wits,
    And more, as with our nimble mirth best fits.
    What thing soe'er this changeling Queen may wish,
    Be it for robe, or crown, or spicy dish,
    Or milk-white horse to ride, or page to wait,
    Or such like folly fancied for her state,
    We will attend and straight fulfil her mind
    In what preposterous way we best can find.
    We will amaze these mortals.
FAIRY KING.   Spritely said!
    Fairies, begin the charm; some at the head,

Some at the feet, some touch the hands, the knees,
Be close and corporate as wax-making bees.
FAIRIES. Weave a web of finest air
    All about this sleeping pair,
    Whisper softly at their lips,
    Steal before with finger-tips;
    You to fly, and you to stand,
    Touch a cheek, and touch a hand,
    Semblance without twist or flaw,
    None shall see you as they saw.
    At cockcrow now all who espy you,
    Shall think you her that sleeps close by you.
    You a wench, and you a Queen,
    What you wished for, now be seen!
FAIRY KING. Well thridded, imps; the charm is fairly made.
    Now follow freely through the forest glade.

                                        [*Exeunt*]
[*A Shepherd's pipe is heard. Enter the* SHEPHERD.]

SHEPHERD. Why do my feet bring me ever hopefully to this
    dead forest? There is a mystery here which my gaze
    cannot yet pierce. When I have kindled the sticks from
    these trees, the flames have leapt up like flowers in shape
    and hue, as though the blossoms of seven springs had
    flowered together in one little grate. Yet among the
    blooms appeared ever and again a serpent's head; and
    then the sweet petals curled and withered, and a cold
    blast issued from the heart of the fire. Thus far I can see;
    this forest is neither dead nor sleeping, it is earthbound
    and cannot give back to Heaven its pent-up life. Who
    shall set it free? For unless it come to life again, this
    kingdom will surely perish. I cannot leave these trees
    tonight; once more I must be a wanderer under these
    bare boughs.

                            [*Exit, playing his pipe*]
[*Enter the* GOOD SPIRIT]

GOOD SPIRIT. Immortal Gods I serve, whose face of old
    From rock and leafy wood and mountain green
    Shone clear to mortal seeing, and their Word,
    Breathing omnipotence, through wind and flood,

Sounded, and sounded in the breath of man.
Then, for a space withdrawn, they planned unseen
Through sacrifice – though fall'n in miry ways
And bestial with a Spirit's power – his good.
Now, more than merciful, they bend again
Earthward their earnest gaze on those rare souls
Whose love begets their knowledge. Them I help
Or bring where through their striving help is won.
This Shepherd here, who (for the Gods have seen
And pitied this disordered realm) must read
The secret of this wood, my care has brought
Where he may work their will. I have o'erheard
The prattle of yon fairy tribe, and will
Convert their mischief to this kingdom's gain.
They are our ministers and know it not.
For many deeds in idle mood begun
Find gravest end at last for good or ill.

[*Exit*]

[*Enter a* FAIRY]

FAIRY. Hither hath my fairy master
Sped me on a night-wind, faster
Than the darting dragon-fly,
To watch these mortals where they lie.
What a thing, poor fay to send,
When our revels have not end!
I must find another way
To keep them safe yet have my play.
See, I cast instead a charm
To hold them hid from every harm.
Darkness like a cloud I spread,
Darkness cover foot and head
Forest trees be lost to sight –
Farewell all, till morning light!

[*Exit*]

ACT II

SCENE. *The same, early the following morning.*

[*Enter* SIMON PRATLEY, *uncomfortably dressed for his wedding.*]

SIMON. Here is an ill night to come before a man's wedding
day. Half the folk knocked out of their beds and such a
rumbling of thunder and moaning of the wind that there
was no sleep for them that kept theirs. I would I knew the
Queen were well and safe, for all the old gentleman's
saying she had gone away who came to our house last
night. It was a strange thing now, the way those sticks
burned, the flames spotted with green and blue, and the
wood hissing as it burned, though it was as dry as old
bones. And how the old man laughed when he saw it,
and rubbed his hands together! It looks ill for the
Queen. Margaretta not here yet? I will walk up and
down until she comes, and think it over while I may. It's
little time a man has for thinking once he is married to a
woman. Let me see now. Suppose this forest – why – 'tis
Margaretta sleeping here all the time and I never knew it
[*seeing the* QUEEN]. Now to wake her with a loving kiss!
[*He kneels carefully and kisses the* QUEEN.]
QUEEN [*waking and springing up*].
Fellow, what have you done?
O that I should be so insulted!
SIMON. Insulted! Why I declare she takes me for one of those
courtiers in these fine new clothes. Do you not know
your Simon, Margaretta?
QUEEN. Why it is the fellow I spoke with here last night.
SIMON. It is the fellow you are to marry this day.
QUEEN. Do you know who I am, fellow?
SIMON. Do you know who I am, wench?
QUEEN. You dare to speak this to the Queen?
SIMON. To the Queen! God defend us, the forest has turned
her wits. Come away Margaretta. You will get them back fast
enough once we are married. Come away, I say. [*He drags her
off protesting.*]

[*Enter* DAMOCLES, *and is arrested by the voice of the* EVIL SPIRIT *speaking as from a distance.*]

EVIL SPIRIT. Stay, for you know I may not show my face
    By this day's light, repeat what you must do
    To bring our broken purpose to its end.
    Speak, what are my commands?
DAMOCLES. First, my dread Lord,
    I must procure the jewel from the Queen,
    Touching it with the charm you showed me. Next,
    So guide her steps that she come not to speech
    Or any touch with him our rustics call
    The Shepherd of New Gifts.
EVIL SPIRIT.   Remembering so,
    Perform precisely. Servant of ill, farewell.
DAMOCLES. Farewell, great Master,
    [*seeing Margaretta*] Ha, the Queen. Still here
    And sleeping still. Now may I have the jewel,
    And say some robber took it while she slept.
    Softly! 'tis hidden in her dress.
                      [*A pipe is heard in the distance*]
                    Who's that?
                        [*Enter* SHEPHERD]
    The very man he spoke of. Shepherd, good morrow.
    You come in timely need. A moment since
    There burst a raging fellow from this wood
    Dragging a helpless girl, whose screams made sick
    The very sun. I made what speed I could
    To render feeble aid, but these old limbs
    Serve not for succour. After them, I pray,
    And see no harm befall. This way they went.
SHEPHERD. I'll follow and attempt what destiny
    Gives to my hand to do. Farewell, and thanks.
DAMOCLES. Go and bring back the girl, I will protect her.
                        [*Exit* SHEPHERD]
    All things are for us. First I'll have the jewel,
    Then to remove the Queen another way.
    'Tis hidden well. No doubt she has it hung
    Next to her heart. Gently –
    [*Enter* FAVIL *unobserved*]

FAVIL.   Well, Damocles,
  You keep your watch most close upon the Queen.
DAMOCLES. My good Lord Favil! Slept you well, my Lord?
FAVIL. Not a wink the whole night, believe me. I would I had
  stayed with the Queen. Forty thousand devils were better
  than one such bed. 'Twas a feather bed – stuffed with
  porcupine's feathers. The sheets were old sails with the
  sea not yet dried out of them. A donkey would be glad to
  graze on blankets so rich in thistle. Slept you here with
  the Queen?
DAMOCLES. No, my Lord, she would not suffer it. I was but
  just arrived when you came, and looking to see if she yet
  slept.
FAVIL. Come, be honest, Damocles.
  Do you think I do not know how long
  You have wanted the Queen's jewel?
DAMOCLES. You are ever merry, my Lord. Take care that you
  be not sometimes over-merry.
FAVIL. Is it true, my Lord, what they say of you, that you drink
  every day for your health a pint of ass's milk?
DAMOCLES. Ass's milk!
FAVIL. – and that you season your meat with Fool's Parsley?
DAMOCLES. I do not answer jest with jest, my Lord.
  But see, here comes Ricardo.

  [*Enter* RICARDO]

RICARDO. Good morning, Lords, is the Queen safe?
DAMOCLES. Safe and yet sleeping.
RICARDO. She sleeps late.
DAMOCLES. We must awake her. She is to make progress
  through the countryside to see their sports this Mid-
  summer Day. Already the people await her.
FAVIL. She shall wake most delicately. See, I lift this bough,
  and a shaft of sunlight falls on her sleeping eyes to bid
  them open.
MARGARETTA (*waking*). Simon, Simon –
FAVIL. My second name, I assure you. I was so called after my
  great grandfather, who lost both his legs against the
  Turks and was knighted for being the only man that
  stood his ground.

MARGARETTA. Where are my pigs?

FAVIL. Here, at your service.

MARGARETTA. Why? What is this? Where am I? Three
gentlemen!

DAMOCLES. I felicitate your Majesty on this happy termination
to your night's adventure. The forest now –

FAVIL. See, Madam, how you woke. I lift this twig, a ray of
sunlight falls on your sleeping countenance, the Sun
himself starts to see such beauty, and fearing –

RICARDO. Madam, my errand is happily completed; command me now for what adventure you will.

MARGARETTA. I pray you, gentlemen, make me not your sport
this Midsummer Day. For 'tis my wedding day, and all
should go sweetly with me this day.

DAMOCLES. Your Majesty's wedding day!
Impossible. It is not so notified in any proclamation.

FAVIL. Is there not one here, Madam, whom you would
favour with this fair hand?

RICARDO. This is but a jest. [aside] Yet my mind misgives me
that I should have stayed with her last night.

MARGARETTA. You mock me still, gentlemen. I am no Queen
but a poor swineherd's daughter.

DAMOCLES. A swineherd's daughter! I fear the forest has
turned her head. [aside] My master warned me not of
this.

RICARDO. Madam, you are the Queen. Command what you
will, and I shall perform it.

MARGARETTA. If I be indeed a Queen as you say, gentlemen,
let my robe and crown be brought, and let there be
attendance about me.

RICARDO and FAVIL. I make all haste to fetch them, Madam.
[They turn to go]

DAMOCLES. Ay, it were best to humour her.

RICARDO. Mercy on me! What do I see? O the spell is on me
too!

FAVIL. On us all, man. The Queen will make us her fools yet.
Is this your superstition, Damocles?

[Music. Enter FAIRIES as soldiers, in somewhat oriental dress,
bearing a throne on the shafts of spears. MARGARETTA sits, and
other attendants bring a crown, robe and sceptre.]

MARGARETTA. I ask your pardon, gentlemen. It was a dream, I think, that made me forget I was a Queen. You may kiss my hand.

[*They kiss her hand*]

And now I would have some mirth to begin this Midsummer Day. What merriment have you for your Queen, my Lords?

DAMOCLES. Madam, in yonder village where I slept last night, there is to be seen to-day a performing bear. They say it can count up to eight, spins dinner plates ten at a time, and puts on its own coat and breeches like any Christian, most comical to behold. Let me escort you thither.

MARGARETTA. I will not see it. I hate it when beasts are made to act like men, or men set out to be like the beasts. There are men, and there are the poor beasts, and I will have neither pretending to be like the other in my kingdom. Let it be so proclaimed.

DAMOCLES [*writing it down*]. It shall be done, your Majesty.

MARGARETTA. What other merriment have you? Do you sing? Or play upon the pipe?

COURTIERS. Madam, we cannot.

MARGARETTA. Why, every shepherd in the dales does as much, and you are great courtiers. Can you dance?

COURTIERS. Madam, a little.

MARGARETTA. Show me your skill then. Let music play.

[*A grotesque dance in which fairies lead the courtiers hither and thither to their confusion.*]

MARGARETTA. Enough. I like not your dancing. I see simple folk little know what skill they have. What is there next to do?

DAMOCLES. Madam, setting aside the performances of the bear, which I note your majesty approves not – you are to make progress this day among the sports of your people. It is so written in the orders for the day, and the time set down for starting is already almost ten minutes past – fortunately the precise time which had been allowed for seeing the performance of the bear. Therefore, if your Majesty will start at once, you may yet punctually perform your prescribed duties.

[*Presenting her with a scroll*]

MARGARETTA. Is it so set down?

DAMOCLES. Madam, it is; and well becomes your Majesty.

MARGARETTA. It shall be done, then. You shall come with me, old gentleman, and in every village that we pass you shall proclaim our royal will about the poor beasts. And further to make it the more to show, you shall lead that same dancing bear by the hand as you go, that all folk may see how much more noble a bear may be than a man.

For you, Sirs, there shall be honest work found for you. Call yonder farmer.

RICARDO. Ho, there, fellow! [*Enter* ROBERT]

FAVIL. The Queen would speak with you.

MARGARETTA. It seems you have too much skill in your heads gentlemen, and not enough in your arms and legs. Good farmer, what work have you to do this day?

ROBERT. The mowing must be finished, your Majesty, and the hay here turned; and my man is to be married this day, so there is short time before the wedding and no help.

MARGARETTA. These two honest gentlemen will mow and rake for you. Show them what is to be done, and then away to your wedding.

ROBERT. I thank your Majesty. This way, gentlemen.

MARGARETTA. Why do you stand, Sirs? Must I send my guards with you?

[*The guards take a step forward*]

FAVIL. }
RICARDO. } Nay, we go, your Majesty.

MARGARETTA. See the work be done before evening. And now, old gentleman, lead me to the bear.

DAMOCLES. To the bear, your Majesty!

MARGARETTA. Ay, to the bear.

[*Exeunt,* MARGARETTA *carried in her throne by the guards*]
[*Enter* FAIRIES *laughing and capering*]

FAIRY QUEEN. How like you this our mirth? Is't to your mind?

FAIRY KING. As honey to the bear such sport I find,
My Queen, for this I yield you up the sway.
Rule o'er our revels each Midsummer Day.

FAIRY QUEEN. I shall find sport, believe me. But go, two,

Follow these Lords unseen, and take with you
Teasel and speary reed to prick them on,
See that they slack not. In a breath be gone.
Come, good my Lord, we will away and see
How Counsellor and dancing bear agree.

[Exeunt FAIRIES]

[Enter QUEEN and SHEPHERD]

QUEEN. How can I thank you, what bestow on you
    Who rescued me unaided, when the rout
    Conspired to call me wench, and would by force
    Have dragged me to the altar with a swain.
    How shall I serve them!
SHEPHERD.   Lady, blame them not.
    Believe me, some delusion had o'ercome
    Their simple sight, some spell of the forest here,
    Which I, more skilled through use against its charms,
    Could penetrate, and with a clearer eye
    But not more honest heart, behold the truth.
QUEEN. What truth beheld you, Sir?
SHEPHERD.   I saw the Queen,
    Wrapped in that cruder semblance, as a flower
    Shines from the husky seed, or butterfly,
    Gleams from the sleepy woven chrysalis,
    Creature of light; or as a sculptor sees
    Diana in a stone.
QUEEN.   I thank you, Sir.
    So speaking, you have given me back my Self,
    Who else was all distraction and base fear.
    O let me speak your name! Who are you, Sir?
    And where your dwelling?
SHEPHERD.   Lady, I am a shepherd
    And dwell close by this Forest, in that glade,
    Where first our Mother in her dream of Spring
    Visits the light with golden daffodils,
    So favoured is it.
QUEEN.   Are you not he they call
    The Shepherd of New Gifts?
SHEPHERD.   The country folk
    Call me by many names. For I have none

From parentage, who as a babe was brought
From whence none speak who know, nor by what hand
Left sleeping in this wood.
QUEEN.   I know you now.
You are that Shepherd I have sought for long,
And by heaven's mercy proved before I found.
Sir, being what you are you have taught me much.
O teach me further, if this forest hold
The secret of our ruin; and be not
Like some physicians, surer to prescribe
The sickness than the cure, but say what help
Sleeps in these hands, what must I feel and think
To fight against an influence so dread
I cannot name him?
SHEPHERD.   Little can I say,
But gladly speak to one so charged to hear.
Know then the most that, wandering in this wood,
I have beheld and heard. There was a spring,
Deep in the midmost glade, whose waters gushed
So musically from a bank of flowers
That all who heard where charmed to silence. Thither
Last night I passed, mourning its absent voice
When, as the sudden opening of a door
Sheds light and clamour on some still dark road,
The air was rent with riot; from mine eyes
Scales fell, and I beheld angelic forms,
Wrestling with demons that kept not one shape
But grew by change more frightful; so will rage
The battle huge when Michael shall put down
That dragon old who thinks to sway the world.
I stood amazed, when from the general din
One voice rang out, whose stern and pleading tones
Live yet about my ears, "Where art thou, Man?
Why fightest thou not with us? Man, where art thou?"
Crying "I come", I forward stepped, with sling,
And shepherd-staff made ready, but the words
Melted to mockery, my weapons dropped,
Silence and utter dark rushed back. I fell,
And scarcely knew I fell, repeating still
The Spirit's warning words. "Where art thou, Man?

Why fightest thou not with us? Man, where art thou?"
Thus near I came to help, but could not win
What lies not in my fate.

QUEEN.   I thank you, Shepherd,
You teach me what's to do. I know that Spring,
Oft with my father have I wandered there
And drunk a quickening draught. Thither I go,
To bring what force I may in this great need.
Rest you here, Shepherd. You have given me back
More than my life in mending my poor faith.
Take then this jewel. Wear it for me. Farewell.

[*Exit*]

SHEPHERD. Go, and the Gods be with you. I would follow
But cannot move. I feel some great event
Hangs on her deed this day. Heaven prosper her,
She has a brave heart. I will wear the jewel.

[*He puts on the jewel. Music. Enter the* GOOD SPIRIT, *attended.
A dance, after which the attendants melt away.*]

GOOD SPIRIT. Shepherd, dream not. Thou hast a work to do
That needs a deeper wakening. Look on this stone
And say what there thou seest.

[*The* SHEPHERD *draws a sword from the Stone*]
                          Thou hast done well
To act and not to speak. Take thou this blade,
Touch every spring in the forest till thou come
Unto that midmost issue which they call
Fountain of Life. Strike deeply at its source,
Then be prepared for that thou knowest. Farewell.

[*Exit* SHEPHERD]

Now hither bend your sweetest influence,
Ye starry hosts, and every human heart
Prosper his courage with your warmth of love.

[*Exit*]

[*Enter* ROBERT, *followed by* SIMON PRATLEY]

ROBERT. Come Simon, pluck up your heart! We will find this
Margaretta of yours yet. Meanwhile tell me about the
new proclamation.

SIMON. Master Robert, have you heard it?

ROBERT. Not yet, Simon. Let us rest here awhile and you shall tell me of it. [*They sit*] Now let me hear it.

SIMON. First, Master, there are to be no bears dancing.

ROBERT. No bears dancing!

SIMON. Nor no men sitting out; for all are to learn to dance by next Quarter Day, and they that cannot are to be taxed by the leg.

ROBERT. What else, Simon?

SIMON. All men are to be in bed by nine o'clock in the evening, or half past nine on Saturdays and holidays, and up before six in the morning. And all men are to do honest work for their living, or show good cause to the contrary.

ROBERT. What think you of this proclamation, Simon?

SIMON. What think I of this proclamation? I think it to be madness, and I think it to be murder. 'Tis madness to make some folk dance, and murder to make others work. You can take it from me, Sir, this is none of the Queen's doing. The Lord Chancellor is behind this. And why is he behind it? Because, Sir, to speak without detraction of any one, the Lord Chancellor is mad.

ROBERT. Mad is he?

SIMON. Why else does he go about the countryside arm in arm with a great bear, as though he had found his long lost brother? If such a man be not mad, then say it is I, Simon Pratley, that is mad.

ROBERT. Very like.

SIMON. Very like? Nay, 'tis certain. Tell me, Master Robert, which is the more like to be mad; the Lord Chancellor that is so learned that when he is dead, they say not a man will be left alive can understand a word he says; or honest Simon Pratley that never had a ha'porth of learning to turn his head?

ROBERT. Why, 'tis hard for him that never had any wits to lose them.

SIMON. Exactly; and therefore it is proof presumptious that the Lord Chancellor is mad.

ROBERT. Well, mad or not, Simon, we must find this Margaretta of yours. And if she still will not marry you –

SIMON. Master, my mind is made up. If she still will not marry me, I will have the law on her.

ROBERT. Say you so?

SIMON. Ay, the Queen will give me the law. It is better to have Margaretta at the hands of the law than not to have her at all.

ROBERT [*rising*]. We must find her first, Simon. Come let us be going.

SIMON. We must find her first indeed, Master, but my comfort is in the law. Truly the law is to be respected when it gives a man what he wants.

[*Exeunt*]

[*Enter* RICARDO *and* FAVIL *limping, and bearing a scythe and hay-fork*]

RICARDO. What means the Queen by playing us this trick? Where got she this witchcraft? Every time I stopped swinging this frightful scythe, an ague took me that bent my back as crooked as this blade.

FAVIL. And every time I stopped wielding this fearful fork, ten thousand devils began prodding at me, each armed with a pair of prongs sharper than Beelzebub's at the day of judgment. Yet if it be witchcraft, Ricardo, confess it is honest witchcraft.

RICARDO. Honest witchcraft!

FAVIL. Ay, there is not a pang you and I have endured to-day that we do not richly deserve to suffer tenfold to eternity. For my part I will think no more evil thoughts against the Queen. I will not even wish to marry her. She is above me. I will serve her.

RICARDO. Say you so?

FAVIL. I will say it to her face, and confess my villainy. I am for the Queen now, to ask her pardon.

RICARDO. Then I am with you too. O Favil, would that you had my back!

FAVIL. Nay, I will carry your back, if your back will carry my legs. Come, to the Queen.

[*Exeunt limping*]

[*Enter the* QUEEN]

QUEEN. O it was frightful! Be my mind henceforth
    Feeble as water, that it not retain
    The impress of what I saw. Let me not know
    Nor be myself, if so I may forget.
    All beauty now is bleared, the sure earth reels,
    A rush of blood is in the sky. O Shepherd!

                                         [*She falls*]

[*Enter* DAMOCLES]

DAMOCLES
    These are my master's wages. I have given
    My blood into his hand, addressed each sense
    To serve him only; been his eyes, his ears,
    His hands for villainy, mixed his poisoned cups,
    Smelt out his minions like a rat in the sewer;
    Brought him the King – yet for a moment's lapse,
    A hairbreadth hesitance, he calls me fool,
    Threatens me torment from a hand not slow
    Nor feeble to fulfil. How has he served me!
    Twinn'd to a bear, by clowns rough handled, mocked
    In every lane and alley. I serve no more.
    Let him come on, I will defy him now.
    Each limb and member of his being I
    Curse and abjure.
    If he be Body, worms corrupt his flesh,
    If he be Soul, burning desire consume him,
    If he be Spirit, let him not see the light!
    What thing is this? the country maid? asleep?
    So might the Queen have slept, had I but brought her.
    This is no evil chance. The girl shall serve
    To mock my Master, who shall think, vain fool,
    He has the Queen at last. [*Covering the* QUEEN] Then to
      reveal,
    And spite him to his face. I call him now.

                         [*Invoking the* EVIL SPIRIT]

[*Solemn thunder. Enter the* EVIL SPIRIT. DAMOCLES *neither turns
round nor speaks.*]

EVIL SPIRIT. Speak, slave, what hast thou done?

DAMOCLES. For answer look,
On this thou seest. Shall I lift up the robe?
EVIL SPIRIT. In time thou shalt. But first mine art takes off
A spell that lies beneath it. Now remove,
And be thyself amazed.

[DAMOCLES *lifts the robe, and the* QUEEN *rises as though in a trance.*]
DAMOCLES. Whom do I see?
The Queen! Ye Gods strike off these hands, that are
To evil so inured they cannot leave it,
Though willing good.
EVIL SPIRIT. Call not upon the Gods,
But take her by the hand and come. You are
A faithful servant. I shall repay you well.
[*They begin to go out slowly*]

[*Enter the* SHEPHERD, *and thrusts his sword between* DAMOCLES *and the* QUEEN]

SHEPHERD. Stay, by the unrelenting might of truth
I bid you stay; and interpose my sword
Between you and this soul. Know, evil ones,
Your spells are scotched, the demons of this forest
Are fallen every one, and all your power
Is but a pictured dream. The springs unchoked
Flow with reviving moisture; from the ground
Flowers spring; and every green-capped forest twig
Is more exalted than your diadem.
You know your sign, being wise though evil. Take
The warning of the Gods and go.
EVIL SPIRIT. That I
Should live through them! Yet where the living breath
In creature shape, or thought of mortal mind,
Congeals not to its end, nor any form
Is fixed beyond resolve, I cannot know
Nor be myself. My feet already slide,
The way is dark for the sun.
[*To* DAMOCLES]
Follow thou me,
We shall be fellows yet.

DAMOCLES.   O Shepherd, save me,
    Stretch out thy sword between us. Let me not be
    Cast off for ever.
EVIL SPIRIT. Thou canst not do it, Shepherd,
    There is a bond between us past your power.
SHEPHERD [*putting up his sword*].
    He honours truth who speaks it. Yet, old man,
    Be this your comfort; if the Gods spare him,
    They do it for his servant, who may yet
    For all you sink, find out the more to rise.
    Your helper too is cared for. So fare hence.
                  [*Exeunt* EVIL SPIRIT *and* DAMOCLES]
QUEEN. Sir, there are thanks past words. If all my life,
    And what lies after life, I serve you only,
    Remember you in every waking act,
    Dream you and seek your spirit when I sleep,
    It were small gratitude.
SHEPHERD.   They thank the best
    Who serve, with him they thank, the powers he serves.
    Sit with me then. The rear of death being fled,
    The ministers of life press on even here.

[*Music. A dance of nymphs or of fairies, bearing green boughs
with which they deck the bare trees of the Forest.*]
[*Enter* FAIRY KING *and* FAIRIES]

FAIRY QUEEN. My love, what do I muse on I have seen?
    Canst thou remember what our mirth has been?
FAIRY KING. I do forget it quite. 'Tis nothing now,
    See, high in Heaven the Huntress bends her bow;
    Her shining shafts are silver, but her dark
    Are purest gold. Follow, and we will mark
    Where most she shoots them. Think not of the day,
    Seek new delight for ever. Come, away.

SONG

    Away and away,
    Think not of the day,
    But seek new delight
    In the paths of the night;

But run, but run,
And never be done,
With the moonshine hoar
A glimmer before,
And echoing laughter
That follows after;
But dance to the jig
Of the topmost twig
On the tallest trees
As they bend in the breeze;
But drop with the dew
The soft night through,
To sink in a bower
At the foot of a flower,
In the clear green light
Of a glow-worm bright;
Or slip with the rains
Through the earth's rich veins,
But run, but run,
And never be done,
Through earth and through air,
It matters not where,
Away and away –
Think not of the day
But seek new delight
In the paths of the night.

[*Exeunt*]

SHEPHERD. How little sure are sights that constant stay!
   Those visions are more true which melt away.
   See, yonder come your friends. They know you now.

[*Enter* RICARDO *and* FAVIL]

FAVIL. Madam, here are two that never thought to be mowers
   and hay-pitchers, and never hoped to be penitents. Yet
   mowers and hay-pitchers they have been perforce, and
   penitents they are by persuasion; and being convinced of
   their own knavery against you, they kneel and humbly
   ask your pardon.
QUEEN. I scarcely know what you say, gentlemen; yet if you
   have offended against me in anything, I forgive you

freely. Come, I have need of all my friends about me
[*raising them*].

RICARDO. |
FAVIL. | We humbly thank your Majesty.

[*Enter* ROBERT *and* SIMON *with* MARGARETTA]

ROBERT. We trust not to intrude, your Majesty, but here is a
man would have the law on this maiden, who will not
make her promised marriage with him, and the maiden,
it seems, has grievous complaints against your courtiers
who mocked her this day by pretending she was a
Queen, and carried her away by force from her wedding.

FAVIL. I begin to see some meaning in this, Your Majesty. It is
no shallow meaning either. My legs are witness to it.

RICARDO. It is in my bones too.

QUEEN. Trust me not if I cannot make all well. Your hand,
dear maiden, and yours my honest friend. You have
both been cruelly used, and recompense shall be made
to you. For you, though you cannot be a Queen yourself,
yet you shall have a Queen at your wedding, and for you,
I make you now the keeper of this Forest which
henceforth is free to all that love it and will venture to
walk in it. What say you now, my friends?

SIMON. What shall I say, Margaretta?

MARGARETTA. You must thank the Queen.

SIMON. Nay, we must thank her together.

QUEEN. You do me honour. And now what hinders us from
setting out for the wedding?

SHEPHERD. It ends not here the harvest of this day,
The flower is wanting. Take, O Queen, this sword
And strike (for so he ordered whom I serve)
On yonder oak. Fear not the event, it shall
Be more for happy than for bitter tears.

[*The* QUEEN *strikes on the tree which opens and the* KING
appears.]

QUEEN. My father, how you come to be the crown
Of all this matchless day!

KING.   Be not amazed

Nor think it strange, who know this Forest's power
To see me thus delivered. I have suffered
Not without merit, whose scant watch has brought
Evil not on myself alone.
QUEEN.   Not dead,
Ev'n as my heart foretold me! [*kneeling*] O my father,
A thousand morning welcomes for each day
Our loves were sundered. Friends, salute the King.

[*All kneeling as they speak*]

RICARDO. Noble in Wisdom.
FAVIL. Gracious Lord.
SHEPHERD. Most Good.
ROBERT. The Father of your people.
SIMON. Lost and found.
MARGARETTA. Our sweetest sovereign.
ALL. We salute the King.
KING. Call me not King, my friends, who will not now
    Take up the sceptre left these seven years.
    I have another work, and must be gone,
    To help where my unhelp has ruin made.
    One spirit above all, whose root of evil
    I watered with my folly, I must pursue –
    My still loved Damocles – to him I go,
    I leant too hardly on him, thinking him sound.
    He broke, I fell, but from that ruin restored
    I trust to be his prop. For not alone
    Our deeds of ill, but all that scorn of truth
    Called Ignorance, seeks out its due amend.
    I was the slippery place on which he fell,
    Poor Damocles, and needs must bring him aid.
    Speak not against it: Come my dearest child,
    One kiss is Welcome and the next Farewell.
QUEEN. My heart goes with you.
KING. Fare-you-well, my friends.
ALL. Farewell, great King.
                                    [*Exit the* KING]
QUEEN.   It is a bitter loss,
    That comes so near the finding. Yet in thee
    We have new treasure, Shepherd, passing all

Save that we lose. Be still our friend. Go with us,
Our flock will need thee.
SHEPHERD.   Lady, I may not come,
I am the hired man at this harvesting,
And when the crop is garnered, take my staff
With sad content and go. Yet first this jewel,
Which not without the Gods you gave me, I
Give back into your keeping. Wear it well,
And see your hand sleep not upon this sword,
So shall your Kingdom prosper. You are a Queen:
Become that which you are.
QUEEN.   Go you too, Shepherd?
A life's farewells are crowding in this day.
You came, in drought a Heaven-sweetened shower,
A silence in this noisy world – so go
In silence and in sweetness. Fare-you-well.
[*Exit the* SHEPHERD. *His pipe is heard in the distance. The*
QUEEN *gazes after him.*]
SIMON. The sun is setting, your Majesty, and if it were not to
disturb you overmuch, Margaretta and I would fain be
married this Midsummer day.
MARGARETTA. There are bakemeats too, Madam, which will
sadly spoil for the keeping, and a great dish of cream
with strawberries in it, that will surely turn, if you have
not mercy on it.
FAVIL. Your Majesty, my head tells me you should not stay in
this place another night, my heart cries out that this
loving couple should be married before the day is over;
and if after this day's work there is anything left of me
which is neither head nor heart, it will not sit idle to the
spoiling of a bakemeat, nor be over-stern with a dish of
cream and strawberries.
QUEEN [*rousing herself from her reverie*]. Ricardo! Favil! Why do
you stand here? We must away to the wedding. Your
hands, my friends. You shall have a royal wedding and
there shall be dancing after for all the countryside.
Ricardo, let the priest be warned.
Favil, see that my fiddles are fetched.
There never came such marvels, men shall say,
Nor e'er such wedding on Midsummer Day.

[*The* QUEEN *leads them all out. As they go out the* FAIRY QUEEN *enters and looks uncomprehendingly at them.*]

[*Exeunt* FAIRIES, *except one who remains behind. To her re-enters the* FAIRY KING.]

FAIRY KING. What, little one, why come you not with us to the forest?

FAIRY. I cannot tell, Monarch.

FAIRY KING. Why do you not smile on me?

FAIRY. I cannot, Monarch, I am sad.

FAIRY KING. Sad! How come you to be sad? Are you not a fairy?

FAIRY. Yes, but I have seen tears shed to-day. They are not like the dew and the rain; they taste of the earth and are bitter. What are tears, Monarch? And who are the creatures that shed them?

FAIRY KING. Think not of them lest by thinking you become like them. They are called mortals and are by nature both sad and stupid. Believe me, there is not a creature on the earth that knows his business there less than these mortal men, though they say the Gods help them. Therefore meddle not with their fates, little one; but if you meet with any, say to them (as I would say now, were there some in this place): "Go you your ways, and I will go mine." Come, to the Forest.

[*They run out.*]

CORONATION MASQUE

*

CHARACTERS

ARIEL
CALIBAN
MASTER OF CEREMONIES
MR. ADAM, a builder
SIR JOHN CHAYNOR
LADY CHAYNOR
PROFESSOR REEDLE
MISS PANSY VISAGE
MOTHER
SMALL BOY
EARTH SPIRITS
AIR SPIRITS
WATER SPIRITS
A SPIRIT OF LIGHT

PROLOGUE

SCENE: *The island of Shakespeare's* Tempest.
[*Enter* CALIBAN *followed by* ARIEL]

CALIBAN. I do not like to go in. I tell you I do not like
    To go in.
ARIEL.   You went in often enough, didn't you,
    When Prospero told you to. What did you do? Sweep,
    Dust, make the beds, O you brave, fetch
    Water, logs, anything, and all the time
    The great book lying there. Now it's sunk,
    No more spells or pinches, and you're afraid.
CALIBAN. What do you know? He may have done something
    dreadful
    In there before he went. You've heard his voice,
    The book wasn't everything. The rocks may close if
    someone
    Goes in. I'm not taking risks with my freedom.
ARIEL.   Freedom!
    Then aren't you free in the earth and under it, free
    To go where you like, as I am free in the air?
    Free? and you stand in front of a silly hole
    In the rock, and daren't go in.
CALIBAN.   Do you really think
    That it's safe, now the book's gone?
ARIEL.   I tell you Caliban,
    Were Ariel free of the earth, as you are, what things
    I'd do in yonder! dance, exult, shout, make
    The cave one mouth to cry freedom, freedom.
CALIBAN. I'd like to see inside. But what's the good?
ARIEL. There may be something left there – it's you I'm think-
    ing of –
    Honey, or what not else, a blanket for warmth
    When the wind blows mist from the sea. You'd better
    get it,
    There may be frost tonight.
CALIBAN.   It looks empty enough.
    I'd rather it wasn't. Suppose he came back and found me.

ARIEL. He can't. He won't. He broke his staff and threw it
    After his book in the sea.
CALIBAN.   It's dark inside,
    The lamp's gone out, and it feels cold.
ARIEL.   Hurry, hurry.
    You're in for it now. Bring out what there is.

                          [*Exit* CALIBAN]
                            O Master,
    Master, I feel you still. What have you left?
    A breath, a touch on the wall, a tress of the child's hair,
    Beautiful, hateful – one whom you loved as you never
    Loved me. You promised me freedom, and yet you linger
    Like the sound of the sea in a shell. I hear you always.
    You wrap me about like a cloud, stifling me, choking me,
    Clogging my wings and my words. What have you left
      here?
    Some part of yourself to remind me and bind me? Free-
      dom.
    You promised me freedom unsullied. I am chained,
      chained
    Like the birds to the season and sun. I am chained to a
      cell –

    [*Re-enter* CALIBAN]

ARIEL. Why are you trembling?
CALIBAN.   O dreadful, dreadful!
ARIEL.   You saw?
CALIBAN. O worse than nothing, his table and chair, empty,
    Sideways turned, as he always sat. I touched.
    They were cold, they were stone. There was nothing else;
      I fled.
    I feared to be stone, Caliban stone, no more
    Mouth for the berries and springs, no ear for the sounds
    Giving delight in the night, surprising the day.
ARIEL. Nothing you say, there was nothing?
CALIBAN.   Only a white
    Leaf, four-cornered and flat, such as Master used
    For the signs of his magic, dropped on the floor, all
      scratched
    With devils in black. I saw them dancing.

ARIEL.   Fetch it,
    Fetch it, fetch it.
CALIBAN.   I dare not, will not.
ARIEL.   You must.
    Do you know what it was you saw? A page from his book,
    Part of the master himself. The island's not ours,
    No freedom for us while it's there. Fetch it, fetch it.
CALIBAN. Who's going to read it there? I'm not such a fool
    But I know that a book needs a reader. It can lie in the cell
    Till doomsday for me.
ARIEL.   Supposing a ship, like the last one,
    With men, women perhaps, men who can read,
    Comes to the shore. I see them often, when you
    See only the crabs on the beach. One comes to the cell,
    Enters and reads the spell. You know what follows.
    Thunder and riving flashes. Cramps and agues
    On your poor body. The old toil again,
    Logs, water, fish-dams, a master calling.
    All for a moment's fear of a white leaf.
    Well, you will suffer for it.
CALIBAN.   You think I'll not
    Be turned to stone?
ARIEL.   No fear, if you don't touch it.
    Carry it on a stick. You'll be quite safe then.
    One with a sharp prong point. There's one by your foot.
    In with you.

                                              [*Exit* CALIBAN]
                      O Master, Master over the sea,
    Why did you do this? What is your plan? Your wisdom
    Never has failed. Speak to me. Be once again
    Wind to the leaves of my thought. I tremble. Your will?
    Yet once again! On the sea to cast it, secure
    From the drench, the waves to float it, the vessel at hand?
    Farewell for ever? Ariel echoes – you hear it – for
    Ever farewell.

    [*Re-enter* CALIBAN]
CALIBAN.   Look. I have brought it. It tried
    To jump when I pronged it. Take it. But mind, it
    wriggles.

ARIEL. One thing more. The vessel that hangs round your
neck,
Empty, the drunken sailor's. There's bad luck in it,
Cold fire for hot, the spawn of fiends, that will,
Unless you find other food, bite in your flesh
And suck you dry to the bone.
CALIBAN.   Mercy, what food?
I'll search the shores. Must they be masters too?
ARIEL. Stop, fool. Not all the crabs in the pools, mussels
That blue the rocks, and starry limpets will sate
Their appetite. Fiend feeds on fiend. Give them
This leaf of devils. Quick. Stuff it in the throat
Of the father of them all. [CALIBAN *stuffs the parchment into*
Now, seal it again,   *the bottle*]
And pray that none escaped. Next, down to the waves,
Hurl it beyond the surf. Don't look, but turn
Your head to the land. Run, Run.
CALIBAN.   I go.
More masters – O Setebos!
ARIEL.   The waves and winds
Fulfil your wish, dear Master. O, I miss you.
Can freedom hurt? Grows Ariel half man,
Hungry for friend and bondage? O that splash!
Your last command performed. I will go bathe
In the light-filled spray, and wash the mortal from me.
Freedom! O how I hate that word!

THE MASQUE

SCENE: *The village of Much Newil during the Coronation celebrations for Her Majesty Queen Elizabeth II.*
[*Enter* MASTER OF CEREMONIES, MR. ADAM *a builder*, SIR JOHN *and* LADY CHAYNOR, PROFESSOR REEDLE, *and* MISS PANSY VISAGE *an actress.*]

M.C. Ladies and Gentlemen. Before we enjoy the excellent tea, which Lady Chaynor and the Committee of the Women's Institute are kindly providing in the marquee, we have brought you together for a surprise item, which we venture to prophesy will make the coronation celebrations of Much Newil unique in the whole length and breadth of our glorious country. I believe it is no exaggeration to say that when the news of this astonishing event is published, the eyes of the whole country will be turned with envy, astonishment and admiration on the village of Much Newil. Ladies and Gentlemen, we are able to bring you today a message direct from the glorious and heroic reign of Elizabeth I to a reign which we are now inaugurating, a reign which we trust will be no less glorious and no less heroic, the reign of Her Majesty Queen Elizabeth II. How is it that we are able to perform this amazing feat of bridging the centuries? To satisfy your curiosity, the principal actors in an astonishing chain of circumstances will tell you in turn the parts they played in it. And first I call upon our friend Mr. Adam, the builder. Is Mr. Adam there please?

MR. ADAM. Well, Ladies and Gentlemen, it was like this. A fortnight ago come Saturday Sir John Chaynor he dropped in at my yard, and he told me the roof at the Old Hall was a-leaking again. I says, Sir John, I says, it's a main leaky old roof, and if you ask me it won't be long before it will have to be stripped and rebuilt top to bottom, I says. Not in my life-time, he says, it's got to last me out. I'm sure I hopes it will, I says, and I'll come along on Monday and see what I can do about patching of it.

Well, I comes on Monday, and first I goes up into the
attic to see if the timbers is sound, and I have to clear
away a lot of old rubble and junk to get a clear view, and
terrible worm-eaten they were, but that's neither here
not there, only I says it will be a neck-and-neck race
between you and old Sir John and I hope Sir John won't
win, I says, asking his pardon, but that's not to the point
either, but what I've got to tell you is that, buried in that
junk and rubble, I finds an old bottle, and takes it to the
light to see it better. That's an old bottle, I says, as soon
as I sees it, and what's more it's got an old label round it,
and I tries to read the label and can't, because the
writing's all loops and squiggles. So when I comes down
to tell Sir John about the timbers, I takes the bottle with
me and tells him how I found it in the rubble under the
roof. And Sir John he takes it and pulls out the cork, the
same as you and I might, to have a sniff like, and then he
says —

M.C. Thank you very much, Mr. Adam. You have given a
wonderfully clear account of how you found the bottle. I
think we should now ask Sir John Chaynor to tell us what
he did with it. Thank you again Mr. Adam.

Sir John. I suppose everyone's instinct when they find a bottle
is to pull out the cork — I confess mine is. Well, as our
friend Mr. Adam has said, I pulled out the cork and had
a sniff, and musty enough it was. Then I noticed the label
and, as far as I could make it out, it said: Found by ye
fishermen of Plymouth in their nets and given to me in ye
month of May — then came a date and signature which
were too faded to read, but I thought I could make out
the name Chaynor, and there was a Chaynor, Admiral of
the Fleet at Plymouth in the reign of James I, so that
would account for his being given the bottle, which is
certainly a very old one. But now comes the important
part. When I looked down the mouth of the bottle, I
could see something like a roll of paper stuffed inside it.
With the help of one of Lady Chaynor's hairpins I
managed to get it out, and found it was an old sheet of
parchment covered with an ancient form of writing
which I could make very little of. So I took it to our

friend Professor Reedle, and I think I had better leave the story to him now.

M.C. Thank you, Sir John. I'm sure what you found in the bottle more than made up for your disappointment when you first drew the cork. Will Professor Reedle please continue?

PROF. REEDLE. First a word about the bottle. I consulted the ancient glass department of the British Museum and they tell me it is of Italian manufacture of a kind made in Naples in the sixteenth century. No doubt they were common enough then, but they are rather rare now and the museum only has one specimen. So the bottle alone is an important find. But still more the parchment. It is written in a court hand of the time of Queen Elizabeth I, and seems to be a copy in MS. taken from some contemporary Book of Prophecy – the equivalent of Old Moore's Almanac – of which several specimens have survived from the sixteenth century. The one that is best known, as you are no doubt aware, is *The Princes' Prognostick*, or *The Parfait Mirrour of Futuritie*, a work of great importance in literary criticism, because it contains a doubtful allusion to a lost poem by the Earl of Northampton, which there is some evidence for believing contained a reference to a certain Sir James Prosper, who is believed to have been shipwrecked in the year 1607 and may have given his name to Shakespeare's character of Prospero in the play of *The Tempest*. There is no doubt that our document is authentic, and owing to the excellent state of its preservation it was not too difficult to decipher. The astonishing thing is that it records a prophecy which might well be taken by the superstitious to refer to the happy event which we are now celebrating. The prophecy contains some passages of considerable literary merit, to which I feel my voice would hardly do justice. I am, therefore, going to ask our talented actress, Miss Pansy Visage, to read you the actual text, of which I now hand her this copy. Please don't forget it was written in the time of Elizabeth I – I should say from internal evidence soon after the defeat of the Armada in 1588.

M.C. Thank you Professor, that is all very interesting. I will now ask Miss Pansy Visage to read us the MS.

PANSY VISAGE. It is really a very great honour to be asked to read this quite wonderful piece of writing for the first time in public. I really feel very diffident about doing so, especially as it starts with a kind of magic invocation in Latin – a language which I don't pretend to know much about – which Professor Reedle tells me was meant to summon up certain elemental spirits with quaint names like Sylphs and Undines and Dryads, in which people used to believe in the old days. He also tells me that Latin was thought to be a more magical language than English, I don't know why. Of course it would be much better if the Professor read this part himself, but he insists on my doing so. I only hope you will all be able to hear me and that it won't have any extraordinary effect. [*She reads*]

Terram manentem,
Aquam fluentem,
Aër ridentem,
   Vos invocamus.
     [*Thunder*]

Caelo iucundo,
Ponto profundo,
Imo ex mundo
   Huc festinate.
     [*Thunder*]

Faunos et Dryadas,
Nymphas et Naiadas,
Pleiadas, Hyadas
   Verbo mandamus.
     [*Thunder*]

Claris coloribus
Blandis odoribus
Summis honoribus
   Nos visitate.
     [*Thunder*]

[*During the Invocation the different characters severally put up their umbrellas, the* MASTER OF CEREMONIES *gallantly holding a large one over* MISS PANSY VISAGE. *At the last verse enter from different directions* SPIRITS OF EARTH, AIR *and* WATER. *By this time all the human characters have disappeared behind their umbrellas, except one* SMALL BOY *who escapes from his* MOTHER *and glues his eyes on the newcomers.*]

EARTH SPIRITS. You finer spirits of air, what is your charge
      Since now a maid is queen, and time's at large
      To form new schemes beneath the zodiac,
      Speak first your care, we rest give answer back.
AIR SPIRITS. We are too free of the world. You elfs of earth,
      Veined in the rock that gave Eliza birth,
      Not wanderers like we, your rooted work
      Most prime to this land declare.
EARTH SPIRITS.   We nothing shirk,
      But there's a middle way, for this dedicate isle
      More genial. You freshet nymphs, that while
      Sport in her streams, while wash her rocky shores,
      Your service tell. What notable help is yours?
WATER SPIRITS. In Saturn's age we trenched a sundering rift
      And from her dominant mother cast adrift
      This island ship, new-suited with cloud sail
      To queen the seas. The sequence does not fail.
      Eliza's sailors turn contemptuous backs
      On tidal straits. Not Saragossa's wracks
      Nor sightless mists of Newfoundland can stay
      Their ocean landfalls. Tempests are their play.
      They know their island strength. And each one, grown
      Himself an island, trusts his strength alone.
      Thus far our tale; we start auspicious things.
      Take up the word, you spirits of winds and wings.
AIR SPIRITS. Our task, O nymphs, to raise or lull your seas;
      We blow to scatter, with miracle of no breeze
      (Warding the perilous hour's too quick despair)
      We waft the scattered home. From peaks of air
      We shepherd clouds and down this island's hills
      Drive them transfigured to sweet founts and rills.
EARTH SPIRITS. Spirits, you work greatly. Hear next our toil.

All seeds we foster in this island's soil,
Roots, tendrils, cleaving bulbs – a shield of green
With argent flowers, fit blazon for a Queen.
Our rocks are whispers from old Saturn's reign,
Our stones mutter of life. In every vein
The pulse of ancient power sleeps all unguessed,
Wild heart-beats stilled beneath this delicate breast.

[*During this speech a* SPIRIT OF LIGHT *enters.*]

LIGHT SPIRIT. No island, but a Paradise you tell.
Your gift of prophecy use. Is all thus well?
Already a dark wind shivers the calm
Of your fair words. What is this lurking harm?
WATER SPIRITS. Your name, stranger?   [Powers?
AIR SPIRITS.   Sent hither from what
EARTH SPIRITS. You seem not of our troop.
WATER SPIRITS.   Nor ours.
AIR SPIRITS.   Nor ours.
LIGHT SPIRIT. I am a spirit of light. Each several flower
Grows to the sun, yet in due place and hour.
I am the beam of Albion. My task
To raise this island flower. No further ask.
WATER SPIRITS. We see through mists of centuries, yet feel
This island race each in himself congeal,
Prisoner to thought, the liberal soul sense
Withered, a centre sans circumference.
EARTH SPIRITS. We see him drudging in earth's veins, and still
Slave to the force he wakens, all his will
Bowed to a chthonic measure, to disembower
Careless, if so he multiply a power.
AIR SPIRITS. We see him ride the clouds, yet not more near
To heaven or self, scattering greater fear
The more he greatly dares, our sheltering breath
An impotent fence against the flying death.
WATER SPIRITS. All this we see darkly, because we see
Pleased with new powers and earth's rich mastery
His vision sets new horizons, and we slide
Over the viewless rim, forgot, denied.
And we once lost, how shall his limited eye
Feed on a spirit more infinitely high?

LIGHT SPIRIT. Sad words but true you speak. I backward sent
    By potent spells declare great Time's event,
    Bringing from one far off auspicious day
    A Torch word from a Mother to a May.
    You serve a Virgin Queen. An age shall be
    Queened by a Mother not less loved than she,
    Both from a third bearing a syllabled name
    Whose son did in the wilderness proclaim
    That hearts be changed with fierce prophetic breath,
    A name of honour rare, Elizabeth.
    O would this island heed that prophet's cry
    And with new heart seek out an empery
    Beyond the Western main, beyond the skies,
    Bartering love for wisdom's merchandise,
    That were a reign to equal in renown
    The days when great Eliza wears the crown,
    To whose large age a suppliant are we
    For favouring grace and help that this may be.
EARTH SPIRITS. What shall we say?
WATER SPIRITS.   He speaks beyond our scope.
AIR SPIRITS. Yet shines the sun more brightly with this hope.
EARTH SPIRITS. ⎫ Stranger, our word is pledged and still shall
WATER SPIRITS. ⎬   be
AIR SPIRITS.   ⎭ To keep these treasured acres fresh and free.
    The rest between this island people lies
    And your great powers. We know not mysteries.
    And yet we know, should all your wishes flower,
    And souls rise equal to their spirit's hour,
    What joy would be, when every rose should sing
    And all the steepled trees in triumph ring.
    Then, token of our pledge, join hand to hand
    With solemn dance to consecrate this land.

    [*Here follows a dance, after which the* SPIRITS *vanish severally,
    the* SPIRIT OF LIGHT *alone remaining.*]

LIGHT SPIRIT. None but the wise and innocent have known
    This sight. The rest have heard a voice alone.
    [*As he goes out he gives the* SMALL BOY *a rose and a lily.*]
M.C. That is the end of the MS., Ladies and Gentlemen. The
    storm seems to have passed away now. In fact I think we

need hardly have put up our umbrellas. We are all most grateful to Miss Pansy Visage for reading so beautifully to us in spite of the difficult circumstances. Her rendering, you will agree, was so dramatic that we could almost see the characters before our eyes. We owe her a deep debt of gratitude. I am sure you are all now ready for a cup of tea, which (as I said before) has been kindly provided by Lady Chaynor and the Committee of the Women's Institute in the marquee. Thank you all very much.

[*All leave except the* SMALL BOY *and his* MOTHER *who is fast asleep in her chair behind her umbrella.*]

BOY. Mother – mother – mother. Who were they?

MOTHER. You naughty boy. You've been picking the flowers.

BOY. No, I haven't. One of them gave them to me, the tall one in the yellow dress. Who were they, mother?

MOTHER. What are you talking about, you silly boy?

BOY. The people who danced. Who were they, mother?

MOTHER. Bless my soul! The boy's been dreaming. I don't wonder either. Such a long lecture, I nearly fell asleep myself. Come along quickly, or we shall be late for tea. But don't go picking any more flowers that's all.

BOY. No, mother. But one day I *shall* find out who they were.

[*Distant thunder as they go out.*]

THE MASQUE OF MIDAS
or
ASSES' EARS

*

CHARACTERS

MIDAS	APOLLO
HIS QUEEN	PAN
CREON, his Counsellor	DIONYSUS
TIMON, a Barber	SILENUS
PRAXINOE, his Wife	TMOLUS
VINEDRESSERS	NYMPHS
CRIER	SUN SPIRITS
TRUMPETER	SATYRS
SLAVES	REEDS

There are two legends about King Midas, which have been joined together in the Masque here presented.

The first legend is that when the old Satyr Silenus, who had been foster-father to Dionysus, was found wandering in the King's vineyard, Midas sent him home to Dionysus, who, in return, granted Midas any gift he might choose to ask. He asked that anything he touched should turn to gold, not foreseeing the consequences of his wish. Ultimately, he was able to get rid of his magical power by washing his hands in the waters of the river Pactolus, whose bed from that time bore golden sands.

The other legend is that Midas was once present when Pan and Phoebus Apollo held a musical contest of lyre against pipes. Old Tmolus, the god of a neighbouring mountain, who had been asked to act as judge, had no hesitation in giving the prize to Apollo — but Midas preferred the music of Pan. Apollo thereupon changed his ears to asses' ears — a change which Midas endeavoured to keep secret, but which was discovered in the manner portrayed in the Masque.

The lyre of Phoebus Apollo represented to the Greeks the harmony of the great universe, while pipes, which are informed with the breath of man, expressed purely earthly and human forces.

The Sun God was still in the heavens, and man had not yet witnessed the Word that became flesh. It is worth remembering that, though Apollo is the God of Light, he is not the God of the physical sun. The oracle of Apollo at Delphi was open only in the summer; but in the winter, when the sun god Helios went to the South, Apollo departed to the North.

PART 1

SCENE. *King Midas' Vineyard by the River Pactolus.*
[*Enter* VINEDRESSERS *and* BOYS]

STREPHON. As soon as the king comes, lads, start working like
  seven devils. No easing your back or mopping your
  brow while he's about. If he speaks to you, don't look up
  when you answer or your back will be the sorer for it.
DAMON [*to* FIRST BOY]. Have you got the basket of weeds, boy?
  Spill them round the roots of the vines, and pick them up
  like mad when he comes.
PHILEMON. Pull some of the vines down there, and have your
  knives and twine ready to tie them up if he looks this way.
DAMOETAS [*to* SECOND BOY]. You boy, here is a jar of grubs and
  caterpillars. Put 'em on the leaves and take 'em off again.
  And don't whistle.
FIRST BOY. Father, why must I spill the weeds just in order to
  pick them up again?
DAMON. What? Do you think you can just stand about idling,
  when the king's inspecting the vineyards? You just try it,
  my boy.
STREPHON [*pointing*]. That's the way the king will come –
  through the palace gate. I shall see him in good time
  from up here. So when I cough – like this – you just go to
  it. We'll try it out. Ready now.

[*He coughs, and they all work. While they work* SILENUS *staggers
in unobserved and collapses among them.*]

SILENUS. Help, help, good people!

[*They stop work and gather round.*]

FIRST BOY. Father, it's a satyr! I've never seen one before. Can I
  touch him? He's all hairy, like Uncle George.
DAMON. Hold your tongue, boy. Here, fetch a flask of water.
  Lads, we're in luck. The vines will flourish now.

[*The water is brought and poured between the satyr's lips.*]

SILENUS [*coughing*]. Apollo, Apollo, what a drink is yours! I

would give six skins of this for a noggin of good wine.
Where is my master, Dionysus? Give me some wine.

PHILEMON. We have no wine, O Satyr . . . King Midas takes it
all from us.

DAMOETAS. We tend his vineyards but do not drink his wine.
He sells it overseas for gold.

SILENUS. Are these the vineyards of King Midas? I have been
wandering, then, like my old wits. Help me home, good
people.

STREPHON. Alas, we dare not leave the vineyard. King
Midas——

[*The* KING *with his attendants has entered unobserved.*]

MIDAS. Why are these men not working, Creon? Let them be
severely beaten for idleness.

[*The* VINEDRESSERS *begin to work.*]

And what is this old rascal doing in my vineyard?

STREPHON. He is a satyr, your Majesty. He came while we were
dressing the vine and called for help. If he will touch the
vines, there'll be a rich harvest.

MIDAS. Is this true? Bring the satyr before me. It may be worth
our while to humour him. What do you think, Creon?

CREON. A satyr's touch is very potent, my lord.

MIDAS. Your name and business here?

SILENUS. I am Silenus, the old Silenus, who reared young
Dionysus when his mother died. Quick Hermes brought
him to my valley and set him on a bank of flowers and
left him there. I found him lying among their scattered
petals, with his little fists crushing wild strawberries to
his mouth. So I took him to my cave and reared him –
the great teacher of the crafts of life. From him you have
the threefold harvest, corn and oil and wine. Now I am
old he cares for me as well as I once cared for him. Send
me back to him, O King, and he will grant you whatever
wish is dearest to your heart.

MIDAS. What shall I ask for, Satyr?

SILENUS. This is the wisdom of man, O King. So fickle is his
fate that not to be born is the best thing he can wish for;

but if he cannot wish for that, the next best is to die. Ask
my master for the boon of death, O King.

MIDAS. What, Satyr, Midas with all his gold to die? Let him
rather ask to be exempt from age and death. But first you
must touch the vines in my vineyard. I hear your hand
can make them yield as never before.

CREON. Indeed, my lord, he has a golden touch.

MIDAS. A golden touch! You have said the word, Creon. Satyr,
this is my wish – that whatsoever I touch shall turn to
gold.

QUEEN. O my husband, this is folly. You have gold enough in
your treasury. Think only——

MIDAS. Silence, the king has wished, and will not unsay his
wish.

SILENUS. The king has wished. I bear his wish to my Master.

MIDAS. But first to my vines, Silenus. You must touch my
vines.

SILENUS. And you will then send me home, O King?

MIDAS. Assuredly, my slaves shall bear you.

SILENUS. Then I will touch your vines. And let the vinedressers
sing, while I put out my hand.

[*They sing a song while* SILENUS *touches the vines.*]

SONG FOR SILENUS

Satyr with the cloven heel
    Leave your print upon this land,
Bud and stem and tendril steal
    Life abounding from your hand.

Half of you is mother earth,
    Through your veins her secrets rise,
What is human knowledge worth?
    Leave it, satyr, and be wise.

Fingers green have life and power
    More than books or brain can own;
Touch a bud, it grows a flower;
    Touch a flower, the fruit falls down.

Earth's a berry ripe and round,
Cloven heel can pierce its skin;
Satyr, tread upon this ground,
Draw the wine of life within.

SILENUS. Your vines are touched, Monarch. Your promise.
MIDAS. And yours from your master Dionysus, Satyr. Slaves
carry him away. A golden touch, Creon, a golden
touch. . . . Apples of gold shall fall around me in my
orchards, the fountain in my palace shall run gold, the
walls of my treasury shall be themselves a treasure. How
slow and toilsome seems now the work of these slaves in
my vineyard. But work slaves, work. I must have gold. I
must have gold.

[*Exit* MIDAS]

QUEEN. I have a heavy heart, Creon. If he gets his wish, it will
be a black day for my husband. Why did the satyr bid
him ask for death?
CREON. Perhaps to try him, Lady. A black day indeed.

[*Exit* QUEEN, CREON *and attendants.* STREPHON *whistles and
the* VINEDRESSERS *leave their work.*]

FIRST BOY. Father, will King Midas get the golden touch?
DAMON. Silenus said so, boy.
SECOND BOY. Then what will he do when he wants to eat and
drink, Father? He can't swallow gold.
PHILEMON. Dang it, the boy's right; but it won't do to tell him
so, or he'll get a swollen head. Did you never see a
conjurer swallow a poker, boy?
SECOND BOY. Yes, Father, I saw it with my own eyes last
Vintage Fair.
PHILEMON. And if a conjurer can swallow a poker, do you
think a king can't swallow a morsel of gold, eh?
SECOND BOY. But the conjurer didn't live on the poker, Father.
I saw him tucking in afterwards in the kitchen and it
wasn't pokers.
PHILEMON. And how do you know what kings live on, boy?
Hold your tongue.

[*A sound of piping is heard in the distance.*]

ALL. It's the God! It's Pan himself! Pan, Pan, the mighty Pan,
etc.

[*Enter* PAN *with* NYMPHS *in attendance*. PAN *plays his pipe and*
VINEDRESSERS *and* NYMPHS *dance*.]

PAN. Fellows, will you stare and sigh,
    When these nymphs are standing by?
    Join your hands and dance your pleasure,
    Pan will play a tripping measure.

[*They dance*]

    Nymphs and dressers of the vine,
    Heard you ever tunes like mine?
    Could Apollo better please?
    Can he harp you airs like these?
ALL. Down with Phoebus and his lyre,
    Your pipes alone have life and fire.
PAN. Then Apollo, come and try
    Against my reeds your minstrelsy,
    Through their vents a spirit sings
    Mightier than your seven strings.
    Answer, or for aye be dumb.
    Pan defies you. Will you come?
ALL. Answer, or for aye be dumb.
    Pan defies you. Will you come?

[APOLLO *appears high up*.]

APOLLO. Who calls me from my tower of light
    Where I hide from human sight?
    Throngs of mortals here I see
    Met in high festivity,
    Nymphs by swains from dancing led
    And one with horns upon his head –
    Pan, by thunder! What's your will?
PAN. Phoebus, try with me your skill,
    Wake your strings to sweetest sound,
    I will answer with a round.
    Paris gave the prize to Venus,
    Choose we, too, a judge between us,
    Which can lovelier music breed,

Golden strings or hollow reed?
Though your lyre has built up cities,
I'll wager I've the sweeter ditties.
APOLLO. Pan, this is a foolish game,
So you'll find it to your shame.
In my seven strings resound
Echoes from the crystal round,
Every planet bears his tone –
Will you pit your pipes alone
Against the music of the spheres?
Have you pipes, and have not ears?
But, to please you, I'll agree
To harp a measure 'gainst your glee.
Tmolus here shall judge our skill,
Ancient Lord of this green hill.
I'll go beg of him this boon –
Meet me here to-morrow noon.
PAN. Farewell Phoebus, see you soon.
By to-morrow,
Lord Apollo,
The wreath on your head
I'll wear it instead,
And by the same token
Your lyre shall be broken,
Your music forsaken,
And Pan pipes shall be
The sole minstrelsy
For ever and aye,
Hurray, Hurray!
Come nymphs, away.

[*Exeunt* PAN *and* NYMPHS]

PHILEMON. Tmolus will never do such a thing, he's far too wise
an old bird. Panpipes are all right for a country dance,
but when it comes to real music, I've heard Apollo
playing in the hills of a summer evening till every bone in
my body began singing for the sweetness of it. 'Twould
be madness to give the prize to Pan.
DAMOETAS. But that's his artfulness. Did you never hear of
Midsummer Madness? All the folk go mad at mid-

summer, and no one madder than old Tmolus; so
naturally he'll give the prize to Pan.

DAMON. What an artful rogue Pan is! Apollo will never think
of that.

DAMOETAS. And the beauty of it is, 'tis Lord Apollo himself
makes the folk mad with all the sparkle and joy of a
midsummer day.

STREPHON. Lads, the king's returning. Back to work. Quick.

[*They work. Enter* MIDAS *and his train with* DIONYSUS.]

MIDAS. Send these slaves away, Creon. Now, Lord Dionysus,
tell me again what must I do?

DIONYSUS. Here in this vineyard drink this charmèd cup,
'Tis bitter-sweet. But spare not, drink it up.
Silenus, my old nurse, you found and saved,
Then with this drink I grant the boon you craved.
The longed for alchemy your hand shall hold –
What thing you touch, that thing shall turn to gold.
Treasure and King, farewell. Long may you live
To take your pleasure of the gift I give.

[*Exit* DIONYSUS]

QUEEN. My Lord, you have your wish. Be careful what you
touch.

MIDAS. Now am I the richest monarch in the world, if the
word of Dionysus be true. Gently, gently, I will enjoy the
new feast delicately. [*He plucks a vine leaf which turns to
gold.*] Behold – Dionysus is a god of power. The intricate
pattern of this leaf in purest gold! My Queen, a golden
vine leaf for your hair. And now these young grapes shall
bear a bloom no autumn sun could ever bring them. [*He
plucks a cluster of grapes.*] Ha! The first fruits of my harvest.
I give them, my Queen, to you as well. Wear them in
remembrance of this happy day. A stone at my feet. The
King stoops to a stone, and raises on high a nugget of
gold. O joy! O joy! All things I touch are gold. Lord
Dionysus, what a gift you have given. O lucky day! O
happy king! Kiss me, my Queen. Your hand, my Creon.
[*They start back.*] What is this? Do you start away from me?

QUEEN. My husband, it is enough to-day that you have won
the golden touch.

CREON. Your servants are bringing you refreshment, Sire. You will need to rest after your labours.

[*Enter slaves with a table of fruit and wine.*]

MIDAS [*looking perplexed for a moment, and then breaking into a laugh*]. Ha! Ha! I see they are jealous. The whole world will envy you, Midas, as these two are envying you now. Slaves, set the table here. I have a strange hunger on me – and a thirst as well. Sit, my Queen. Let us eat and drink. Forget your jealousy. You have but to ask, and any little thing you bring I will touch and turn it for you into gold. [*He puts an apple to his mouth.*] Slaves – what joke is this? My teeth will break. What, gold as well? Lord Dionysus, I did not mean this. I must eat and drink like other men. I cannot eat this gold. Slave, put a goblet to my lips. (*He spits out.*] Gold, gold, gold. Dionysus, Dionysus, what have you done to me? What have you done to me? [*He storms out.*] Dionysus! Lord Dionysus!

QUEEN. After him, good Creon. He may do mischief to himself.

[*Exit* CREON]

Take this food away. Leave me alone. Stop. Take these too. [*Giving the vine leaf and grapes.*] This misbegotten gold burns my head like fire. O Midas, Midas, could your touch quicken this leaf to green again!

[*Exeunt* SLAVES]

O my husband, had you not gold enough? Where has your greed led you? Lord Dionysus, take away your gift, and let my husband live. [PAN's *pipes are heard in the distance.*] Who comes piping here? I will hide and see. It may be some messenger of the gods.

[*Enter* PAN *with* NYMPHS *singing.*]

SONG FOR PAN

Who comes piping here
With an alien note,
On a sun-dried reed
Mimicking a throat?
With his crafty knife

Moulding sharp and clear
Half the breath of life –
Who comes piping here?

Gods gave tongue to birds
And the crooning beach,
Winds and waterfalls
Use a godlike speech;
But this hollow stalk
Breathing sad or gay,
This the gods had not,
Who has found this way?

Who has found this way?
Why, the mighty Pan,
Making reeds rejoice,
Giving gifts to man.
Blow, Man, blow your will,
Phoebus' reign is done,
Walk in your own light,
Go against the sun.

QUEEN. Pan, Pan – you serve the Lord Dionysus.
PAN. He is my master, Lady.
QUEEN. Can you take me to him, good Pan?
PAN. What for, Lady?
QUEEN. For my husband, King Midas, who is in deadly peril unless the Lord Dionysus will help him.
PAN. Are you the Queen then?
QUEEN. I am indeed.
PAN. Then promise me one thing and I will take you.
QUEEN. Anything, good Pan, if you will lead me to him.
PAN. To-morrow at noon in this place a mighty contest will take place. Apollo will play and Pan will play and Tmolus will judge between us, and all the people will be here in their places to see. Bring King Midas here, Lady. I know his voice will be for me, and Tmolus will never dare to give the prize to Apollo in the presence of the King. Promise me this, Lady, and I will lead you to the Lord Dionysus.

QUEEN. I promise.

PAN. Follow me then. But stop. He is visiting the vines to-day, and cannot be far away. He will surely hear if I blow the harvest call.

[PAN *blows a call on the pipes.* DIONYSUS *enters.*]

DIONYSUS. Who paeans harvest on a lusty pipe
Before my clustered grapes are purple-ripe?
Is there some monstrous need? Or are you quite
Drunk, ere the vintage, with the summer light?

PAN. The lady's is the need, though mine the call.

QUEEN. Great Dionysus, at your feet I fall –
My husband Midas craved a foolish boon,
He asked too rashly, and you gave too soon,
In torment now he learns this truth to hold,
One living grape is worth a world of gold,
From his parched throat the dusty metal cries,
Take back your gift, great Lord, or else he dies.

DIONYSUS. Then from King Midas' wish I charge you learn,
Ask not unthought the thing for which you yearn.
The fruit you crave some hidden worm may hold,
Your golden dream may wake to Midas' gold, –
The gods give better when the gods withhold.
This foolish husband, lady, if you'd save,
In waters of Pactolus bid him lave
Five times the palms of his gold-itching hands –
The golden gift will sink upon the sands,
And barren shall those gleaming sands remain,
But Midas eat the living fruit again.

QUEEN. My thanks, Great Lord. He in Pactolus here
His hands shall wash to cleanse the golden smear.
And dry them, when each perfect washing's done,
In the bright rays of the restoring sun.
Farewell! Ah, would the gods might still refuse
Those gifts to men that men will still misuse.

[*Exit* DIONYSUS]

PAN. And will you bring King Midas here to-morrow as you said, Lady?

QUEEN. Assuredly, good Pan. You have faithfully performed your part, and I wish you good-bye.

[*Exit the* QUEEN]

PAN. Farewell, Lady. And now, one favour, good vinedressers, and Pan will promise to play for your dances
for evermore.

VINEDRESSERS. What is it, Pan?

PAN. When I play my pipes to-morrow, begin the dressing of
your vines. It will please King Midas, and he will give his
voice for me. Will you do this?

VINEDRESSERS. We will, we will.

PAN. Then the prize will surely be mine. Nymphs and all good
people, scatter and take your ease. When you come
together again, it shall be to-morrow. It will be worth
your coming for, I promise you, you shall see the
Triumph of Pan.

PART 2

SCENE. *The King's Vineyard.*

[*Enter two* SUN SPIRITS, *with chalices of water.*]

FIRST SPIRIT. Sister, why has the Lord Apollo sent us to scatter the heavenly dew upon this place?

SECOND SPIRIT. Hist, speak quietly lest some mortal hear. We must perform our task before the sun comes out from yonder cloud, or Midas and his train will return and mar our rite.

FIRST SPIRIT. Sprinkle your dew on this side, and I will take the other. And while you sprinkle, whisper your secret in words as gentle as the drops that fall upon the flowers.

SECOND Spirit. Then know that, as a fire goes dull and grey when the bright sun chances to fall upon it, so when the midsummer light floods the world, the little light of man's wit grows pale and thin. Mortals at this time give themselves to all manner of folly, and quite forget what small store they have of sense and judgement.

FIRST SPIRIT. I have heard they call it Midsummer Madness. And they say those men are the wisest who at this season can most play the fool. So strange is the life of these mortals.

SECOND SPIRIT. So it is, sister. But in this place there must be no folly. For the Lord Apollo will here compete this day, string against pipe, with the mighty Pan; and there must be no foolish judgement in those who hear him play. This dew we scatter will keep their wits cool, that no light from the world without may darken the light of their understanding.

FIRST SPIRIT. All save those who are born foolish?

SECOND SPIRIT.All save them. Such must be led where they see their own folly as in a mirror. But even then it is hard for them to know it and to change.

FIRST SPIRIT. I have heard that this king – but see, the edge of the cloud is already gilded, and my bowl is empty.

SECOND SPIRIT. And mine too. Our work is done and the sun returns. Away.

[*Exeunt. Enter* MIDAS, QUEEN, CREON *and train, including* CRIER *and* TRUMPETER. MIDAS *is holding his hands out before him. A servant is carrying a tray with fruit and wine.*]

QUEEN. Your hands are dry again, my husband, and the sun shines once more. Now for the fifth time wash them in the waters of Pactolus.

MIDAS. And may the word of the Lord Dionysus prove as strong to take away as to bestow. [*He washes.*] Look! Do you not see flashes of gold in the water.

QUEEN. The gold is sinking to the bottom, and see, the sands are turning yellow. O my husband, you are saved. Praise the Lord Dionysus!

MIDAS [*rising*]. I think his art fails not. But I must prove it first. Bring me fruit and wine. [*He takes a grape.*] What! purple still? And the taste? Ha! Eat, my wife; eat, Creon. What do you taste? A drink, there. I live again. What do you taste?

CREON. My lord, it is only a grape.

MIDAS. I thought it was ambrosia. But do not say 'only', Creon. Say it is a grape. Say 'only' and you lose the world.

QUEEN. And is not gold only gold, my lord?

MIDAS. Not if you show it to the sun from whence it comes. Why do I keep my gold in vaults beneath the ground? Why dig it from the earth, to put it there again? I will have it beaten into torques, chains, necklaces, rings – what you will – and all fair ladies in my kingdom shall wear them. Dionysus, what have I not learnt from you in one short day? More grapes there!

QUEEN. Long may you keep your present mind, my lord.

MIDAS. Hope not for that, my Queen. Men soon forget the lesson they have learnt. Already these grapes lose their ambrosial taste. To-morrow, like Creon, I shall call them – only grapes. And next week I shall change my mind, and keep my gold in the cellars of my treasury as before. Now to work. What must I do to-day, Creon?

CREON [*looking in a scroll*]. It is the Midsummer Holiday, my lord. Your Majesty has only to show yourself on the palace balcony to the people. But stay. There is one appointment first. At twelve noon your Majesty's principal Barber will attend to cut the Royal Hair – before your Majesty appears on the balcony.

QUEEN. But that is the hour you promised to grace the contest between Pan and Phoebus, my lord. I gave my word to Pan, and it is to him you owe your rescue from the golden death.

MIDAS. All that is over, and I wish it to be forgotten. But I will keep my word. Creon, send someone to bid the barber attend me here. Hurry. I hear the sound of pipes already.

[*Enter* PAN *attended by* SATYRS *and* NYMPHS. PAN *plays and the* NYMPHS *sing.*]

SONG FOR PAN

Noontide approaches,
  Shadows grow small,
The Midsummer sun
  Rides high over all;
Man's little shadow
  Can darken sunfire,
Pan's little pipe shall
  Outwarble a lyre.
Strings cannot sing to
  The breath of a man,
This is the day of
  The Triumph of Pan.

PAN [*to the* QUEEN]. Lady, I thank you that you have kept your word. Will the King give order for all his people to come and see my triumph in the contest? [*The* QUEEN *whispers to* MIDAS.]

MIDAS. Let my Crier proclaim a holiday for this day. It will cost me dear, but the Queen will have it so.

CREON. Crier, stand forth and proclaim a holiday.

CRIER. Oyez! oyez! King Midas bids all his people make holiday, and come together for the contest of Phoebus and Pan.

[VINEDRESSERS, *etc., enter.*]

MIDAS. I see the rogues were waiting for this. They are always
   ready for a holiday.
QUEEN. I hear another music. Apollo comes.

   [APOLLO *enters and speaks to soft music. He is attended by*
   planetary spirits.]

APOLLO. I come, great Mischief, at your call,
   To grace this solemn festival.
   Not mine the will, or mine the blame,
   If in this trial you suffer shame.
   My strings are stretched. I claim decision.
   Come, take your pipes and make division.
   Tmolus awaits the summoning voice.
   Call him, and he will make his choice.
MIDAS. Lord Apollo, let the task of summoning Tmolus be
   entrusted to my royal Trumpeter and my royal Crier.
   They are idle wretches, and have not enough to do.
   [APOLLO *signs agreement.*] And they draw double rations
   for it.
CREON. Let the King's Trumpeter and King's Crier stand
   forth. [*The* TRUMPETER *sounds a call.*]
CRIER. Tmolus, lord of this fair hill,
   We summon thee to try the skill
   Of Pan and Phoebus, who submit
   Themselves to your all-judging wit.
   Each has pledged him to abide
   By the doom you shall decide.
   Both stand ready to appear.
   Come and give your verdict here.

   [*All sing a song during which* TMOLUS *enters suitably attended.*]

SONG FOR THE ENTRY OF TMOLUS

   Tmolus, lord of this fair hill,
      Leave your upland steep,
   Where the sudden song-borne lark
      Goes up among the sheep,

Where the winds are never still,
Where the white clouds mass,
And starry flowers lie close to earth
Among the quivering grass.

Leave the wild and spongy waste
Where brackish marshes bleed,
Leave the outcrop's ferny break
Where the springs are freed.
Leave the dell, and leave the rill,
Leave the waterfall,
Tmolus, Tmolus, judge and sage,
Answer to our call.

TMOLUS. Not lightly do I leave my ancient seat:
But when, my lord Apollo, you entreat –
And you, good neighbour Pan – an old man's ear
To judge the contest of your music here –
Though little thinking, with my centuries bowed,
To walk abroad and see this noble crowd
(A sight that brings me back my salad days
When oft young Tmolus bore away the bays) –
Gladly, despite these locks, I leave my hill
To judge in pipe and string your rival skill.
Come then, begin. But who? Have you made choice?
If not, and you will heed an old man's voice,
I say, Apollo's art is older reckoned,
Let him begin, and Pan shall follow second.
PAN. Ay, let him start, or else he'll not be heard,
He'll break his strings when once my pipes have skirred.

[APOLLO *plays, and the* PLANETARY SPIRITS *dance with solemn
gaiety. At the end much applause and cries of 'Apollo', 'Phoebus
Apollo', etc.*]

PAN. Now it is the turn of Pan,
Listen gods, and listen man,
Listen Tmolus, while Pan plays on
His enchanting diapason,
Once you've heard it, you'll swear roundly
Pan has beaten Phoebus soundly.

[PAN *signs to the* VINEDRESSERS *to work. He plays and* SATYRS
dance grotesquely. MIDAS *rises and half joins in the dance.
General and uneasy laughter, until* TMOLUS *rises from his throne
and speaks.*]

TMOLUS. O what a noise! For God's sake stop it,
    And Pan, with all your satyrs, hop it.
    I'd rather hear a sucker squeal,
    Or a rusty shrieking wheel,
    Or a cow that's lost its calf,
    Or forty mad hyenas laugh, –
    Apollo, without more ado,
    I give my voice, great Lord, to you.
MIDAS. And I give my voice for Pan. His music is worth the
    money. My men can work to it. Music while you work.
    There is something in this music after all. Who votes for
    Pan with me? [*Silence.*] I say, who votes for Pan with me?
    [*Still silence.* APOLLO *steps forward.*]
APOLLO. King, if you would rightly hear,
    You must grow a better ear.
    Lightly on each lobe I tap
    Hidden by your Phrygian cap.
    You have given Pan your voice,
    I give you ears to fit your choice.
    Farewell, Pan, and farewell all,
    The heavens grace your festival. –
    And when, too soon, the bleak days follow,
    Remember you have seen Apollo;
    Then with fire of thought and love
    Raise your sprite to spheres above,
    Till you climb the golden stair
    To realms beyond the upper air,
    Where the lords of morning dwell
    In glory of light invisible.
    Come, bright spirits, we must part.
    What Phoebus says, write in your heart.
              [*Music while* APOLLO *and his* SPIRITS *exeunt*]
PAN. Write it down a pack of lies.
    I've been cheated of my prize.
    This is all midsummer folly

That warps men's wits and makes them silly,
Till they choose the melancholy
Strings of Phoebus, when the jolly
Pipes of Pan with music fill ye
Like the wine at vintage, till ye
Cannot choose but dance a jig.
This Apollo is a pig.
What care I? 'Twas all a jest,
And Midas liked my music best.
He is for me; and I know,
When winter comes and brings the snow
And yon high sun has fallen low,
Humans needs must dance and sing,
Pipes are then the only thing,
And Pan shall be their Winter King.

APOLLO [*appearing above*]. Pan be wise, and give no scope
To another foolish hope.
In the darkest winter's night
Shall be born another light,
Greater light, and greater love
Than Apollo sways above.
Out of the weak is born the strong,
Out of silence comes the song, –
Lord of pipe, and Lord of string,
Heaven and earth shall call him King.

[*Exit.*]

QUEEN. Apollo's voice is hard to spell,
He speaks like his own oracle,
Yet must I think his mantic word
(So deep the heart within me stirred)
The best thing that I ever heard.

MIDAS. You are right, Pan. This is Midsummer Madness. The
greatest light in the winter is the log fire in my great hall.
Come to me again later, and I will hear more of your
music. But leave me now. I have business to attend to.
Do not let this verdict worry you, Sir Pan. Critics always
condemn the new art.

PAN. Farewell King, and farewell people.
Though I cannot climb the steeple
Like our friend so light and airy,
Or pretend to be a fairy,

Give me a smooth and solid floor
And Pan will dance through any door.
                              [*Exeunt* PAN *and* SATYRS *dancing*]
TMOLUS. Fair Hill, no other god shall Tmolus wrench
  From your delights to sit upon a bench.
  But since they wrangle in the valley still,
  Tmolus will seek again his quiet hill.
                                                    [*Exit* TMOLUS]
CREON. My lord, the royal Barber, whom you sent for, is in
  attendance, and it is almost time for your Majesty to
  show yourself on the balcony.
MIDAS. I will have my hair dressed alone. (*Enter* TIMON *the*
  barber.] Leave me, my Queen, and prepare yourself in the
  palace. I need no attendance.
                              [*Exeunt all except* MIDAS *and* TIMON]
  Come here, barber. My hair feels strangely heavy about
  my ears. Is it longer than usual?
TIMON. Your Majesty, I cannot see till I have removed your
  majesty's cap.
MIDAS. Remove it then. [TIMON *removes cap and yells*.]
TIMON. O Chronos, what do I see?
MIDAS. What *do* you see? What *do* you see, fellow?
TIMON. My lord, I dare not say what I see.
MIDAS. You villain, tell me the truth. What do you see?
TIMON. O my lord, your Majesty has . . . your Majesty has . . .
  your Majesty has . . .
MIDAS. Has what, fellow?
TIMON. O forgive me, your Majesty, but you have . . . I cannot
  take my eyes off them, your Majesty.
MIDAS. Off what, you idiot? For the last time, what have I on
  my head?
TIMON. O your Majesty, you have – asses' ears.
MIDAS [*grimly*]. Asses's ears. This is your doing, Apollo.
  This is worse than the gift of gold. Fellow, put on my
  cap again. One word of this to anyone, and I'll have
  you cut into pieces with your own shears. Can you be
  secret?
TIMON. Yes, your Majesty. I promise.
MIDAS. Then keep your promise, or you know your fate.
  Apollo, Apollo. Asses' ears, asses' ears.
                                                    [*Exit* MIDAS]

TIMON [*crying*]. Boohoo, Boohoo, what shall I do?

[*Enter his wife,* PRAXINOE, *who hits him smartly on the head.*]

PRAXINOE. There you are, husband, rhyming again. And what's the matter now?

TIMON. Is that you, Praxinoe dear? How did you find me? Boohoo Boohoo, what shall I do?

PRAXINOE. There you are again. Can't you stop these dreadful rhymes? You're a barber, not a poet. You'll be losing your job, and where shall we be then? You know the king won't have poets or other useless things at court.

TIMON. But I wasn't rhyming, Praxy dear.

PRAXINOE. Yes, you was. You said Boohoo Boohoo what shall I do? If that doesn't rhyme, I should like to know what does.

TIMON. O my dear Praxy, nothing rhymes these awful times. (*She hits him.*] O dear, I didn't mean it, I really didn't mean it.

PRAXINOE. But I mean it, Timon. I mean you to stop it, sir. Do you understand?

TIMON. O dear Praxy, don't get waxy.

PRAXINOE. Praxy, waxy – there you are again [*hitting him*]. Praxy, waxy: topsy, wopsy: pudsy, mudsy – I'll knock them out of your head.

TIMON. I wish you'd knock one thing out of my head, my dear. O what a surprise to see with your eyes!

PRAXINOE [*bursting into tears*]. O why was I born, married to a man like this! Why didn't I get yoked to some natural creature that talks prose like kings and queens and the royal ministers? O my stars, what a fate you've brought me to!

TIMON. Why, dear wife, what have I done? You stopped me when I'd just begun –

PRAXINOE. There you are again! Done! Begun! And must you have your 'done' before your 'begun', Sir? These poets make everything topsy-turvy. And the wretch hasn't told me what he was boohooing for yet.

TIMON. Dear wife, I was trying but couldn't for cr . . . no, no, no, – I mean I couldn't because you kept interrupting me, Praxy. O my dear, it's the secret – the awful secret.

PRAXINOE. What secret, Sir?

TIMON. Why, King Midas' secret. He's got – O dear, O dear, I nearly said it.

PRAXINOE. Now then, husband, what has King Midas got?

TIMON. I daren't tell you, Praxy dear – I daren't really. The King will cut me in little pieces with these shears if I do. It's something awful. He's got as . . . O dear, I nearly said it again. I can't get it out of my head. I'm sure to say it one day – it's too awful to forget. O Praxy, what shall I do?

PRAXINOE. What shall you do, Timon? I know what you must do. But if I tell you, will you promise me two things, first?

TIMON. What are they, Praxy?

PRAXINOE. Not to make any more rhymes – and to tell me the secret.

TIMON. I promise both upon my oath – there, don't be angry, that's the last time, dear. Now tell me, what must I do?

PRAXINOE. Very well, then. Sit down and listen. You must do what the King's butler did when he wanted to forget about the bottle of wine he'd taken from the King's cellar.

TIMON. And what's that, my dear?

PRAXINOE. Well, he'd taken lots of bottles before, and forgotten them all quite easily. But this particular bottle stuck in his throat, so he couldn't forget it, poor man. And why? Because when he was coming along the passage from the cellar to the side door, he happened to look in a mirror that was hanging on the wall, and there he saw himself, large as life, walking away with the bottle. Now, if he hadn't seen himself, he would have forgotten it as easily as the other bottles, but he naturally couldn't forget the sight of himself with the bottle in his very own hands. And the bottle lay so heavy on the poor man's chest, that at last he asked the cook, and the cook told him what to do, and he did it, and forgot all about it. And now he always shuts his eyes, when he goes past the mirror, and so he has no more trouble. There! that's what you must do, husband.

TIMON. But what did the cook tell him to do, Praxy dear?

PRAXINOE. Can't I tell a story without being interrupted in every sentence, you aggravating man? She told him to dig a little hole in the earth, and whisper the secret into the hole, and then cover it up. And he did, and forgot it at once.

TIMON. Wife, I'll try it. Quick, my shears. [*He digs a hole.*] Now stand over there, while I whisper. Mother earth, I give my secret to you. [*He whispers into the hole, and then fills it in.*] There! it's covered up now, and nobody will ever find it.

PRAXINOE. And now, what was the secret, dear?

TIMON [*scratching his head*]. Blow me, if I haven't forgotten it. Let me see. However did it begin?

PRAXINOE. You said it began: 'Midas has as . . .'

TIMON. Midas has as . . . ? Midas has as . . . ? Midas has as . . . Midas has as . . . What could it have been? Midas has as . . . I've got it. Midas has asymetrical earrings. I must have noticed them when I was cutting his hair. That's it – Midas has asymmetrical earrings! And an awful thing to have, too.

PRAXINOE. And what are assy madrigal earrings, husband?

TIMON. What King Midas has, my dear.

PRAXINOE. But the king doesn't wear earrings at all.

TIMON. Blow me, neither does he. Then I must have forgotten the secret good and proper. Thank the gods for that. Hurray! Hurray! Midas's murky mystery no more in memory I maintain. I say, that's fine! I shall take up alliteration now. No more rhymes for me. Come wife, to supper. [*Declaims.*] In the sweet of the summer when supper is set. And the barber has broached his barrel of beer –

PRAXINOE. Husband, what is this?

TIMON. Peace, Praxinoe, it isn't poetry. Rhymes are rotten, and there is reason in everything.

[*Exeunt. Enter* CHORUS OF REEDS.]

SONG FOR THE REEDS
[*to be spoken in chorus*]

We are the rushes and
  Reeds by the river,
Like spears in the sunshine
  We sparkle and quiver;
But half way to Hades
  Our roots have their birth,
And we know the seminal
  Secrets of earth.

The King's barber dug a
  Small hole with his shears,
And whispered: 'King Midas
  Has grown asses' ears,'
Asses' ears, asses' ears,
  Our roots heard the history,
Whenever the breeze blows,
  We whisper the mystery.

Midas has asses' ears,
  He shan't dissemble,
We tell the secret,
  As soon as we tremble,
Asses' ears, asses' ears,
  His cap never shows it –
But we whisper the secret,
  And all the world knows it.

[*Enter* MIDAS, QUEEN, CREON, TRUMPETER,*etc.*]

MIDAS. Base wretches! Devils! Slaves in soul and body! Will
  they jeer and hoot at me? Have I not made the kingdom
  famous? Is not my treasure of gold known all over the
  world? Have I not an immortal name for the wealth and
  weight of my gold? This is their gratitude for a holiday!
  But they shall work the harder, they shall work the
  harder.
CREON. Let me entreat your Majesty. Listen again to the
  divine music of Apollo. How can you turn against the

order of heaven, and hope to maintain the order of your kingdom? Untune Apollo's string – and all harmonies are marred.

QUEEN. You are the sun, the Apollo, of this land, my lord. Give your wealth to your people as freely as the sun gives his light. So you will become their sun and king.

MIDAS. Are you too against me? Must I be baited in my own vineyard? But I will see if I have any loyal subjects left. Trumpeter, summon my vinedressers. No more words. They will be faithful to me. [*The* TRUMPETER *plays a call, and the* VINEDRESSERS *enter.*] Good vinedressers, have you no thanks to me for this holiday?

STREPHON. It is the first holiday we have had since the old king died, your Majesty.

DAMON. We could do with more holidays.

FIRST BOY. Lots and lots of holidays.

PHILEMON. We work very hard, your Majesty.

DAMOETAS. And we get very little pay.

STREPHON. And there's very little to buy.

SECOND BOY. Not enough sweets.

DAMON. And not enough to buy it with.

PHILEMON. And the taxes are too high.

DAMOETAS. We need better homes.

STREPHON. And better food.

DAMON. And stronger wine.

DAMOETAS. And cheaper clothes.

ALL [*shouting*]. We need everything better and cheaper and bigger and stronger.

[MIDAS, *who has been somewhat cowed by these speeches, suddenly collects himself and rises.*]

MIDAS. Silence. I am your king, and will be obeyed. Can I command half the gold in the world and not command the tongues of a parcel of slaves? Silence, I said. Who dares to raise his voice now?

[*During his speech the* REEDS *have begun to whisper.*]

REEDS.   We are the rushes and
                  Reeds by the river,
              Like spears in the sunshine
                  We sparkle and quiver,

          But half way to Hades
          Our roots have their birth
          And we know the seminal
          Secrets of earth.

MIDAS. Who is that whispering when I have commanded silence?

CREON. It is only the wind in the reeds, your Majesty.

QUEEN. It is the reeds talking in the wind, my husband.

MIDAS. Talking! What are they saying?

REEDS.   The King's barber dug a
          Small hole with his shears,
          And whispered: 'King Midas
          Has grown asses' ears.'
        Asses' ears, asses' ears,
          Our roots heard the history,
          Whenever the wind blows
          We whisper the mystery.

MIDAS. Stop them! Stop them! For God's sake stop them!

CREON. We cannot stop the reeds, your Majesty.

QUEEN. The wind blows when it wills, husband. Listen, they are beginning again.

REEDS [*louder*]. Midas has asses' ears,
          He shan't dissemble,
        We tell the secret
          As soon as we tremble,
        Asses' ears, asses' ears,
          His cap never shows it –

[MIDAS, *who has been pressing his hands to his ears, involuntarily throws the cap off.*]

        But we whisper the secret,

ALL [*pointing*]. **And all the world knows it.**

MIDAS [*storming out*]. A mirror! A mirror! If I never saw myself before, I must see that sight now. Apollo, you teach me to see myself. A mirror, a mirror!

                                  [*Exit*]

CREON. My lady, it is an ancient law of this land that no man may sit upon its throne who suffers from any disfigurement of his person. Therefore until our late king Midas recovers the true shape of his ears (which I pray Apollo he may) the throne is vacant, and I call upon your Majesty as next in succession to ascend it and rule this kingdom.

QUEEN. Is it the will of all dwellers in this land that I become its ruler?

CREON. Let all who inhabit this valley come forward to declare their will. And first I call upon Apollo and his spirits. [*They enter.*] Is it your will that this lady shall rule the land?

APOLLO AND SPIRITS. It is our will, and we add thereto our blessing.

CREON. And next I call upon old Tmolus. [*He enters.*] Is it your will, O Tmolus?

TMOLUS. It is my will. And may there be peace in the valley as upon my hill.

CREON. And now I call upon Pan and Dionysus and all nymphs and satyrs. [*They enter.*] Is it your will, ye gods and goddesses of earth?

ALL. It is our will.

DIONYSUS. And I will make fruitful the vine slopes and cornlands and olive groves, and multiply their crops.

PAN. And I will play music to her Majesty.

CREON. And last I call upon the vinedressers here, and the reeds that grow by the river. Will you take this lady for your queen and ruler?

VINEDRESSERS AND REEDS. We will, we will. Long live her Majesty!

[*Enter* PRAXINOE *dragging* TIMON.]

PRAXINOE. My lord, you have forgotten the most important court official, the royal Barber, my husband. Will you take this queen for your king, Timon dear?

TIMON [*kissing the* QUEEN's *skirt*]. I salute her skirt as a sign of subjection. [*Taking his shears.*] And will quietly consider the coronation cut.

QUEEN. Then at your will, until King Midas mend,
Gladly this empty throne I will ascend.
Good people, do not mock a fallen king,
But you, who saw poor Midas, take this thing
To your own heart, and ask if it appears
You should yourself be wearing asses' ears.

Have you no folly? Have you no blind spot?
Then think (and be contented with your lot)
If Phoebus touched you, it might come to pass,
Not ears, but all of you would turn an ass.
Then show by favour (lest our purpose fail)
That asses' ears make not an asses' tale.

TOBIAS

An Easter Mystery

*

Part One – Blindness
Part Two – The Journey
Part Three – Marriage
Part Four – The Return

PART ONE

BLINDNESS

THE EASTER SPIRIT SPEAKS

To those who live beyond my Master's death
I speak, whose backward-gazing eye can see
The hollow of time, and that small eminence
Called Golgotha, whence man begins to raise
His fallen nature to the throne of God,
Learning to say, Not I, but Christ in me.
Such know my Master's path, how he received
The Spirit in Jordan, made the blind to see,
Cast devils out — Physician to sick man,
Guide to the lost, a Fisherman of souls.
Let them behold, before my Master came,
He sent his Messengers to light his way
And comfort souls without the greater hope.
Of one this story tells, a glorious power,
Raphael, His healing Angel, before whom
I bow in worship, and pray my Master, Drive
The Evil Spirit from Man, restore his eyes,
And lead his feet to ways of light and love.

THE NARRATIVE

In Nineveh old Tobit lived, the son
of Tobiel, there brought from Thisbe's town
With Anna and Tobias, wife and child,
When the ten tribes who bowed the knee to Baal
Were carried captive by Sennacherib.
But Tobit had not sinned; each year he took
Alone his first-fruits to Jerusalem,

And still in Nineveh he kept the law.
For when one day there's plenty for a meal,
He sends his son Tobias to the streets
To find a hungry brother. Awed and pale,
White rose for red, he's back at once, crying,
'A man, a brother, slain, strangled outside.'
The meal's pushed back, old Tobit leaves the house,
And drags the body to an outer room,
Then, being polluted, lies under the eaves.
Sleep comes not, but upon his eyes the birds,
The swallows chattering at sundown, mute their dung,
And with their dawn-song Tobit knows he's blind.
Old Anna thinks bitterly, All this comes
From meddling, putting spokes in others' wheels,
(He always did), not leaving well alone.
But manfully, for now she's man and wife,
She takes in work from the rich houses round.
   The money's poor, but often scraps of food
And oddments find their way into her bag.
One day she brings a kid, but cannot say –
Or will not – clearly how she came by it.
Old Tobit, sick with shame, cries out, 'A thief,
My wife a thief, even this I am not spared,'
And holds his head and will not speak all day.
At that same hour when Tobit chid his wife,
His kinsman Raguel in Ecbatana
Reproached his child Sarah, and called her witch.
Seven bridegrooms had she had, and not one lived;
But in the morning on the bridal bed
Each one lay stretched, by an evil Spirit slain
Called Asmodeus, and Raguel buried them,
Even the seventh, and cried, 'A witch, a witch,
My child a witch, even this I am not spared,'
And cursed the day when he begot a maid.
   So those old men were joined in misery,
Kinsmen, though now remote in foreign lands,
Old Tobit and old Raguel, sad souls,

Hopeless, and trusting not that God would send
Archangel Raphael to lift up their feet
And give them light, light spiritual to both,
And to blind Tobit healing for his eyes.
      For in the old King's reign, whom Tobit served
With wealth and honour, fearful then of change,
He sent ten talents into Media,
Silver, to Gabael, brother to Gabrias,
With tallies cut, to hold it there in trust
Against bad times. And now he sadly thinks,
Groping to find the tally in some drawer,
'The boy must go, Tobias, my dear son.
Our only hope. I say he must. No matter
What Anna thinks. I feel it as much myself.'
But dares not for a time speak out his mind.
Daily he feels the tally. Then one night,
The plain meal done, Tobias sent to bed,
He tells his mind to Anna. She, angry,
Cries, 'You've lost wealth and sight and all, you fool,
And now you'll lose Tobias. Not while I live.
Never. He shall not go, our only child.
What are ten talents weighed against our son?'
      They quarrel late that night; but the next day,
When Anna, half worn down, goes out to char,
Tobit calls, 'Here, Tobias, I want you boy.
Go to the market-place, where the guides stand
At the north end, and find a likely man
That knows the ways to Media. Bring him here.'
And tells his son of Raguel and the bond.
      Tobias, all eager to see the world,
Calls to his dog and goes, while Tobit prays,
'O Lord, have pity on a blind old man,
Let not his seed be withered. O, if ever
I took an offering to your sanctuary,
If ever raised the fallen, fed the poor,
Kept pure ever my hand, my heart, my eye,
Account it Lord for righteousness. O let

Your Angel lead Tobias on his way.'
So Tobit prayed, and knew not what he prayed,
But young Tobias found among the guides
A Guide indeed, who knew the Median ways,
And knew the ways of God, and spoke His word,
And brought him home, a comely man, brown-eyed,
Wonderfully light of foot. 'I like his voice,'
Thought Tobit, 'and his hand feels good. He'll do,'
And asked his name and tribe. 'Seek you,' he said,
'A Tribesman or a guide?' but told his name
Was Azarias, Ananias' son.
   So Tobit hired him for a drachma a day
And all things necessary, as for his son,
To guide the boy to Rages, there and back,
And knew not it was Raphael whom he bought,
Chaffering with money for an Angel's hire.
   Then, while the boy listened all ears, they fell
To talking of the road. 'The best way lies
Through Ecbatana, a fine town,' Tobit said,
'Where Raguel my kinsman lives. Poor man
He has his troubles too – a sad story –
His daughter has an evil spirit. Enquire him out,
He'll welcome you, boy, for your father's sake,
Give him my greetings. We were close friends once.'
So while they talk, Anna returns, all ice
To freeze this going, and she sees the guide.
But Raphael turns his marvellous eye, and melts
The cold fears in her heart with looks of love.
   That night the lamp burns late, while Anna sews,
And even old Tobit plies polish and brush.
With morning come farewells, tears choking smiles,
Quick laughter, rippling on the soul's surface
To hide the tragic depths. But now they've gone,
The boy's step lengthened to the Angel's stride,
The small dog nosing on. The old pair turn,
She to her work, he to his chair. All day
And many days he sits, his inner eye

Painting the way: thus far they've come, and now
They cross the Tigris: now – a rough stretch that –
They reach the Median border: now they've won
To Ecbatana – pray God Raguel live
To give them shelter. Thus he maps their course,
With lids so drooping on his blinded eyes
That Anna, back from work, fancies he sleeps,
And makes no meal, but sits till the night comes,
And the small room is dark and still as death.

PART TWO

THE JOURNEY

THE EASTER SPIRIT SPEAKS

Life is a journey and the travellers choose
What road and pace they will, but come at last
To the one centre, Death. Who knows not this,
Though wishful to forget? But O how few
Know that the centre is the infinite
To one who rightly sees. And such are they
Who take my Master as their guide. He leads
Their steps to living waters, whence they drink
Healing for body and soul. He knows all roads,
And why the traveller chooses this or that,
Not knowing himself, although he thinks to know.
I pray my Master teach you on your way:
Let Him but touch your eyes, and you shall see
In that small centre, Self, the infinite Christ.

THE NARRATIVE

For three bright days they walked the river road,
Dog, Man and Angel, till they reached the ford
Where the great road goes up to Media.
Tobias ran to swim, while on the bank
The Angel sat and watched the boy's white legs
Kicking a lace of foam on the blue stream,
The small dog barking anxious at the edge.
Suddenly Panic came. 'A fish, a monster,'
Tobias cried and beat it for the land.
But when his feet touched bottom he felt ashamed,
And Raphael's voice came with a calming power,

'It will not hurt you. Take it by the fins,
And draw it to the bank. This fish shall be
Fruit of the water of life for more than food.'
The boy seized fin and tail, and with strange ease
Drew it upon the bank, subdued to touch
As a horse yields, feeling behind its ears
The master's hand, and meekly takes the bit.
And Raphael, as the fish lay on the bank,
Twisting its silver scales among the flowers,
Touched it, and quietly it gasped out its life.
'Now take your knife,' the Angel said, 'and slit
The belly underneath. Cut out the heart,
The liver and the gall, and put them up
Safely.' The boy obeyed, much wondering why,
But dared not ask, so changed was Raphael's voice
Like music moving to a harsher key;
And with the Angel's help, and his new knife,
Opened the fish, and from its belly drew
Heart, liver and gall, and put them in his bag.
    Then Raphael sends him up the sandy shore
To search for sticks and driftwood from the stream,
Or fallen from dry trees, gnarled lumps of thorn,
And slender branches, barkless, white as bones,
That break with a sharp crack across the knee.
    Meanwhile the Angel takes tinder and flint,
Builds carefully a cage of twigs. The fire
Soon kindles, and when stouter sticks have blazed
To make a heart of embers, they spit the flesh
And roast it, while the dog runs circles round,
And the great sun moves down the arc of heaven.
    That day they walked in silence, but the next,
The Angel's voice being sweet as the blue sky,
Tobias asked, 'Why did you make me cut
Gall, heart and liver from that fish I caught,
And keep them in my bag? What use are they?
Tell me, good Azarias,' – but asked with fear,
Remembering his voice of yesterday.

But Raphael answered, 'You do well to ask.
As for the heart and liver, if one have
An evil spirit, or be possessed by fiends,
Burn but a little before him, and the smoke
Will drive the fiend away: and for the gall,
If one be blind with whiteness of the eyes
Smear it upon those eyes, and he shall see.'
So on they walk: the dusty road has gone,
And now sharp stones lead up to Media.
Sometimes they turn to mark the river plain,
With cities shrunk to toys; the camel trains
Like beads along a thread; the river's glint,
And riband of lush green that marks his bed,
And dust-cloud on the road from Nineveh.
But the boy, seeing his home so far away,
And he alone, with none but a hired guide,
Doing his father's work, felt every day
His manhood grow upon him; new thoughts and aims,
And pictures of new worlds danced in his heart.
One day the Angel said, 'This night we reach
Ecbatana – and Rages is not far –
Where Raguel, your father's cousin and friend
Will make us welcome; and, Tobias, this
I speak to you as man, no more as boy –
He has a daughter, very sweet and fair,
Sarah her name, and he must marry her
Within his tribe. Who then so fit as you,
His old friend's son? Ask boldly for her hand
And he will give it. You will love her much.'
Tobias said, 'My father warned me of her,
A witch that has an evil spirit, who slays
All that go to her. Seven has she killed
Already. I am my father's only son.'
But Raphael answered, 'Judge her not unseen;
The girl is fair, and good as she is fair,
The spirit alone is evil. Did I not tell you
To make a smoke, if any were possessed,

Burning the heart and liver of the fish,
And void the fiend, and let the true self in?
Do so to Sarah, and pray. All will be well.'
Tobias said nothing; but suddenly
The maid stood like a vision everywhere,
Making all sights unreal. He never saw
The city gates, or heard the street babel;
But when the Angel stopped a girl, and asked
The way to Raguel's house, his senses woke:
He saw, he heard; and knew that it was she
Even before her words, 'He is my father,
Come, I will take you home.' She was his soul
Walking beside him, lovely as a star
And he her sphere. Quickly they reached the house,
The old man opened, and they told their tribe,
The sons of Nephthalim, captive in Nineveh.
'Welcome, young man, we come of the same tribe.
So Sarah met you. Call your mother, girl.
And you, sir, you come of a fine stock too.
Come in. You must stay a week at least. My wife
Shall make you welcome. Come in, and bring the dog.
You will have news to tell of Nineveh.
A fine dog you have to travel all that way.'
The old man led them in, echoing still
'Come in.' They followed, and the door shut to.

PART THREE

MARRIAGE

THE EASTER SPIRIT SPEAKS

Think not that death comes once and all at once.
You die with every breath. When first you see,
Hear, touch and taste, you gnaw the bone of death.
To find the world is death; and death to know
The soul and spirit within. My Master died
With every act and word; and Golgotha
But finished what began on Jordan's stream.
The tree of death grows in you and spreads its roots
Sucking the sap of life. But by that death
You think and are a man. Let not the fiend
Drag you to death. Quicken your thoughts. Transcend
The dying brain, and let Love's thinking in.
So, like my Master, dying you shall not die,
But heal life's sickness in the body's grave.

THE NARRATIVE

How cool and rich was Raguel's house; the walls
With carpets hung, and floors so thick with rugs
That voices softened to the noiseless tread.
It was as quiet as a sanctuary
Between the last bell and the voice of prayer
And to Tobias it was a holy place.
They washed and drank, and sat in marvellous peace,
While Raguel gave orders for the meal,
And Edna came with Sarah, and took their hands
And spoke them words of love. But Raguel
Whispered his wife, 'How like the young man is

To Tobit, my good cousin'. Then aloud:
'You come from Nineveh – you surely know
My cousin Tobit. Lives he, and is he well?'
Tobias answered, 'He is my father and well.'
Then Raguel leapt up and kissed the boy,
And blessed him, crying, 'You have a good father, son.
Said I not, Edna, he was like my friend?
But why these wet eyes, lad? Is something wrong?'
'My father is blind,' Tobias said, and told
How Tobit brought the body from the streets,
And slept beneath the eaves and was made blind.
But Raguel wept and said, 'How like himself!
He ever went about doing good things.
And now he's blind. Poor Tobit!' And wept again.
And Anna wept and Sarah, and the boy
No more held back his tears, but cried aloud,
While Raphael's eyes brimmed over with pity and love.
So sorrow bound them closer. But when soon
The servants brought the meal in, Raguel said,
'Come, he is blind but lives, and he is well.
Be thankful for that, and wipe your tears. They take
Your sight away, and cannot give back his.
We must find ways to help him. So, to eat.'
    But, while they rose, Tobias drew the guide
Deftly apart, and whispered, 'Speak to him,
Good Azarias, speak of what you said
Upon the journey. I love Sarah so
I cannot eat, unless she shall be mine.'
So Raphael spoke, urging the young man's suit
For fitness and for love. But Raguel said,
'These things must not be hurried. Time enough
Later to speak of this. We will eat first.'
Tobias ventured all. 'I cannot eat,'
He answered, 'till I know.' And Raguel, pleased
To see the young man's spirit, and how he stood
Half fire, half water, between will and love,
Replied, 'To no man living would I give

My child more gladly. But I'll tell you all:
My daughter has an evil spirit, that slays
All those that come to her. I would not bury
My old friend's son.' Tobias said, 'If she
Will take me, let my death be on my head,
But still I trust in God.' He placed his hand
In hers. She took it sweetly. He had won.
　　Once more they wept, but now for joy, until
Their host first dried his eyes and made them sit.
But while they feasted, sometimes in the dish
Tobias' hand touched Sarah's, and he ate
To feel that touch again and not for food.
　　The meal was rich, with sweets and talk prolonged;
Tobias told of Nineveh, and all
His father suffered when the old king fell
Until his blindness (here they wept again)
And of the talents left with Gabael.
'The guide shall fetch the money,' Raguel said,
While you stay here and hold the wedding feast
Two weeks – my wife will not have less – our friends
Must come to share our joy.' Tobias turned
To ask the guide, but saw his eyes agree,
And thought with tears, How good all people are!
Then Raguel joined their hands. 'Take her,' he said,
'Lead her unto thy father. She is thy bride.'
And took a book, and wrote an instrument,
While Anna made the chamber ready, and spread
New coverings, and lit the incense bowl.
But when the door was shut, the old pair turned
Like those who turn at sunset to behold
Eastward a night of clouds, and sought their beds
As they had seen a dear child die in pain.
　　But with his bride alone, Tobias took
The fish's heart and liver, as Raphael said,
And threw them on the incense bowl, and made
A smoke which rose and curled in dragon forms
Down the four walls; and Asmodeus knew

His Master, and to Egypt whence he stemmed
Fled, but escaped not; for the Angel came
With chains and bound him, hungering for souls,
As a cat hungers, seeing on a branch
The bird it all but caught, and from its mouth
The envious juices slobber to the ground.
   Meanwhile Tobias rose upon the bed
With Sarah, hand in hand, and prayed to God,
And said, 'Have mercy, Lord, who gavest Eve
To Adam for a helpmeet. Not for lust
I take this woman, but in truth. O grant
We grow together old and die in peace.'
With that the smoke cleared to a little flame
That watched the darkness where those lovers slept.
   But in the morning early Raguel rose
And took a spade and dug a grave and said,
'Lest he should also die': then called his wife
To send a maid and wake, if both could wake,
The sleeping pair within; or bury one
Secretly, no man seeing. The maid returned,
And from the chamber door, like sun and moon
Fronting each other in the morning sky,
The lovers came. O then, what joy, what tears,
What pressings to the heart, what words of love,
What thankfulness to God! And first they ran
To tell the guide, but, finding he was gone,
Praised him because he went, the Prince of Guides,
Sent like an Angel of God, of great despatch,
Not idle like the guides of these bad days.
   Two weeks they kept the feast, till he returned
Bringing the talents, and with him Gabael came
To share the feasting. But Tobias said:
'My father counts the days till my return
And listens to each footfall. Let me go.'
   Then Raguel gave him half of all his wealth,
Goods, cattle, servants; and Anna, at the last,
Drew him aside and said, 'I give my child

To you in special trust. Entreat her well.'
They watch them go, believing not they've gone,
Then turn to their strange home, where every room
Is desolate of a spirit. But on the road
Tobias rides with Sarah, the small dog
Barks at the camel's legs, a pace ahead
Grave-lipped and smiling-eyed the Angel goes.

PART FOUR

THE RETURN

THE EASTER SPIRIT SPEAKS

Sorrow and gladness, Mansoul's weight and wings,
From what a flux of change they reach their poise
After wild ebb and flow, calming the heart;
Nor find their balance in one life, one soul —
Your side the furrow is burnished with the sun,
Then yours must bear the shade, that light and dark
Stand even in the field. So that old pair
In far Ecbatana bear the heavy load
That those young lovers go light in the light;
Type of my Master who made grief his joy,
His flood our ebb of woe, that with light feet,
His Angel leading, we take the homeward way.

THE NARRATIVE

In Nineveh the leaden days went by.
They filled the measure; then o'erbrimmed the cup
Spreading a poison in the house. Tobit
Put on a mask of hope. 'No doubt', he said,
'They have missed the way: or they are tired and rest:
Or they have met a brother who holds them back
Feasting;' or, later, raising a lesser fear
To quench a greater, 'Gabael is dead
And his affairs unproved. None can dispense
The talents without order — the law is long.
But doubt not they are safe and will come soon.'
    Anna would only say; 'The boy is dead.
I knew how it would be. My child, my child,

I cannot live without you.' She hid her face,
And would not eat or speak for all those days
Tobias feasted and life was very dear.
But when the fit was done, she went each day
Beyond the gates, to sit where she could see
The road to Nineveh, while Tobit stayed
Alone in the dark house, nor any more
Listened, but in his dead heart hope was dead.
   But the day dawned when they saw Nineveh,
Tobias and his guide. And Raphael said,
'Brother, thou knowest thy father, how he is.
Let us run forward and prepare the house,
Leaving thy bride to follow. But take the gall.
Thy father, when he hears thy voice, poor soul,
Will open wide his eyes. Take then the gall
And streak his eyeballs, till, to ease their smart
Rubbing, he rub the white film off and see.'
   So they went forward, and the young man's dog
Ran after them. But Anna in the gate
Saw him, and knew her son, and ran and fell
Upon his neck and cried: 'Now let me die,
Since I have seen my child.' Weeping they went
Towards the house, and Tobit heard and rose,
His beating heart loud as the noise without,
But stumbled at the door. Tobias ran,
Caught him about to fall, and turned his head,
And strake the gall upon his eyes, crying;
'Be of good cheer, my father. It is I.'
The old man rubbed to ease the smart; the film
Scaled from his eyeballs, and he saw his son.
   Then first he wept and said; 'Blessed is God
With all his holy angels, who did scourge
And then have mercy on me. I see my son.'
Tobias poured his tale out, the great things
That had befallen on the way, the fish,
Raguel's house, his daughter and their love,
The evil spirit fled, the marriage feast,

With praises for the guide. He told not half,
But Tobit rose and led them through the streets
(Amazed were all that saw) and at the gate
Welcomed his daughter, giving thanks to God,
And held her in his arms; and she forgot
Her secret fear, and whispered cheek to cheek,
'You are my father now. I have come home.'
　　So they returned with light hearts to the house
Where Tobit sat in darkness those long weeks.
Then to his son he said, 'Fetch here the man
That went with thee. Give him the wages due,
No harm to give him more.' Tobias called
The guide into the house and bade him, 'Take
The half of what you brought. You led me safe,
Gave back my wife's spirit, my father's eyes;
You shall not part with less.' But as he spoke,
They saw it was an Angel and were afraid.
But he said: 'I am Raphael, of the Seven
God's Angels, who present before his throne
The prayers of men. It is wisdom to keep
The secrets of a king, but to reveal
Gloriously the works of God. I heard your prayer,
And Sarah when she prayed. I was with you
(For deeds are prayers) when you brought home the dead.
From God I brought this health for sight and soul.
Give Him the thanks, and tell what you have seen.'
　　The Angel went; but in his light they sat
That left a golden summer in the room,
Tobias' hand in Sarah's hands, Anna
Gazing into his face, old Tobit's eyes
Not seeing, though new-quickened, the small dog
Stretched all along the mat, dreaming their bliss;
Till from his vision waking with a song
The old man's heart and voice flowed out with joy.

THE EASTER SPIRIT SPEAKS

Joy is my ending, and I pray your song,
As Tobit once sang joy in Nineveh;
Joy for the spirit healed, the sight restored,
The love of souls, the God revealed in man.
O Master Christ, Physician Son of God,
Water of life, the salve of eye and soul,
Look on this people, those who seek thy Sun,
And those who think their darkness to be day,
Rise from thy grave this hour, unfreeze their blood,
Go with them in thy spiritual form,
Their bride and Guide, their Way and Journey's End.

Fantasia on Three Voices

It is probably best to describe this particular experience in the way it came to me. There is an unconscious art, only too little perceived, in the unfolding of the whole life of a man, and within it isolated experiences or chapters have often a dramatic development which is generally forgotten when the whole landscape of events becomes plain. Occasionally, however, even to the less perceptive, the form of events is so striking that it becomes inseparable from the events themselves. For me this was the case with the particular experience which I wish to describe. I shall therefore try to recapture its growth and clarification, even more than the historical or moral lesson which I afterwards saw that it seemed to convey. Indeed, the latter is so unimportant compared with the mood which the experience created that I shall probably say nothing about it at all.

I suppose everyone has at some time lifted the receiver of a telephone to make a call, only to find himself a dumb participant in an intimate conversation. That was precisely the sensation that I had when, waking from a particularly deep sleep in the middle of the night, I first became aware that I was listening to a conversation between three voices. The difference, however, was that whereas on the telephone one's better self tells one to overcome curiosity and slap the receiver down, I knew on this occasion that I should be an auditor; in fact that the conversation could not take place unless I was myself listening to it.

On the first occasion this amounted only to a feeling or intuition; I had no idea of the reason. Later, however, when the conversation, which almost always ended abruptly, was continued at irregular intervals, I became fully conscious of why I had to be present. The three voices were not all speaking the same language, and could communicate with each other only through my mind.

Each of them, also, had a different relation to my consciousness, which took me some time to discover. The first was certainly speaking Greek – ancient Greek – but with a pronunciation quite unfamiliar to me, which it would have taxed my utmost efforts to understand or translate. When I tried to do so, however – and even on the first occasion I did distinctly catch a few words like "city", "king", "palace" and "child" – the voice became fainter, and the more I tried to understand it intellectually, the more it dwindled until it reached almost complete inaudibility. If, however, I gave myself up entirely to pure listening, merely devoting myself to the sound and form of the words, the voice itself underwent some magical change, and began to speak in a kind of broken English, though broken only to the extent that I was unable to repress my normal habit of listening for the sense in the sounds of the words.

This was extraordinarily difficult to do, so that on the first few occasions the conversation was extremely fragmentary, and I often had the impression that the voices were impatient with me. Even when the first voice became English, I still had to listen to the sounds and not think of the meaning, and in my own language this was even more difficult. You will, of course, at once ask, How then did I know what the voice said? The answer is that for the most part I remembered the sounds afterwards, and so worked my way backwards to the sense. No doubt there was much that I missed, but it never failed to astonish me that I remembered so much.

In the first few conversations the first voice did most of the talking, though the balance afterwards changed. From this voice I began to form a very clear picture of a small town, not much more than a collection of farms, but among them was one larger farm built of stone, which was dignified with the name of a palace, where the speaker's father had lived. He was sufficiently important to be called the king of the community, and his palace was the wonder of the whole district. The voice spoke very much of a happy childhood there, of going out to the hills with his father's shepherds and goatherds, and of the glory of standing by his father, whom he plainly adored, when the community gathered together for some sacrifice or festival, in which his father played the leading role.

But there was a cloud in all this sunshine. I gathered that when he was still quite a young boy, this beloved father had left him – whether through death or for some other reason was not at first clear. At all events, from that time onward the place became partly deserted. The roofs of houses and farms fell in, and grass began to grow in some of the streets. The voice seemed especially anxious to impress this change on the other two, who at first spoke only occasionally, and indeed the early conversations were mainly a monologue from the first voice.

I must mention that from the first the voices seemed to come from different directions of space, yet the direction was not so much conveyed by a three-dimensional sense of the place or origin, as by a peculiar tone or colour in the voice. The first voice, even when it was loudest and most insistent, never failed to give me an impression of the blue haze of distant hills seen across a broad valley from a great height; the third had in it the quality of clear and bright sunshine, as of a yellow sun between snow clouds on a frosty day; the second was marked by a kaleidoscopic change of tone colour, and sometimes struck me as being almost chameleon-like in taking on the tones of the other two. The voice had also the property of speaking the most perfect English but always with something of a foreign intonation, as though a most gifted linguist had learned the language with absolute mastery, but too late in life to acquire the native accent.

Those conversations were always the easiest for me in which the second voice predominated, because it made no special demands on me, except that of not being confused by the quickness of its speech and the constant metamorphoses of tone. It was like listening to an air played on a number of successive instruments, though of course the transition was not abrupt, but organic.

At first this second voice seemed principally interested in establishing a kind of communion or identity with the first voice and the eagerness of its agreement came with the overwhelming suddenness of torrential rain. The similarity which developed between the histories of the first two speakers was remarkable. It appeared that the second had also been the son of a king and had been intensely devoted to his father. He also spoke of a dream childhood: there was a castle or palace, too (in both cases they were near the sea, and ships were always coming and going), and then there came the same strange and tragic disappearance of the father. Here also it seemed there had been a journey or visit abroad, which caused a separation before the final catastrophe occurred, though in this case it was the son who went away.

They spoke at first very guardedly of the catastrophe, partly as though they wished to shelter someone who had played a particularly disastrous part in it – I gathered that this person was a woman – and partly because it seemed they were afraid of giving offence to the third speaker. It seemed that this speaker was not in the same position as the first two, but had been an actor, in a different role, in a similar catastrophe. As the first two speakers established more and more firmly their identity of situation and interest, they turned with ever-increasing eagerness to him, as though he could do something tremendous for them – giving *light* was the phrase mostly used by the first speaker, while the second spoke chiefly of death, and the need for *life*.

The third speaker was for me the most exhausting of the three to understand and interpret. This was not because he spoke a foreign language – he spoke English with the same mastery as the second but also with a native accent – but because his thoughts came with such rapidity and compulsive power that they almost seemed to shatter the words in which they endeavoured to express themselves. They forced their way into the words like the lightning that rives the oak which gives it passage to its home in mother earth.

With this speaker I found nothing but incoherence if I

listened to the sounds, as with the first. But if, as far as possible, I tried to neglect the sounds and go direct to the thought of the speaker, the voice then spoke a language more or less intelligible both to me and to the other two voices. This was, however, exceptionally hard work, and it was some time before I gathered anything more than that the voice was that of an older man, and that he had himself suffered the same catastrophe which had befallen the fathers of the other two, but whether by natural death or violence was not at first clear.

I have said that there soon emerged an extraordinary similarity of situation between the first two speakers, but this similarity did not extend to their thoughts and feelings. Indeed, some conversations were little more than the repetition of opposite statements by the two. One of the earliest of these was when the first kept saying, "the god told me", which the second countered with "the god told me nothing", and finally, "there is no god". On another occasion the first voice said, "We are nothing; the blood is all", while the second repeated, "Nothing but I, O God, nothing but I" and this conversation ended with the first voice repeating "Infinity", and the second exclaiming "a nutshell, a nutshell".

During these altercations the third voice spoke very little. I think now that he was waiting for the full sense of identity of circumstance to establish itself between the other two. This came only later, in a very passionate and overwrought conversation in which the first voice spoke of a tremendous conflict of impulses he had undergone in connection with the sinister figure of the woman who had played a decisive part in the catastrophe. His actual words were: "The blood said strike, and the blood said leave. The limbs and entrails were torn apart. Father blood fought mother blood."

It was at the sound of the word *mother* that the second voice made one of those shattering changes of tone which were more terrifying than the leap of a tiger. "You, you," he shouted, and his voice became almost identical with that which he addressed. "You, you." And then, "A mother, a mother". Lastly, in his own voice. "Me". That was all. There was no repetition, and the conversation ended. But I knew that the two had established a fellowship beyond anything they had dreamed before.

After this the conversations became longer and more fluent, probably because I was already half certain of who the first two characters were, and they therefore found it easier to converse with each other through me. In proportion as they became easier to understand, however, the third voice became more difficult. This was all the more trying because, as the conversation came to a climax, it was plain that he had now the most important contribution to make. Indeed, the first two now hung on his words as though their lives or the salvation of their souls depended on him.

At this stage I made little headway with the third voice until I realised that to what he said I had now to attribute not one, but two, levels of meaning. The voice was telling the story of real events which had happened in his life, but these events had a validity far beyond their immediate application. They had the light of a revelation and the force of a redemption. It was this for which the first two speakers were so earnestly seeking, and which they hoped to gain from the third.

I mention this now, somewhat before its place, because I realised it in a dim kind of way even at the time of the critical dialogue I have described, and it gave me a clue to the relation of the first two characters which helped me a good deal in establishing a full connection between them. The fact was that they had not expected to meet each other, and had come together only because each of them was seeking the third. At one time it even seemed that each of the two regarded the meeting as a misfortune which hindered his true quest. At the slightest suggestion of this, however, the third voice always intervened. I had the impression that he claimed some magical power by which he believed he had brought them together. I think that my realisation of the relation between the three helped the conversations to develop, quite as much as did the new sense of fellowship established between the first two.

From this time onwards these two spoke to each other with complete frankness, and every detail fully confirmed my conjecture as to their identity. They never named themselves, and because I wish to convey as far as I can the exact impression which the conversation made on me, I will not do so either. A name can be very potent in taking away a man's mystery. But the first spoke of the sack of a great city, of a king returning in triumph to be murdered in his bath. The second caught up the tale with a picture of death lying in wait in an orchard. Almost in unison they told of an absent son, of a wife's treachery, of marriage to a murderer, of revenge on a mother for a father's death. But how hard it was for them to understand each other's sequel!

The first spoke of the bond which bound sister to brother, made stronger by the common will to vengeance. Who could understand the killing which came from killing and led to more killing? But it was the will of the gods that blood must be redeemed by blood. They who commanded would punish the deed, but it was glorious to stand in the chain which stretched to eternity, which neither gods nor men could break. All would go into the darkness, but in the darkness the memory of the deed would give a little light, a little warmth, a little sense of life. "The god thinks thus in me", the voice concluded.

Of course it was often interrupted and I have concentrated the general sense of a number of conversations into one short paragraph. The second voice denied nearly everything which the first affirmed. Indeed, as they argued, or rather asserted their convictions, it seemed as though the feeling that their encounter was a misfortune had been justified, and they had really forgotten their quest.

I fancy this was what the third voice intended, and that the conflict of their opinions was being more educative to them than they themselves imagined. The second voice, for instance, was immensely scornful of the chain of the generations. "Birth and death, the beginning and the end," he kept repeating. And as you had to die alone, so you had to live alone. There was no glory in the deed, only shame and remorse.

"Shake yourself free of all others," this voice said, "do not drag them into the shame. Let them find their own death, even as you will find yours, but do not take them with you into your own darkness. For there is light on the earth, light in the mind on the earth, but it shows only the corruption and the darkness to come. Happy is the man who can live in darkness on the earth, and cannot see the infinite darkness ahead. The light is all, but the light cannot live without generation and the blood; yet the blood is death and corruption, and swallows up the light. The only glory is to say 'the light is me'; but the light has no life, the light is eaten by the worm that devours the blood."

It was plainly very difficult for the first voice to understand anything of what the second said. Particularly hard was the saying, "the light is me". "The light is me," it kept repeating, "how can you say, the light is me? The gods are the light, the men have only the darkness." But it went on repeating, as though it were savouring a new taste, "the light is me, the light is me".

It was from this point that the third voice began to intervene more and more insistently. Generally it seemed to speak in a kind of allegorical language, as though there were no words in which it could immediately express itself, and it seemed that often the first voice understood this more easily than it understood the more direct language of the second. "You cannot find your own light," the third voice would say, addressing itself to the first, "because you are not yet on the island." And to the second, "You cannot find the life without death because you are on the hard island." Then to both: "Come to the enchanted island."

From this time onward all three voices began to speak in the short gnomic sentences which were mainly characteristic of the third. Certain terms also became current among them which plainly had a meaning beyond the ordinary. I will not attempt to explain or alter them because again I wish to give as far as possible the exact effect which the voices themselves produced.

For instance, the first voice asked: "Did the vengeance bring light and warmth? Did it reach the shadow in Hades?" The second: "What are you that demand the vengeance? Are you the shadow of the light? Where is the life?" As they asked these questions, they grew more and more insistent, till I began to feel them like children crowding their questions into the ears of a wise old man. There was a mellowness in the answers of the third voice which carried conviction, even when they were not immediately comprehensible. To the questions I have given, the older voice had always the same answer: "With me there is no vengeance, and no instrument of vengeance. There was only the picture of the deed, the remorse and the return. The picture was the vengeance. The picture spoke to the life within, which is beyond the death. Come to the enchanted island and you will understand."

This last sentence was the refrain which ran through all the answers of the third voice. At first it was a whispered pleading like the distant call of a bird, and when it ceased I sometimes thought I heard the noise of hovering wings attending it. It grew more insistent and powerful every time some perplexity on the part of the first two voices was cleared away, and the perplexities were many and various.

The first voice, for instance, could not understand the saying, "The vengeance is the picture of the deed in the light," and was still more troubled when the third voice kept saying, "The picture is from within." "But the vengeance is from without," the first voice objected. "How then can the vengeance be the picture? Where is the death and the darkness which the vengeance brings?" "The picture is the vengeance in the light," the third voice insisted. "The deed is in the darkness, in the blood; the picture of the deed is in the light. The picture brings the suffering and the remorse. It brings the death in the warm light, which is harder than the death in the darkness. But the death in the warm light does not kill like the death in the hot blood.''

It was the last statement which seemed most to trouble the second voice. "There is the death in the light," it said, "and the death kills. It kills the heat, it kills the life, it kills all." "You are on the hard island," was the response, "where the light is cold. Come to the enchanted island where the light is warm, and gives the life." "But the heat is in the darkness, in the blood." "Not the heat, the warmth; the heat is of the blood, but warmth is of the light. Come to the enchanted island, where the picture is in the light, and the light is not in the cold but in the warmth."

It was this last idea of the light in the warmth which seemed to give the greatest difficulty to the second voice, and the third voice returned to it again and again. It insisted on the difference between the heat and the warmth; it developed the idea that it was the warmth in the picture which gave both the vengeance and the desire for the return. "The warm light wishes to enter the darkness," it often said. "It wishes to redeem the deed in the dark blood."

Another idea which the first voice found very hard to grasp was that the deed in the cold light is as bad as in the hot blood. "To slay in the cold light is as though one slew in the hot blood. My brother and his friend slew me in the cold light, but I was not slain as your fathers were slain". This last statement brought a cry of horror from the second voice. "But your daughter," it said, "how could she mingle her blood with the son of the slayer?" "She did not see the son of the slayer," was the reply. "She saw the warm light in the son, and she loved the warm light in him."

It was at this point that the second voice suddenly assumed almost completely the tone and character of the third. "And the son," it cried, "did he see the warm light in her?"

"He loved her," the third voice replied, "because he saw the warm light in her. And she loved him because the warm light in the son conquered the dark blood in the father. The return was not in the darkness but in the warm light. The father and the son found the return together in the warm light."

When the voice finished speaking there came the sound of waves falling lazily on level sands, mingled with snatches of aerial music. For the first and only time a fourth voice intruded, a voice of extraordinary clearness and purity, like sea water lying unruffled in a rock pool on a sunny day. But it had also a tang, a resistance, like the sea air. It said only one word: "Master."

Drama at Bockley Manor

A Hallowe'en Story

Some of you will probably remember the minor sensation that was caused thirty years ago when young Michael Fairtrees left the stage to become a barrister. There were indeed one or two critics who maintained that his acting, in spite of its formal perfection, lacked inspiration; but most of them, and certainly the public at large, were already hailing him as the genius of the century. The mystery – and therefore the sensation – was all the greater because Fairtrees himself obstinately refused to give one word of explanation, merely quoting to the newspaper men who besieged him a line from *Julius Caesar*: 'The cause is in my will, I will it so'.

If I tell you that I was one of three people who knew the reason for his decision, you will probably imagine that I was among his more intimate friends. I therefore hasten to assure you that I only met him on two occasions, and I doubt very much whether he even remembered my name for long. Nor did he take any pains to impress on us three his desire for secrecy. 'I shall give no reasons for this,' was all he said. But I think that both Sir John and Lady Hilton and I realised immediately that his secrecy was also binding on us. However, it is now nearly a year since the newspapers announced the death of Mr. Justice Fairtrees, an event which naturally led to a revival of the mystery of his retirement from the stage; and, as one or two quite false theories have almost been accepted with regard to it, I think I have the duty, as the only living person who knows the truth, to tell the whole story as it occurred.

It began with my friendship at Oxford with a Canadian called Trask. There were half a dozen of us who were special friends – exactly how such sets arise is always a mystery – and Trash (his inevitable nickname) was certainly one of us. But I think none of us felt entirely at home with Trash. We used to say he had Red Indian blood in him, and his black smooth hair and high cheek-bones certainly suggested it. He would suddenly become extremely wild without any provocation, and he loved to disappear for a week or two and re-appear without explanation. It was typical of our relation to him that no one ever asked him where he had been. It was also typical that he should choose me – the least likely member of our set – for the special favour of sharing the secret of his disappearances. For one day he put his head in at my room to throw me a book he had borrowed and announced: 'I'm going to Bockley at the week-end to stay with a sort of aunt I have there. Come out and have lunch on Sunday – you can cycle it in an hour. It's the last house on the right past the church.' So that was how I came to arrive at Bockley Manor one fine Sunday in May in an old pair of flannel trousers and an old sports jacket, and riding a rusty old bicycle.

Dressed like that – Trash had added 'Wear what you like' through the door – it was rather a shock to find myself in front of a beautiful three-gabled Elizabethan Manor House and to realise that I did not even know the name of the people on whom I was calling. I think I would probably have fled if Trash himself had not come out at that moment, dressed no better than I was, and carried me off to bathe in the stone pool beneath the terrace.

It was the first time I had been in the garden of so lovely a Cotswold House. We swam among the water lilies ('everyone bathes naked here,' said Trash): then, while we dressed, he told me he had a distant relative called Hilton, whose father had made a fortune in Canada and got a baronetcy for something or other before he died, and the son wasn't much good for anything, but had a pot of money and a perfect wife, and they had bought the place only a year before. 'Lots of people come to lunch on Sundays,' he added, 'so you just grab what you can.'

The lots of people turned out to be half a dozen or more of the kind of person I was not accustomed to meet – indeed had never met before. There was at least one literary lion, a Peer of the realm, and a not very minor politician. Trash himself said very little, but looked perfectly at his ease and dreadfully distinguished with his black hair and eyes. I was in the abject misery of social inferiority, not knowing how to help myself at the buffet (lunch was always served there on Sundays) or how to join in a conversation in which life was approached from an angle with which I was totally unfamiliar. How I envied Trash his ability to sit still and not care. I hardly know how I got through the lunch, or how I had the courage to go up to Lady Hilton after it and tell her that I feared I must be going. It was then that I first appreciated what Trash meant when he said his aunt was perfect. 'Oh, don't go', she said, 'I'm afraid these people have bored you terribly. Stay to tea and we'll have some real conversation.' I suppose it was the first time that I had been put at my ease – and flattered – by a beautiful and gracious lady. I know it produced in me a mood of gratitude and devotion which has lasted all my life.

It is perhaps significant that I have not yet mentioned Sir John Hilton. The only positive thing about him seemed to be his devotion to his wife. I learnt afterwards that as a young man he had had a severe accident to his head from which he had never entirely recovered. He was always planning little surprises for her, and she behaved to him as though he were the most wonderful and adorable of men. She did not allow herself to believe anything other.

Of course I stayed to tea, and Lady Hilton walked with me in the garden and loosed my tongue to talk of my youthful enthusiasms. Perhaps my exceptional innocence appealed to her. But I should add that I had a tolerable voice and she shared my devotion to Elizabethan music. It was not long before she was at the harpsichord – then a newly re-discovered instrument – demanding song after song. Whatever the reason, from that time on I became a regular visitor, and even the Sunday lunches lost their terror. When Trash went back to Canada in the autumn, I took his place as a kind of adopted nephew – the Hiltons had no children of their own – and Bockley Manor became my real home. It was there that I spent most of my vacations, reading in the great library in which many of the books had been bought with the house. This library – the largest room in the house – had a typical Tudor fireplace, over which hung a portrait of some young man of the seventeenth century with a pair of foils stuck over the frame. One evening, when he found me looking at this rather dingy and wooden picture, Sir John became unusually communicative and told me it had been a condition of the purchase of the house that the picture, with the foils over it, should be allowed to hang there until it fell. His lawyer had laughed at the condition, but whether legally enforceable or not, he and Lady Hilton had determined to abide by it, in spite of the completely undistinguished nature of the portrait. For such, it appears, had been the condition of tenure of the property ever since the seventeenth century, though it had remained in the hands of one family until the Hiltons bought it. The founder of the family – whose name was Shipley – had made his fortune in the wool trade, like so many Cotswold families of the time, had built the Manor House and half re-built the Church, and left his descendants 'spacious in the possession of dirt.' Antony Shipley, from whom the Hiltons had bought the house, was the last of his name. The picture was supposed to be of an ancestor, but no one knew of whom.

I got a chair to examine it closely, but it made very little impression on me. I did, however, notice one thing; one of the two foils had a button on the end, the other had not. The wire on which the picture hung appeared pretty weak, and I remember remarking that it wouldn't be long before it fell of its own accord. In that I was wiser than I knew.

As I grew a more and more familiar inmate at the Manor, I began bringing my friends, many of whom, like myself, were members of the College Dramatic Club. It happened that the year after my first introduction to Bockley we had put on a specially good production of *Twelfth Night* (I was the Clown, and *The Times*, while approving of my voice, described my acting as 'the one weak spot in an otherwise impeccable production') and I suggested to Lady Hilton that we should ask the Company to give a candlelight performance in the library at Bockley. It was to be a late performance at the end of the summer term, and beds were to be somehow found for the whole cast.

It was a memorable occasion. I think I have never been so deeply moved by the poetry of the play or so little hurt by its cruelties. I saw with delight the radiant happiness on Lady Hilton's face, which was as responsive to her moods as a field of hay to a June breeze. When we got to bed, after a splendid supper, about 2 a.m., I was too tired and excited and happy to sleep. I heard the clock strike three, and soon after came the first pale glimmer of dawn. I rose and looked out of the window at the still grey birth of the day. It appeared I was not the only one who could not sleep. Wilson, who played Malvolio, was walking in the garden, still dressed in his doublet and tights. I did not call out to him for fear of waking the rest of the house, but I watched him walk round the pool and come up to the terrace. A cock crew as he entered the library, which was generally left open all night in the summer, and I hesitated whether to go out and watch the sun rise, or get back into bed and sleep. The cold wind of dawn settled the matter and I got into bed.

Breakfast was at no fixed time. People arrived down as they chose, but most of them were leaving that day for their homes, and no one was very late. Lady Hilton had wisely said good-bye after the performance, Sir John always slept late, and I was left to see the party off. Wilson was one of the last to go, and it was only as he was getting into the car that I mentioned that I had seen him walking in the garden. He looked genuinely astonished. 'Slept like a top, you ass,' he said.

I went into the Library, slightly depressed, to see the scene of last night's triumph. Most of the curtains were still drawn, but one window was partly bare and the sun was shining through it on to the portrait over the fireplace. It was then that I got my first real shock. There was no doubt that the face bore a most decided resemblance to Malvolio. The more I looked the more plainly I could see it. Why had I never noticed it before? I went to draw the curtains over the windows, and as I did so and saw the terrace and pool, and the exact place where I had first seen Wilson in the dawn (for he had not denied being there in so many words), I had my second shock. For I remembered that, when I had seen him walking as Malvolio in the garden, he had been cross-gartered – villainously cross-gartered. Now Malvolio does not wear cross-garters at the end of the play, and I was sure Wilson had been ungartered at the final curtain. It was unthinkable that he should have put on his garters in order to take a solitary walk in the garden at dawn. With some trepidation I turned to the picture again. Now that the light was different I could not see the least resemblance to Malvolio. It was the old wooden young man's face. I wanted to draw the curtain again, and get the sun on the picture as before, but the servants came in to clean up the room and I had no excuse for doing so.

I was decidedly uneasy after this, and none the less so when at lunch Lady Hilton remarked that she also had seen 'young Malvolio' walking in the garden in the grey dawn. She was in great spirits from the success of the performance and I had to pretend to be equally elated, as indeed I had been till a few hours before, though I think I have never felt so strongly a feeling of some coming disaster. The blow fell at supper time. It was the butler's day out, and we were waited on by a maid. She had just taken some dishes out of the room, when we heard a scream and the noise of breaking crockery, and she rushed back into the room. 'If you please, my Lady,' she said (it was natural for the servants to speak to her rather than to her husband), 'there's a black man in the house – he's just gone up the stairs.' Sir John and I both seized a fire-iron and went in pursuit. We searched all the bedrooms, but there was no trace of anyone, and nothing had been disturbed. Of course I thought the girl had meant a man dressed in black like Malvolio; but when we came to question her I found to my surprise that she meant a man with a black face – he had turned on the stairs and she had seen the whites of his eyes 'like a real nigger's'. He might have been dressed in black or it might have been in blue – she couldn't say which. The face was quite enough for her, she hadn't noticed much else.

This proved to be only the beginning. By the end of the following week most of the servants had seen something. What surprised everybody was that mostly they saw different things. The butler had seen a fat man with white hair as he came up from the cellar: two housemaids had seen what they called 'a real ghost – all in white' by the front door, as they came home late one night. But the commonest appearance, which Lady Hilton saw twice in the week, was a figure in black crouching in a corner of the library and gazing with the utmost intensity towards the fire-place.

You may imagine the effect all this had on the household, the village and the whole neighbourhood. The servants gave notice or fled without it. At week-ends parties arrived to peer through the yew hedge. Gentlemen interested in psychical research begged to be allowed to investigate the phenomena. Worst of all, Lady Hilton's health began to be affected with worry and loss of sleep. Sir John begged her to go away, but she had fallen deeply in love with the house and garden, and she declared that to go now would be like deserting a friend in trouble – an action of which no one could dream her capable. I felt dreadfully guilty because it was I who had first suggested the unhappy performance which had started the whole thing off. I was also certain – though I kept this to myself – that it all had something to do with the portrait in the library, though I could not guess what.

It was quite by accident that I got my first clue. We were thinking of putting on the first part of *Henry IV*, and I settled down one night in the library to read it with a view to suggesting parts. I came to the scene where Falstaff is acting the Prince and making his defence of sweet Jack Falstaff. You will remember that at this point they are interrupted by

Bardolph, and Falstaff turns on him with *Out you rogue. Play out the play*. I dropped the book to the floor. There was no doubt about it. Another voice, a strong resonant voice, had echoed the words: *Play out the play*. I sprang up and looked round the room. There was nothing to be seen. But as I turned to pick up the book, my eye fell on the picture. Falstaff's face was looking down on me.

From that time I was certain that the picture was that of an actor whose spirit for some reason had been awakened by the performance of *Twelfth Night* and had begun to haunt the house. My theory was curiously confirmed by an event that occurred only a few days later. I had gone into Oxford to read in the Bodleian for a thesis I was writing, when I ran into Wilson, who had acted Malvolio and of course knew all about the haunting. He told me he had something of importance to tell me, and we went out to lunch together. He said he had been to a coming-of-age dance at the house of some people called Blakeley – descendants of the unfortunate admiral who had been disgraced in the Napoleonic wars. They still had a uniform of his in a glass case, and Wilson had a sudden impulse to put it on and appear as the Admiral in the middle of the dance. The effect was not quite what he intended. It appeared that the Admiral had been known to walk before – and when Wilson appeared on the stairs, several of the guests screamed and at least one fainted. 'And since then,' he said, 'the house is uninhabitable. Eight bells sounding every half hour. Bosuns' whistles shrilling in the dead of night. Smell of weevil biscuits everywhere. And the most awful oaths coming down the chimneys and up through the cracks in the floor.' I agreed that he had a most unfortunate effect on ghosts and advised him to emigrate. I also left him to pay the bill.

Back in the Bodleian I knew what I had to do. I took out all the books I could find about Elizabethan acting companies. Had there ever been an actor of the name of Shipley? Had any company ever been known to come to Bockley? I spent all that week in the library following up every possible clue, and on Saturday I returned to Bockley, where things had gone from bad to worse. Lady Hilton was really ill by this time and the doctor had ordered her to bed. Sir John was desperate, convinced that she would die and quite unable to persuade her to move. Not a servant would stay the night in the house or be in it after dark, so we were dependent on two women who ventured to come in from the village during the day. My only comfort was that I had lost all fear of the invisible presence, which I now felt constantly with me. I had taken to the habit of reading Shakespeare and other Elizabethan plays aloud in the library at night, and by watching the portrait and feeling some kind of heightening in my voice, which I could only attribute to his inspiration, I had a shrewd idea of the parts he had acted. In addition to Malvolio and Falstaff he had certainly played Othello and Richard the Second and Prospero. It was in the part of Hamlet, however, that I felt his presence most compellingly. I only once again heard him speak actual words, and they were the same words *Play out the play*; but twice, in reading *Hamlet*, the words; *Rest, rest perturbed spirit*, were followed by a sigh such as Shakespeare must have had in mind when he wrote: 'What a sigh is there! The heart is sorely charged.' I believe that I now wanted to find rest for that perturbed spirit almost as much for his own sake as for my dear Lady Hilton.

Strangely enough it was when I abandoned my search for lists of actors and returned to my thesis that the ultimate clue was put in my hands. My thesis was concerned with seventeenth-century correspondence, and I had secured permission to examine the Woodward Papers, which at that time had only just been discovered. It was a tedious business deciphering the tormented writing which seems to have passed for a fair hand in the reign of Eliza and our James. But there were some good rewards. There for instance Mistress Elizabeth Woodward, a sprightly widow looking for another husband, who regaled a number of eligible gentlemen with the scandal of the county and not a few excellent stories. One of them – she had it from her cousin Toby – concerned a young man of good family who, to the scandal of his parents, had run away to join a company of actors. His father had let it be known that it would be dangerous for such a reprobate to come near the house again. The young man had changed both his name and his company, and when some years later the new company had come to that part of the county and had been invited to play in the father's house, the son, who was now the leading actor, had thought he would pass unrecognised. 'Perhaps he even thought of discovering himself,' added Mistress Woodward, 'and that, being so famed an actor his father might again take him to his heart.' But during the play, in which he had to fight a duel, another actor had accidentally thrust him through the heart. But there were those who said that the father had recognised the son and had bribed this actor (who had fled overseas) to kill him. The young man's name was very difficult to decipher, but as far as I could make it out it was Navager.

Incredible as it may seem to you, when I read this story I saw it only from the angle of my thesis and did not connect it with the ghost of Bockley. The human mind is astonishingly capable of erecting its own iron curtains. Many years later I saw a witness in a court of law so concentrated by a clever Counsel on making a specimen of his handwriting that he forgot he could give himself away by spelling. I suppose it was some such one-sided concentration that led me to return to Bockley without any idea that I had the solution of the mystery in my hand. What made the truth dawn on me was not the story, palpable as it was, but the name.

In the evening I sat in the library reading my notes of the day, when I was struck by the strangeness of the name Navager. It was surely not English. What language could it come from? The form was Latin. Navager. *Navis* – a ship. *Ager* – a field. Had someone been making a composite Latin name? Shipfield – that did not sound like a decent name. God in Heaven, I swear the picture was smiling at me from the frame. Ager – a field – a ley. Navager was Shipley, and there was the actor Shipley staring at me in the very room in which he had been killed and with that sharpened foil over the frame. No doubt his old father had hung picture and foil there in fearful contrition for what he had done, and willed that they should stay there, a constant mystery which might perhaps one day bring to light the deed he dared not confess.

There could be no doubt of the play in which Shipley, alias Navager, had met his death. I took down a Shakespeare and turned to the last scene of *Hamlet*. As I read those final speeches aloud, with their ominous foreboding of death, I knew that the voice was not my own. I came to what I knew must have been the tragic moment:

> HAMLET. *I pray you, pass with your best violence,*
> *I am afeard you make a wanton of me.*
> LAERTES. *Have at you now.*

I tried to read on, but no sound came from my lips. But for the second time Falstaff's words echoed through the room with a deeply tragic intensity: *Play out the play*. I rose and stood in front of the picture. 'It shall be done,' I said.

I was convinced that it had not only to be done but to be supremely well done. Sir John and Lady Hilton, to whom of course I confided my conviction, were equally agreed on this, and Sir John was emphatic that no expense should be spared. Thus it came about that, when that memorable production of *Hamlet* – with Michael Fairtrees in the name part – came to the end of its run, the whole Company came down to Bockley, to perform in the library of the Manor. The rest of the Company imagined that it was the whim of a rich man to please his invalid wife. Michael Fairtrees alone knew the truth. He was not the kind of man (as many a prisoner subsequently found) from whom the truth was easily concealed, and I realised at once that nothing but the full story would bring him down. He took the whole thing with that immense seriousness and concentration which he brought to everything he did. 'If ever I acted in my life, I will act to-night,' he said to me in the room where he was dressing before the play.

I have never ventured to see a performance of *Hamlet* since.

If Fairtrees inspired the rest of the Company, so that the whole play took on a cosmic immensity, he himself was inspired from some source far beyond his own personality. Never were such riches poured out before so small an audience. As the play proceeded, I felt as though we were approaching some majestic mountain which towered higher and higher into the heavens as we drew near, and yet at the same time revealed the intimate beauties of its valleys and forests. When the fencing scene drew near, I wanted to glance at Lady Hilton but found myself unable to take my eyes off the actors. All three of us agreed afterwards that at that moment we felt our very lives in the balance. We were not in our seats, we were in the play, and had the act come to a premature end we could not have continued to live. It was like the crisis of a mortal illness.

At last we reached the words of Laertes: *Have at you now.* Something broke. It was a moment which I can now only compare to the breaking of the sound barrier. Incredibly, the play proceeded. Hamlet came to the poignant words:

> *If ever thou didst hold me in thy heart,*
> *Absent thee from felicity awhile*
> *And in this harsh world draw thy breath in pain*
> *To tell my story.*

We knew that the perturbed spirit was finding his rest.

Young Fortinbras entered, from smiting the sledded Polacks on the ice, and with him came that last cold evening wind which carries the play to its end. The final words were declaimed: *Go, bid the soldiers shoot,* and there came a deep roar which seemed to shake even the solid walls of the Manor House. I looked up to the picture to see if I could detect any change in its expression. A screen had been placed as near the fire as possible to keep the light from the room and some of the firelight was reflected back on to the wall. But I was too late. At that moment, no doubt shaken by the vibration, the picture broke its rusty wire and fell. One end hit the top of the screen which pitched it back into the fire. I was about to rush to rescue it when I was stopped by Lady Hilton's voice. 'Let it burn', she said, 'the perturbed spirit will rest the quieter.'

We were still sitting spellbound in our chairs when Michael Fairtrees came up to us. 'After this,' he said, 'I shall never act again.' Tragic as his decision was, all three of us knew that it was irrevocable and that it was right. Lady Hilton took his hand and kissed it, and he went out to change.

When the news of his retirement from the stage came out a week later, I could not enough admire the indifference of Fairtrees to the scandalous rumours which were circulated and which you all know have been revived with his death. But now that he is dead I feel that I have the duty to protect his memory. Sir John and my dear Lady Hilton have been dead many years now, Bockley Manor is in other hands, and, unless Fairtrees himself told the tale to others (which I do not believe) I am the only person living who knows what caused him to abandon his stage career.

What the Gas Men Found

A Hallowe'en Story

There is one great disadvantage in being known to be interested in the supernatural – as I confess that I am. Friends, acquaintances and even strangers are always informing you of alleged hauntings, visitations, noises by night and by day, telepathic communications, fits of glossolalia, manifestations of ectoplasm, and any other unusual occurrence for which they can give no rational explanation. Most of these things prove on investigation to be insignificant or fraudulent or both, but occasionally the least likely case proves to be of exceptional interest, and I endeavour – as far as I can – to investigate everything reported to me.

Yet I confess to a real sinking of heart when Wilson rang me up last week to tell me that he had moved to a new flat in Chelsea, where a suicide had occurred some years before, and that something had happened which he was sure would interest me. Would I come to dinner that evening and hear all about it?

I had no doubt that he could have told me all about it in two minutes on the telephone – noises under the floor probably coming from the flat below, or furniture shifted to a different place, almost certainly the work of the charwoman. But Wilson shares his flat with a retired Bank Manager, who is a cook of more than professional skill (got from cooking accounts, his friends tell him) which has deservedly earned him the nickname of Brittlebrit. (If you do not know why, you must read your Grimm's Fairy Tales over again.) So I said, 'Delighted' and hung up the receiver.

With extraordinary restraint Wilson said nothing about the suicide until after dinner. So I guessed that something pretty terrific must have happened to sober him so. But I admit I was not prepared for his opening gambit. 'What I want to tell you,' he said, 'has nothing to do with the suicide – I merely mentioned that on the telephone to get you here.' ('Confound your cheek,' I almost said aloud.) 'I want to read you a very remarkable document which came into my possession only yesterday. When we took this flat, Brittlebrit naturally brought his gas stove with all the gadgets necessary to his art, and the gas-men had to come to fit it. Of course they pulled up half the floor – they always do – and there, "hidden in its vacant interlunar cave" (Wilson will always drag in a quotation if he can) one of them found this old envelope which he gave me, no doubt after making sure it contained nothing valuable. I propose to read the contents to you now.'

My depression returned. Wilson loves to hear his own voice, and I suppose he does not know that he has an appalling trick of dropping his voice during every sentence and starting the next one a fourth higher up. But there was no help for it, and I settled down while he began:

My dear Successor,

The first thing that strikes me as I take up my pen to write you this letter, is the extreme strangeness of my writing to you the most intimate and important thing in my life – a thing which I have never told to another soul – in spite of the fact that I met you in the train for the first time yesterday and do not even know your name and address. But if I am certain that the sun will rise to-morrow, I am equally certain that next Sunday evening you will come to my flat in accordance with the verbal invitation I gave you. Your curiosity, your hopes, I will even add your fears, will be too great for you to keep away, nor have I any apprehension that you will forget the address. My landlady will show you upstairs (as she has been instructed to do) and to your surprise you will find an empty flat containing nothing except a largish Box, and this letter tucked under the string on the lid. For by then I will have removed all the rest of my furniture and with it all traces of myself. The rent is paid till the end of the quarter, and you will have plenty of time to examine the Box and arrange for its removal. I have given no address and it is impossible we shall ever meet again. From now on you will become the guardian of the Box. You will possess it, and if I know anything of its fascination, it will soon fill your life as completely as it has filled mine. It may be that you will be the person destined to communicate its secret, and its power, to the rest of the world. But if not – and I do not think the time is nearly ripe for that yet – in another twenty or thirty years you will be looking for your successor just as I have been looking for you. And when you have found him, he will come to call on you on the day and at the hour you will appoint, and he will find the empty room and the Box and the letter, just as I found them twenty-five years ago and as you will find them next Sunday. The excitement, which will by then have become an intolerable nervous tension, and the burden of responsibility will fall from your shoulders. For what little remains of your life you will be a free man again. I hope you will then enjoy your remaining days as I intend to enjoy mine.

With this my prelude ends: and now I must tell you, firstly, how I came into possession of the Box, and secondly why I have chosen you to be its next owner and my successor.

The place where I met my predecessor, and my fate, was a fairground in a West-Country town. I had been sent by the firm of solicitors in which I was the new junior on one of my first professional jobs, and by the time I had arranged matters with our client it was too late to catch the last train back to London. As I write these words a blush still comes over me. For this was what I told the firm on my return the next day. In reality there was plenty of time. But the client had invited me to dinner, and in my professional capacity I knew something of the contents of his cellar. I had also money in my pocket to pay my expenses at the best hotel in the town, and in those days I was more familiar with those hostelries which carry the badge of the Cyclists' Touring Club than with those which bear the well-starred approval of the motorists' handbooks. Anyhow I stayed, and the dinner and the wine were both well worth the staying for. I was certainly not perfectly sober when I left and I felt the need of fresh air and a little exercise before turning into the hotel.

The lights and the shrill music of a Merry-go-Round with its mechanical gaiety drew me to the opposite end of the town. The fair was about to close, but I had one ride on a galloping ostrich and I was the last to come down the mat-slide. I was in no hurry to get to bed, and I stayed and watched the men already dismantling their gaudy apparatus. It is a terrifying spectacle to see the Fair men fall destructively on the machines in which a minute before they were exulting, – worse, I think, than seeing a building consumed by the flames. There is always something magnificent in the destructive spirit of a fire; momentarily it adds a fearful beauty to the object which it destroys, the life rushes from it in torrents of glory. But when the Fair ends, the lights go down: warmth departs with the jostling crowds and a cold wind begins to blow. The glorious creatures who walked at a slant on the roundabout taking the money as though, like gods, they could defy the earthly law of gravity, become sallow devils mercilessly tearing asunder the vitals of the machines by which they live. A revulsion of feeling came over me, and I inwardly wept for the tragedy of the universe typified in the scene before me. Like Chaucer's monk I rehearsed the sad fates of heroes. Mutability and mighty poets in their misery dead were the one theme of a hopeless life. My client's good wine was certainly losing something of its uplifting effect.

I suspect, my dear young friend, that you also are subject to these sudden floods of emotion which seem to afflict all those who possess the particular kind of supernatural power which we enjoy, through which we find ourselves suddenly localising and reversing the natural process of time. I know now that it is always after some excitement or dejection that I have found myself exercising the Power. It was certainly so in this case. I took out a cigarette to calm myself. A gust blew out my last match. Smoking is not a necessity to me, and I was about to throw the cigarette away (they were ten for sixpence in those days), when I saw an elderly man in the act of lighting a pipe only a few paces away, his face showing clearly in the flame cupped in his hands. What more natural than to ask him for a light? Was it not just as natural for you in the train yesterday to ask me if I minded having the window open? Could either of us have foreseen the consequences of these innocent requests?

The stranger seemed startled, as I spoke to him, and as he held the still burning match to my cigarette, I could see that he was trembling violently. Indeed I thought he would have fallen and I put my arms out to save him. But he recovered himself, took me by the arm and started walking with me into the town. He said nothing till we were well clear of the fairground. Then he halted. 'I have found out your secret', he said. You will imagine how my heart beat and what it meant to have to admit to another human being that I was different from other men, that I possessed a power which until then I believed no one else on the earth shared with me. Or would it be that this man before me possessed the same power, that I could have the infinite relief of sharing my secret with someone else? Was it joy or terror I was undergoing at that moment? Whatever it was, one thing is certain. I had not the least doubt that the stranger knew my secret, nor was I at all in the dark as to how he had learnt it. The match, on which I had concentrated more thought than I had realised, had been the phoenix which gave me away. It had gone out before I spoke to him.

'Does it often happen to you?' he asked. 'About

once a month.' 'But it is getting more frequent, and causing you embarrassment in its lowest, and terror in its highest manifestation?' 'Yes,' I answered. 'More frequent and more terrible.' 'I suppose that up to the present (you are still young) it generally works on some ordinary object, but one which has especially impressed itself on your consciousness?' I thought a moment. 'Yes, that is so!' 'And it is always after some intense emotion?' I had not then thought of this either, but it at once dawned on me that it was the case. 'Ah, you must watch your emotions,' he added, reading my thoughts, and there was a pause. 'But that is not enough,' he added, 'that will not save you from the mad-house. If you possess the Power, and do not use it regularly and under proper control, it will devour you. There is much that could be done with it. It could be a source of immense and beneficial energy. But men are not yet ready for it. In their present state of barbarism they would only use it to destroy one another. But one day things will change, and then we shall see.' I began to be suspicious of him. How could this thing, so personal to me, become a source of power for the world? He evidently felt he had said enough and he changed his tone. 'Do you ever come to London?' he asked. 'I live there,' I said. 'I rather thought so,' he replied, 'I live in Chelsea. Would it be convenient for you to come to my flat, say next Sunday week?' He gave me the address verbally (later I understood that he wished to leave no shadow of a clue to his identity, not so much as a scrap of paper) and with a solemn 'goodnight' he shook me by the hand and walked quickly away. I returned to the Maiden's Head.

I was a good bit shaken by the experience and slept badly. The morning was restless with intermittent rain. A feeling of cold discomfort and apprehension pervaded everything. The waiter was surly, the taxi-man grumbled, the station was rain-swept, the London train was late. But on the way the sun conquered. It was autumn; the landscape became

flooded with a deep golden light, every tree flamed
with colour as though it were on fire. I felt like an
ancient Persian who had witnessed the triumph of
Ormuzd over the dark Angra Mainyu. The black
cloud was charmed from my soul. I sat in breathless
ecstasy. Light is indeed invisible, but it is not
incognisable. For me at that moment the visible
landscape was a secondary thing. I did not need what
light revealed – I was immersed in light itself. I had
forgotten the advice of my new acquaintance to watch
my emotions. (Our fellow men are only familiar with
the blow which knocks them out of time into
unconsciousness. We – you and I – are familiar with a
different sort of blow, which knocks us into a higher
consciousness in which past, present and future
change their normal relationships.)

The train stopped at a junction, and a porter
entered the compartment to remove a suitcase from
the rack. It was a suit case belonging to a middle-
aged lady and I had helped her to put it up when she
had got in with me. Not only was it a very
extraordinary suitcase, being painted with vermilion
stripes, but it bore the most unusual name of
PIMCOX printed large on two yellow labels. I had
therefore paid rather special attention to it and I
suppose it had been living in my sub-conscious mind
all the time I was rejoicing in the light of the sun. The
train began to move out of the station, and I glanced
up at the rack. You, my friend and fellow-sufferer,
will appreciate my horror when I saw that the strange
suit case was still there. I seized it, and quickly thrust
it through the open window. I shall not soon forget
the look of panic on the face of the porter holding up
his empty hands, and staring first at the suit case lying
on the platform twenty yards beyond him, and then at
his hands, as though to assure himself that they at
least were still there. The woman's face was away from
me, but there were other people on the platform
whose faces of blank amazement followed my
carriage as the train gathered momentum. By the

grace of God, the other two people in the compartment were buried in their magazines and saw nothing.

Whether or no I would have gone without it, this incident determined me to keep my appointment with my friend of the fairground. Any chance of release from such sudden visitations of the terrible Power would have taken me to the Antipodes, and I found myself counting the hours till the time appointed. By the time you have this letter in your hand you will know what I found, because you will have found the same – the empty room, the Box, the letter, and with them the passionate hope of relief and the foreboding of some unknown responsibility.

Now as to the Box and its uses. You will find full instructions printed on the various parts. I had no difficulty in mastering its more elementary uses in a few hours and I do not anticipate that you will either, once you have grasped the fundamental principle. The geometrical forms in it are without doubt copies or expressions of the geometrical forces which manifest themselves in the world of plants. The secret of the Box is that it enables those of us who possess the Power to apply it *at will* to the growth and ungrowth of the plant world. Think what energy can be generated when, by the simple use of the Power which you and I possess, a plant can be subjected with incredible rapidity to all its time-space relationships, from seed to flower and back again to seed! What infinite energy would be generated if the same process were applied to the larger trees! I have attempted nothing on such a grand scale – I had no facilities for doing so. But I flatter myself that I have discovered certain adjustments of form to which various forms of plants are peculiarly responsive, and I leave you the legacy of my discoveries.

It is now for you to decide whether this immense source of energy can rightly be communicated to the world. Do not underestimate the opposition you will receive from the controllers of the existing sources of power, and the extreme probability that they will succeed in having you declared insane, and detained during Her Majesty's (or their) pleasure. There is also the dreadful likelihood that the energy would be turned (as it well could be) to destructive purposes, and that in some future war you would find yourself responsible for explosions which would shatter cities and devastate continents.

To whatever use you may put the Box, you may have the assurance that, by using it consciously with some regularity (once a week will be quite adequate), you will entirely escape the embarrassment of unexpected manifestations of the Power in public. There is also no doubt that the Power deserts you as soon as you find a successor. I already feel a difference in my life, which I can only compare to the shutting off of some distant engine whose throb has become so familiar as to be inaudible to ordinary consciousness. I confess I find myself dwelling again and again with indescribable pleasure on the moment at which I found you. I smell the smoke of the tunnel and, as the windows clear, I feel the run of the strap through my hands. Then comes your voice asking if I mind the window being opened, and catching your eyes I see the panic in them, which has so often looked out of mine. For the window is shut; and yet, in the very moment in which you speak, you realise that I have just opened it.

Finally you may care sometimes to meditate on a question which has often exercised me in the past years. Are we – you and I – the precursors of a new race of men with powers as yet undreamed of? Or was the Power once a general possession and do we owe the Pyramids and the monoliths of Stonehenge to its use? In that case you and I are the last decadent survivors of a more gifted race of men. Or are we the links of a slender chain destined to bind two epochs together? I do not know.

Goodbye and good luck.

'That is the end of the letter,' said Wilson,' but there is a footnote in another hand which may interest you.

'The Box has been entirely destroyed. God help me. August 7th.'

Wilson handed me the MS. with the air of an adult allowing a child to hold a fragile and valuable curio. 'What do you think of it?' he asked. 'I think you are wrong in saying that it had nothing special to do with the suicide,' I said. 'Do you happen to know the year when it occurred?' 'The Estate Agent said the year after the war,' Wilson answered. 'He was anxious to impress on me that it was a long time ago and there have been no disturbing phenomena. It appears that many people won't live in a house where there has been a murder or a suicide.' 'The year after the war,' I said, 'that no doubt means the European war. So it brings us to 1945. August 7th, 1945. Our friend had good reason for destroying the Box on that particular day. And I suppose he realised that his life would be insupportable without it, and so destroyed himself at the same time. Yes, I can imagine the agony of those last twenty-four hours.'

'But why on that particular day?' asked Wilson.

'It was the day after Hiroshima,' I replied.

IV

*Essays
and
Recollections*

The Book of Tobit

It would not be easy to determine in what way a story or legend becomes part of a people's accepted religious tradition. The myth-creating genius of ancient peoples doubtless threw up an endless variety of tales of Gods and men, some the product of purely spiritual Imagination, others founded on such physical events as were reflections of spiritual deeds. Only a certain number of them would pass the test of time. Perhaps the general sense would reject one and choose another, as it chooses or rejects a word in a nation's speech; or perhaps some great Initiate would bring form into an incoherent mass of legends, as the Greeks said that Homer was the author of the canon of the Gods.

The book of Tobit, accepted by a simpler age from among the authentic inspired biblical books, was rejected by a more Protestant theology no doubt for a variety of reasons. The story of the recovery of prosperity to Tobit's house by the magical properties of a fish and the intervention of an Archangel could hardly be acceptable to an age which had rejected magic and was inclined to reject Archangels. There is no direct prophecy in the book of the central event of Christianity, nor is it in the historical line of Old Testament history. Indeed it could hardly be accepted as a religious book by an age which had learned to scrutinise historical detail with minute accuracy but had lost the power to interpret the whole picture contained in such stories as the Book of Tobit. When religious feeling expressed itself naturally in creative art, when every church was a bible in pictures, then the scenes of the story of Tobit – the old man waiting, blinded, by the fire, or Tobias his son led by the Angel Raphael with fish in hand and little dog at his side, or the evil spirit Asmodeus fleeing from Sarah 'to the uppermost parts of Egypt' – such scenes were among the most favoured themes for painting, sculpture, or glass. But what could a

Deist do with the liver of a fish? Or a Broad Churchman with a woman who slew seven husbands by witchcraft?

That stories such as Tobit should be revived and presented in different ways to the public to-day is only one among many signs that people are seeking again for a more pictorial consciousness. As a rule, however, all that is understood of these old religious and mythical stories is their dramatic and human element – the moral of the piece is nothing higher than virtue rewarded, and the story as a whole presents no image of spiritual truth.

Yet there are quite plain indications that the writer of the story, in the form in which we have it, does not intend it to be taken *only* as a human story. The book has a close relation to the book of the prophet Jonah, whose prophecies, we are told Tobit accepted and so was able to warn his son Tobias in time for him to flee from Nineveh before it was destroyed. The fish which came out of the river to Tobias was no ordinary fish; we are told it 'would have swallowed the young man up' – even as the fish swallowed up Jonah. And in the thanksgiving of Tobit for the recovery of his son and of his sight there are the words: 'He leadeth down to the grave and bringeth up again.' Such things indicate that the book stands very near to the 'sign of the prophet Jonah' and to begin to comprehend the book we must understand a little of the meaning of that sign, as Rudolf Steiner has portrayed it in many of his lectures.

The going down into Hades, or the going down into the Fish, is the symbol of the way in which the Mystery of Initiation was fulfilled in the times before Christ. The man who was to receive pure spiritual experience came into a trance-like condition resembling death in which he lay for three days. The three days' death of the Christ is the fulfilment in physical fact of the ancient Mysteries of Initiation, and for the early Christians the fish became the symbol of the Redeemer. When, therefore, the young man Tobias takes hold of the fish which rises from the river as he goes down into it, he takes hold of the power of the new conscious

Initiation by which he receives into himself the healing forces of the Christ.

But much more is necessary to understand the Mystery picture presented by the book of Tobit. A double healing takes place. The old man who has been so faithful a keeper of the law, even in the time of his captivity in Nineveh, is blinded by the dung of a sparrow as he lies in his courtyard after burying one of his kinsmen, slain in the streets; and in distant Ecbatana, Sarah, the daughter of Raguel of his own tribe, is possessed by an evil spirit who has slain the seven husbands to whom she has been given, each on the night of his marriage. The Archangel Raphael comes, as mediator and healer, between the afflictions of Tobit and Sarah.

For Raphael, pre-eminently among the Archangels, is the bearer of healing powers, and especially at one season of the year he appears to spiritual sight as the overcomer of the sickness of man. In his description of the spiritual course of the seasons Rudolf Steiner has shown the form in which he appears at the time of Easter as the Archangel who is the ruler of that season of the year. The powers of health are those powers which help man to maintain a balance between two opposing temptations. Man may enter too deeply into earth processes, in which case he will be liable to hardening, ossifying processes in his body, and his thinking will also become 'hardened' and mechanical – this is the Ahrimanic temptation: or he may be tempted to flee away from the earth, when the fluidic processes of his body will become too strong, or his mind will be taken away from the earth and become full of 'vain imaginings' – this is the Luciferic temptation.

At the time of Easter especially, mankind is liable to these two temptations. For with the rising of the carbonic acid from the limestone into the plants at this time, there comes about a kind of ensoulment of the limestone masses of the earth; and by the ensoulment Ahriman has always the hope that he will be able to take possession of the earth and, through the earth, of man himself. But at the same time the Luciferic beings in the atmosphere above the earth endeavour to take possession of the carbonic acid rising in a fine way from the earth, and by means of embodying themselves, as it were, in this fine element, they hope to be able to obtain the mastery over the finer or etheric body of man himself.*

These are the two temptations, the two dangers to which the soul of man has been exposed during the course of the history of the earth, these are the two dangers which appear in the spiritual aspect of the earth in the time of spring. But just as the soul of man was saved or healed from these two sicknesses by the entering of the Christ into the destiny of the earth, so in spring time the Easter Mystery is for ever renewed, the healing forces of the Christ stream upon the earth, and Raphael, the Archangel who bears these forces, stands revealed to spiritual sight between the powers of Lucifer and Ahriman. For Raphael is the Christian Mercury and bears the staff of healing for the sicknesses of mankind.

Easter then, the season of the Archangel Raphael, is essentially the festival of healing when man should learn to recognise the healing qualities in the two polaric elements, the mineralising salt-deposits, and the volatile substances of the earth. Thus it is that in the story of Tobit, too, there is a twofold healing, a healing of the soul which strives to escape too far from the earth region and a healing of the soul which strives to enter too far into it. For Sarah, whose evil spirit brings death to her seven husbands, is the type of the soul which in its sevenfold aspect would flee from the earth; and the old man Tobit, whose self-righteousness will not even allow him to believe that his wife has come by a present in the way of honesty, is dragged by the Ahrimanic temptation into the earth darkness. The dung of the sparrow which falls into his eyes and so causes his blindness is a picture of the 'astral rain' by which, as Dr. Steiner describes it, Ahriman hopes each spring time to ensoul the living limestone masses of the

* For a full description of the spiritual condition of the earth in springtime, see Rudolf Steiner *The Four Seasons and the Archangels*, Lecture 3 (Dornach, 7 October 1923), Rudolf Steiner Press, London 1968.

earth. Raphael brings the healing forces to both these sicknesses. For the old man, recollecting certain monies which he has deposited with a friend in Media, commands his son to find a guide who can conduct him there, that he may show the writing and recover the money. Tobias finds Raphael, disguised as a kinsman of Tobit's, and as they set out the old man says, with happy irony: 'The Angel of God go with you.' On their journey they come to the river Tigris and the young man goes down to the water to wash. It is then that the fish 'leaped out of the river and would have swallowed up the young man. But the angel said unto him, Take hold of the fish. And the young man caught hold of the fish and cast it up on the land.' The angel then commands Tobias to take the heart, liver and gall out of the fish: the rest they roast and eat. So it comes about that Raphael is able to bestow on Tobit the healing forces of the Christ, in the form of the fish, and with the fish he is enabled to heal the woman of her evil spirit, and the old man of his blindness. Students of Rudolf Steiner's spiritual physiology will recognise also the perfection of the details in the picture of the healing. For the woman is healed by the forces of the *heart* and *liver* of the fish – and it is in the liver, of all the inner organs that, in a certain way, the forces of the Ego work with the greatest strength; whereas the old man is healed by virtue of the *gall*, and the gall has the function of paralysing and overcoming a destructive hardening process set up through the combining of carbon with nitrogen in the metabolic system of man. It is the overcoming of the hardening and loosening forces, and the bringing about of a right relation between them, Raphael healing the diseases of Ahriman and Lucifer.

A curious detail in the story has been much commented on. We are told that when Tobias and Raphael set out, 'the young man's dog went with them'. Again on their return, when Tobias has married Sarah and is arriving home with his wife and his father's monies in safety, the Archangel suggests that he and the young man shall run ahead, and 'the dog went after them'. Now in Jewish literature, as in almost all ancient writings, the dog is not looked upon as the friend of man but is the type of everything that is shameless and contemptible. The Homeric heroes call each other 'you dog' where a modern man would be more inclined to employ another animal, and to give your enemy's body to the dogs is the supreme revenge among the Patriarchs. The insistence on the dog in the story of Tobit has led some commentators to refer the whole story to a definitely non-Jewish source; others have been content to remark that the book of Tobit contains perhaps the first mention in history of a dog purely as the friend and companion of man. Yet the dog is not altogether irrelevant to the picture of the whole story. For this change in the attitude of man to the dog is only one among the many minor transformations which have been wrought on the earth by the coming of the Ego to man. Man, by virtue of his bearing the spiritual Ego, has the great task of redemption to perform for the animals from whom he has exacted such great sacrifices and to whom he owes his capacity for so many spiritual qualities. That the shameless dog should become the image of devotion, that Cerberus, guardian of the lower world should be transformed into the Hound of Heaven, provides a type of the work which man has to do in healing the animal world of their premature penetration into the world of matter. It is not for nothing, therefore, that Tobit, who receives the forces of the Christ Ego, should be accompanied by his dog, and that the artists of the Middle Ages and Renaissance, when they painted the healing countenance and gorgeous wings of the Archangel, and the shining fish, and the boy's face full of trustful devotion, do not forget to include the little animal gallantly prancing by his master's side.

'Write in a book all the things which have been done,' says the Archangel to Tobit at the moment when he reveals himself in his real being to father and son. 'Read in the book *all* the things which have been written,' he might say to the modern revivers of these ancient Mystery stories. For it is one of the penalties of advancing consciousness that the picture by itself can no longer work with its old intensity on the human soul. It must be penetrated by a conscious understanding, but by one which can yet develop into a capacity to think pictorially. Stories such as that of Tobit are not to be rationalised, or all the virtue is gone out of them. They should lead to that truly pictorial thinking which stands at the threshold of spiritual experience, that is, into the world of Imagination, where pictures become the objective expression of spiritual realities. In that world Raphael at the festival of Easter stands between the powers of Ahriman and Lucifer, and the healing act of the Christ is for ever renewed.

The Appreciation of Poetry

Children are born to a natural appreciation of poetry, and it is a sad thing that so few of them carry their heritage with them into adult life. In less intellectual ages the poetic faculty survived to blossom in folk-song and ballad. The feeling that poetry was superior to prose – a better and more exciting medium for all sorts of purposes – remained until quite modern times. Sir Walter Scott wrote his tales first of all in verse, and only abandoned this medium when he found himself outdone by Byron; and the elder Mill had the prodigy John Stuart taught to write verse, not because he himself admired poetry, but on the ground that people read verse more readily than prose. The immense number of descriptive and didactic poems of the eighteenth century addressed to sofas or sugar-canes, or describing seasons and shipwrecks, show how long a natural love of rhythm lingered into an artificial age. Not much of that natural love remains to-day. Modern poetry is mostly devoid of rhythm, and young students at the universities are found by their teachers sorely lacking in rhythmical sense. The state of the educator is like that of the gardener; once he has broken the soil and destroyed the harmony of nature he must forever battle to keep the ground clear of weeds. It is only too often a losing battle.

Young children, however, still bring with them into the world a spontaneous joy in all the elements which meet in poetry. They delight in pure sound, and will practise vowels and consonants and intonations hour by hour even in their cradles; their sense of rhythm is gloriously strong; and they think always in images and pictures and dreams. Of course they are completely absorbed by these things. They cannot stand outside them and criticise them as an adult would. It is all the more important that in their younger years they should learn only the best poetry (which does not exclude Nursery

Rhymes) so that in their dreaming days they build up a norm by which to judge the good and the bad when they reach a more conscious age. By the time they have reached fifteen they can begin to appraise poetry more consciously and study this or that element in it so as both to enjoy and to know what is enjoyed. It is not a question at this age of getting them to appreciate hard or subtle things. It is more important that they should first become conscious and appreciative of quite simple matters.

It is easy to begin with rhythm, and in the sphere of rhythm first with slow and fast movement. It is good for the children to learn by heart part or all of a poem in which great variety of movement appears. Tennyson's *Revenge* (Tennyson is a master of rhythm) will provide many fine examples of variation in speed. Compare first of all the orderly, measured movement of the lines:

> So Lord Howard passed away with five ships of war
>   that day,
> Till he melted like a cloud in the silent summer heaven;

with the impetuous rush of the following:

> Sir Richard spoke and he laugh'd, and we roar'd a
>   hurrah, and so
> The little *Revenge* ran on sheer into the heart of the foe,
> With her hundred fighters on deck, and her ninety
>   sick below;

and with the deliberate, almost dirge-like movement of:

> And the stately Spanish men to their flagship bore
>   him then,
> Where they laid him by the mast, old Sir Richard caught
>   at last,
> And they praised him to his face with their courtly
>   foreign grace;

or with the final description of the wave that grew:

Till it smote on their hulls and their sails and their
    masts and their flags,
And the whole sea plunged and fell on the shot-
    shatter'd navy of Spain,
And the little *Revenge* herself went down by the island crags
To be lost evermore in the main.

Notice that in the last line the force of the storm has already
abated. We are left with only the great smooth rollers heaving
over the grave of the *Revenge*.

In these examples you are dealing with elementary basic
rhythms. You can point out the fast movement of a line filled
with anapaests (*Sir Richard spoke and he laughed*) and the
contrasting slowness of the trochee (*And the stately Spanish
men*). You can show how short vowels coupled with light
consonants (*the little* Revenge *ran on*) immensely speed up the
movement, while a massing of consonants, even in a single
word such as 'flagship', will slow down the movement of a
whole line or passage.

You have so far been keeping within the single line, or a
group of lines where each line ends with a concluding pause.
You can next point out to the children, taking again the
simplest examples at first, the extraordinary beauty that can
arise when the sense demands that the rhythm shall not end
with the line but shall flow over the line-ending and be
checked at some other place, when there is something of a
battle or tension between the sense line and the rhythmical
line. It is like an outcrop of rock making first an unexpected
slide and then an obstruction in the course of a stream. The
glory of the stream is to adapt itself to the conditions given it.
You can take, for instance, the beautiful use of the word *down*
in Marvell's description of the death of Charles I:

> He nothing common did or mean
> Upon that memorable scene
> But bow'd his comely head
> Down, as upon a bed.

Or Wordsworth's description of the mountains echoing back
the noise of the skaters from the frozen lake:

> . . . . with the din
> Smitten, the precipices rang aloud.

You could write instead:

> The smitten precipices rang aloud.

but the blow, the hard impact of clear sound on rock, has
gone. The idea alone remains in the head; the heart, the
rhythmical man, is no longer engaged.

With the sounds themselves a third element is added.
Although modern poetry is based on accent and not on
quantity, the difference of effect between a word like 'flagship' or 'canteen' as contrasted with 'borrow' or 'rely' in the
movement of a line is immense. There then arises that
exquisite balance in poetry where rhythm, sound and sense
are in a state of harmonious tension, and have each
contributed their peculiar quality to make a unique line. This
is especially the case with blank verse, which, in English, is
nothing by virtue of its basic rhythm alone. Accompanied by
the musical tinkle of rhyme, verse can amble along fairly
regularly. But in blank verse every line must virtually be a new
rhythmical creation. That is why for every ten good rhyming
poets there is only one writer of blank verse, and why poets
with a great facility for rhyme and an easy metrical gift (like
Byron) always fall down when they attempt blank verse. The
regular rhythm of a poem like Gray's *Elegy* is delightful in
rhyme; it would be intolerable in blank verse.

Of course a line here or there in blank verse may be as even
in its flow as:

> The curfew tolls the knell of parting day,

but such a line can be only a very occasional relief, inserted
for some special end. And how far a blank verse line can

depart from the basic rhythm! – so that if it were met alone, it
would even be hard to know it for what it is; but found in
company it has rich and strong individuality – like the voice
of some deep-sea fisherman or northern mineworker after
the suave and spineless accents of the B.B.C. announcer:

> O how comely it is and how reviving
> To the spirits of just men long oppressed.
>
> Ah me, alas, pain, pain ever for ever.
> Fall battleaxe and flash brand. Let the king reign.

Older children (hardly those of fifteen) will also begin to
appreciate the building of line upon line in one great
architectural spurt of sound. And to this may be added
(especially if the children have learned Eurythmy and are
familiar with the characteristic gestures for the various
sounds) some study of the actual sounds of the words and
their peculiar fitness in the line where they are employed. Two
familiar dicta about poetry badly need revising. Poetry has
been defined as 'the right word in the right place'; it would be
truer to say 'the right sound in the right place'. And when
Lewis Carroll wittily advised the poet to 'take care of the sense
and the sounds will take care of themselves', he was
committing the great heresy of imagining that it is the
meaning – divorced from the sound – that matters in poetry.
Of course the actual imitation of external sounds can
occasionally – very occasionally – be effective in poetry:

> Birds in the high hall garden
> When twilight was falling,
> Maud, Maud, Maud, Maud,
> They were crying and calling.

But it is a far more subtle relationship between sound and
image to which children's attention should now be turned.
To take first a very simple example, Keats's *Ode to Autumn*
contains a beautiful description of something which everyone

has observed – the cloud of gnats falling and rising by water in a still warm evening:

> Then in a wailful choir the small gnats mourn
> Among the river sallows, borne aloft
> Or sinking as the light wind lives or dies.

What incredible aptness of sound is to be found especially in the last half of these three lines! Borne aloft – the 'b' brings the slight effort with which the wind comes out of the calm; the 'l' raises the choir of gnats; in the 'f' the wind is still blowing and they are still rising; but the 't' brings a limit, and, with a last sigh of the wind in the 's' of sinking, the darker, heavier second syllable of that word brings the fall. Up again from the 'l' of light to the 't' once more; down to the darker lower 'd' of wind; only to rise and fall once more in 'lives or dies.'

It is not here a question of *imitating* the sounds of nature, but of catching the essential gesture of each sound of speech, and feeling how marvellously it chimes with the movement of the thing described. There are famous lines of poetry the very meaning of which is in dispute, like Virgil's

> Sunt lacrymae rerum, mentem et mortalia tangunt.

but which from the sound alone everyone admits to be sublime poetry. Chesterton somewhere says that the two most musical lines in Milton – lines which can be repeated again and again with always increasing relish – are those in which he describes the last infirmity of the Middle Ages, when Mr. Worldly Wiseman on his death-bed would put on the gown of a monk and hope to pass by virtue of his dress through the gates of heaven:

> Dying put on the weeds of Dominic,
> Or in Franciscan think to pass disguised.

Why are these lines so exquisite? Notice how the first line is dominated by the heavy sound 'd' which occurs in all the three more strongly accented syllables. We feel that the doom of death is already upon us, and the soul is in despair. Then with the last breath, as it were, comes the wind of hope – 'or in Franciscan think to pass.' The lighter sounds waft us to the gate of heaven; we catch a momentary glimpse of the angels of God, but with the heavy 'disguised' the door is shut in our face, and the two 'd's double bar the door. We know, even without Milton telling us, that the hope is vain. The sounds alone are eloquent.

It will encourage children to read poetry for themselves if you ask them to find out and bring passages where they specially admire the rhythm or the sound. Their choice will sometimes be strange, but sometimes the worst choice will lead to the most fruitful discussion. The children must realise that rhythm springs from the heart, and that what is deeply and truly felt will always clothe itself in the right rhythm. A paltry, doggerel rhythm is a sure sign that the poem is insincere. Sir Philip Sidney truly wrote:

Fool, said my Muse to me, look in thy heart and write.

When we turn to the sense in poetry, the first thing we have to realise is that the poet is trying to do the thing which is of all things most difficult for a modern man; he is trying to make every experience unique and personal. It is not the moon or hunger or tumult he wants to convey to you, but a particular moon or a particular sky, some real person feeling hunger, some scene of riot in an actual city. Sometimes he will do this by calling your attention to fine details. Many superb examples of such description are to be found in Coleridge's unfinished poem *Christabel:*

The one red leaf, the last of its clan,
That dances as often as dance it can,
Hanging so light, and hanging so high,
On the topmost twig that looks up at the sky.

It is not just a twig from which the last leaf of the autumn hangs, but the *topmost* twig *that looks up at the sky.* It is this detail above all which makes us see the jaunty leaf crowning the tree skeleton, and in the contrast we feel the very end and death of summer's life. The one living thing no longer has life in itself. It moves like a puppet, only when a power outside it jerks it into an imitation of life. It dances *as often as dance it can.*

> The thin gray cloud is spread on high,
> It covers but not hides the sky.
> The moon is behind, and at the full;
> And yet she looks both small and dull.
> The night is chill, the cloud is gray;
> 'Tis a month before the month of May,
> And the spring comes slowly up this way.

Notice here the swift and accurate description of a particular sky and its effect on the appearance of the moon. The simplest words are used, and not one is unnecessary. But the supreme genius of the passage lies in the last two lines which bring us straight into the very innermost sensations of the person there. He is longing for the warmth of spring – but the clouds are still unpropitious, and we have the repetition *the cloud is gray.* He is thinking, 'next month will be May, when surely spring will be here'; so we are not told it is April, but the *month before the month of May* (as children think 'three days to the end of term'). And finally we have the master-stroke – the sigh with which he remembers the reputation of the place and resigns himself to fate – *spring comes slowly up this way.*

Poetry which *merely* describes is almost invariably bad; it is like photographic art. If it describes the visible it must do so in order to reveal the invisible. But young poets (Keats for instance) exercise themselves in description, and it is far from a bad exercise for children who will indeed generally make their first poetic efforts in this kind of poetry.

A direct description, indeed, rarely conveys the essence of a thing. We are always trying to describe one thing in terms of another in order to convey the flavour of what we experience or mean. The shiny knobs on drawers are like a usurer's eyes; or our hair stands on end like quills upon the fretful porcupine; or life is a dome of many-coloured glass. The poet, indeed, is always trying to see things not in their isolation but in their interdependence, looking for a common colour, flavour, gesture, essence, with which to make one thing reveal another. Shelley in his *Ode to the Skylark* explicitly asks the question (which all poets are always asking implicitly), 'What is most like thee?' And the reason he gives for asking it is, 'What thou art we know not' – a statement true of all things considered in isolation. The stanzas that follow are therefore a kind of meditation on the skylark, a seeking for its essence in other things. It is interesting to see what new qualities each comparison adds to the bird and its song. The first comparison is to a poet 'hidden in the light of thought'. Shelley is a rather exact poet. He here calls attention to the fact that while most things hide themselves in darkness, the lark actually hides itself in light. We literally cannot see it for the light. In what way is the poet hidden in the light of thought? There is the simple interpretation that he withdraws himself – we meet him, and see the man but not the poet. But I think Shelley may have had a further thing in his mind. The greater the poet – the more *light-filled* his work, the less we find his personality in it. You can read all Shakespeare and all Homer, but Shakespeare and Homer remain as mysteries. You can read a few pages of Byron and you know him very well. The lark's song is at its most thrilling when you do not see the lark; the poet's song is more splendid when you do not see the poet.

The second comparison is to a high-born maiden in a palace tower:

> Soothing her love-laden
> Soul in secret hour
> With music sweet as love, which overflows her bower.

It may seem a little obvious to compare a human voice to a bird's voice, and even to put the lady on a tower to raise her like the lark into the sky. But this is not the point of the comparison. The lady is singing *in secret hour*, and the music *overflows* her bower. She is not singing to anyone. We, the hearers, only hear her song by grace; we are not in her secret; we catch, without her knowing it, the overflow of her heart. The skylark does not sing for us, we do not know why he sings, his song belongs to another sphere; it is by grace alone that some of it spills over on to our terrestrial world.

The third comparison seems at first sight as impossible as the second seemed obvious. The skylark is actually compared to a glow-worm. To compare the most ethereal of birds to a *worm* seems a strange idea, till we find that we have returned to the thought in the former stanza. The glow-worm is also hidden in the light of its own creation.

> Like a glow-worm golden
>   In a dell of dew,
> Scattering unbeholden
>   Its aërial hue
> Among the flowers and grass which screen it from the view.

The dell of *dew* certainly brings a new thought. The dew drops gladly receive and reflect the light, as the earth (fresh as a dew-drop in the season of the lark's song) rejoices in the notes of the lark and even echoes them back to the heavens. It might, however, be objected that this comparison does no more than the first, and indeed, is not so noble and vivid. It might even be said that it would have been better to begin with the glow-worm and rise up to the poet. I think, however, that the sequence is both intentional and right, because a new thought is thereby introduced. We see the glow-worm's dell of dew from outside, and the image helps us to project ourselves into the heavens, and see lark, earth and heaven from the heavens themselves. We can imagine ourselves receiving the fullness of the song in the upper air, not merely catching the overspill on the earth.

The last comparison introduces a further thought:

> Like a rose embower'd
>   In its own green leaves,
> By warm winds deflower'd,
>   Till the scent it gives
> Makes faint with too much sweet these heavy-wingèd thieves.

Again the rose gives an effect, being itself invisible. But it is *hidden in its own green leaves*, and we suddenly conceive the skylark as hidden not in light only, but in its own song. The song so fills the sky that it does not direct us to any one point, and sight is dazed by the brightness of the glittering sound. But the rose also gives its strongest scent when it is at the full, when the petals begin to fade and its life is near the end. We know that the lark will not sing for ever, that it will suddenly fall from the sky, and an immense quietness will possess the heavens; and, anticipating that moment we listen all the more eagerly. Perhaps, indeed, like *the setting sun and music at the close* we enjoy it most at that moment when we realise, with its approach to the earth, that the song is at an end. We appreciate the miracle only when it is accomplished.

It would not be good to discuss such reflections on a poem on the same day as that on which it is read. There are some things which should be dealt with a day or two before reading a poem, and some things which should only come after, so that the poem may be for the children what it should be – a purely artistic experience. To stop a piece of music in the middle in order to explain that a certain effect has been obtained by using a particular harmony or interval is an outrageous procedure. If you wish to introduce children to a poem and you know there are things in it which they do not understand – unfamiliar words or difficult allusions – try to find a way of bringing these things to their attention before you read the poem. For instance, no one probably will understand at the first reading of *Lycidas* why Milton calls the unworthy ministers of the church 'Blind mouths'. Ruskin, however, gives a beautiful and convincing explanation of these extraordinary words. The officers of the church, he says, are bishops and pastors. The root meaning in the first is to see or oversee, in the second to feed. If the bishop, who should oversee, fails in his duty, he may properly be described as blind. But the bad pastor does not merely cease to feed the flock, he feeds himself instead, he becomes a mouth. Hence a bad bishop is blind, a bad pastor is a mouth.

Blind mouths! – to stop reading the poem at those two terrific words of condemnation would be to break the whole effect of sound and rhythm. Try therefore to find some suitable way of speaking about bishops and pastors, of the keys of St. Peter, of the fountain Arethusa, and smooth-sliding Mincius before you read the poem together. You can then enjoy it as a work of art; it will cease to be a puzzle to be explained. And do not immediately after reading proceed to reflections on a poem. Leave that to another day. Perhaps on the day after reading you will merely see how much the children can recall, and then on the following day, when it has had time to sink more deeply into them, ask them to think about the poem, to say what lines or images they find most beautiful and why – to begin to educate their judgment. Poetry is either a great experience or it is nothing. It is worth while using a little art and care in teaching to try to make it the former rather than the latter.

I have purposely in this article used only familiar illustrations from familiar poems. Children must first walk on the broad highways of literature before they explore the byways. I believe it is better for them to know Tennyson than T. S. Eliot. School time cannot do everything. But it can nurture the children's mind and perception so that they are ready to enter upon their mighty heritage.

Walter Ogilvie Field

I first met Walter Field in a shell-damaged up-and-down little villa in the small industrial town of Caudry in northern France. I can still see the steps leading to the pretentious front door, and down the road the railway bridge which went up by a delayed mine twenty-four hours later. The armies were on the move and I had been pursuing for three days the Headquarters of the Warwickshire Battalion to which I had been detailed. The Battalion was in the line, but it was the custom then to leave a cadre behind on which to rebuild the unit if it were destroyed – and casualties were often enormous at that time. Field, who was then Intelligence Officer of the Battalion, was on this occasion one of those who had remained behind.

Three brothers of mine had been in the same Battalion and had written in their letters of the eccentric, voluble and lovable Intelligence Officer, with his eager mind and immense devotion to the men. Indeed he had achieved something like fame in the whole Division through an action which he himself would gladly have had forgotten, but which achieved publicity through an article, in which only the name was disguised, written in a periodical well-known at that time by A. A. Milne, who had been in the same Regiment and, I think, at one time in the same Battalion.* The story illustrates the great interest which Field already took in the possibility of communication between the living and the dead, an interest which later took him quite far into the world of spiritualism. After the war he often described to me seances he had witnessed, in which he believed he had been in communication with friends he had known.

Field's general character was therefore already known to

* The article, entitled *The Stick*, was reproduced together with this Memoir in the Midsummer number of *Mosaic*, a journal for old scholars of Michael Hall School in 1958. Ed.

me as I walked through the pretentious door and asked an orderly for the Officer in charge. A tall thin Captain wearing pince-nez appeared. I saluted and gave my name. To my huge surprise I was embraced with exclamations of delight; bacon and eggs were ordered from the back kitchen, and in the shifting chaos of war I suddenly found the stability of a home and a friend.

Field soon left the Battalion to go on a course, and he did not return. But there had been time for us to have some deep conversations, among which I remember one – I believe it took place on the night of my arrival – on the subject of fear. I maintained that the brave man was he who felt no fear (we were being shelled and I badly wanted to be brave): Field, that he was the man who felt fear to the utmost extreme but overcame it. He was much occupied with the question of fear throughout his life, and it does not seem to me extraordinary that almost the last time I saw him he placed in my hands a passage from a work of Rudolf Steiner, in which Steiner says that the ultimate fear, behind all other fears, is the fear of the spiritual world, and that the man who denies the existence of that fear is closing the door to spiritual perception. Field himself never closed that door.

Short as the first connection was, it was deep enough to make it inevitable that we should meet again. It was on a Summer's day in my first year at Oxford that there came a knock at the door of my room, and to my huge delight a torrent of exclamations brought Field into the room. It was on this and subsequent visits that he told me of his own life at Oxford before the war. He had come up to Trinity with the reputation of social and athletic success at Marlborough (his prize cups accompanied him throughout his life) and the backing of a well-to-do and highly respected Midland family. He described himself as having lived at Oxford the life of a social butterfly in one unending round of dinners, river-parties, house-parties and balls. Perhaps he owed to that time his social adroitness and his perfect manners. But I suspect that even then his manners and conversation had the difference of being sincere; and his friendship with a promising young poet, Sorley (afterwards killed in the war), showed that he was already seeking for deeper things. Mystical poetry especially remained his delight throughout his life. In his last years the spiritual vision contained in Charles Williams' Arthurian poems made an immense appeal to him. For he read poetry, as he read life, for its meaning, and without what Chaucer calls 'high sentence' the beauty of sound and imagery had little effect on him.

Field – I call him this, though from the beginning I knew him by the affectionate nickname of Wof – had interrupted his course at Oxford to join the army. For it must be remembered that in 1914 the army was still an army of volunteers, and he was well among the 'first hundred thousand'. He did not continue his studies after the war, but took a war degree instead. However, he visited Oxford sufficiently often to become a member of a very small group of undergraduates who used to meet together in the search for some meaning in life. Several of that group afterwards became, like Field, followers of Rudolf Steiner.

Five years of war had left Field in a very prostrated condition, and it was a year or two before he took up any serious work. He went first into the law, but, not finding it to his liking, joined a family business in Birmingham. It was a time of great economic depression and social unrest, and Field's heart was torn by the poverty and misery he saw around him, while his head increasingly told him that there was something completely wrong with an economic system which left millions all but starving, while industry was producing masses of goods that no one could afford to buy. It was at this time that he first met Major Douglas and his theory of Social Credit, which placed the blame for this state of affairs on the banking system, which did not (and could not under the existing system) distribute sufficient purchasing power to enable the goods produced to be bought. Yet the banks could – and did for their own purposes – *create* credit, so that it would be possible, by a change in monetary policy, to issue 'dividends for all', which would end the fearful state of poverty amid plenty. Field saw in all this the bright light of social salvation. He threw up business, and became a crusader for the new economic theory with something of the overpowering conviction which had moved his great ancestor, Oliver Cromwell.

At that time I was sharing a flat in Pimlico with a friend who was often away, and Field more or less took his place, often sleeping on a sofa when my friend was at home. He was in a highly excitable state, and would keep us up till all hours demonstrating the Douglas economic theory with statistics from bank balance-sheets and cuttings from newspapers. Even then he was a great cutter-out and underliner. How many of his friends are now missing the periodicals he used to send them with SEE PAGE 23, WOF written boldly on the cover, and the article in question heavily scored, with exclamation marks and comments adorning the margins! In his over-excited state he wore himself out in every possible kind of effort to draw people's attention to the Douglas Credit Theory, from speaking at Hyde Park to lobbying members in the House till late in the night. He would often return quite prostrated, and sleep till midday. Personal difficulties also entered his life at this time, and his friends were even anxious for the balance of his mind.

It happened that about then I had become acquainted with someone* who introduced me to the work of Rudolf Steiner, in which I became more and more interested. Naturally I shared my interest with Field, who himself began to read Steiner's books and lectures. Steiner's exact knowledge of the spiritual world, and his account of the life after death, were immediately and immensely satisfying to Field's mystical thirst and his incessant questioning as to the life of the dead. But he also found in Steiner's conception of the 'Threefold Commonwealth', with its harmony of the economic, political and spiritual spheres, something which went far beyond Major Douglas, even in the limited province of monetary

* The reference is to Daphne Olivier, Harwood's first wife. Ed.

theory. I remember well his excitement when he first read of Steiner's discrimination between different kinds of money – including one kind, which 'dies' – or loses its value – over a period of years. It is only when this is recognised that other forms of money will be able to 'live', or retain their value. Little by little Field transferred his allegiance and enthusiasm to Steiner. We went together in 1924 to Torquay, where Steiner was addressing a Summer School. We were camping in a field outside the town, and as we walked back to our tents after some inspiring lecture, the very stars seemed to us both to shine with the brightness of a new heavenly intelligence.

At Torquay, in addition to his main theme, Dr. Steiner gave some lectures to the small group of teachers who hoped to found the New School.* Field did not join them at once (though I did), but it was not long after the school opened† that he was invited to join the staff. There was some trepidation as to whether his excitable temperament and manner would allow him to manage children. Indeed things did not go too well at first, and he himself used to enjoy telling the story of an early lesson at the end of which there were only two children left in the room and they were beating him over the head with rulers! But character and enthusiasm and hard work soon told – character perhaps in two senses of that word. For children and young people are immensely attracted to 'a character' and Field's mannerisms, the raising of his eyebrows, his 'dear boy' and 'dear girl', will long be remembered by generations of his pupils, as well as his generous comments in their exercise books, and the immense privilege of being taught by someone who was in the highest sense a gentleman.

After the school had moved to Minehead he suffered much from ill-health, and by the end of the war had practically gone into a retirement where he was well tended by his wife, who was devoted to him and died before him. His last years, however, showed an astonishing blossoming of activity. His

* Later re-named Michael Hall. Ed.
† In 1925, at Streatham, London. Ed.

devotion to Steiner's work, and the power of meditation which it had produced in him, brought his life to a wonderfully fruitful close. In addition to much valuable work for the children – individually and in classes – he became the guide, philosopher and friend to a wide circle of parents. His room in the Clockhouse became the social centre of the school community. Young and old could be found there, easy chairs were arranged permanently for study groups, coffee flowed at all times of the day, and at Midsummer Festivals a crowd of old scholars would be regaled with fruit and conversation after the St. John's Fire far into the night.

Some people are fortunate in their birth, others in their death. It was the old practice to examine the position of the stars at birth, because the gateway to the earth was considered of primary importance for human life. Rudolf Steiner has shown that to-day the position is in a sense reversed, and the gateway from the earth to the spiritual world, the gateway of death, is of primary importance for the human soul. If we may judge from the terrestrial disposition of things, Field's death was indeed under favourable stars. After the war he had formed a deep friendship with a priest of the Christian Community, Dr. Doldinger, whom he had taken on a journey to the West Country, especially to such places as Glastonbury and Tintagel associated with the noblest spiritual traditions of England. He had even asked Dr. Doldinger to assist him through his death. In August of last year* he went first to a Summer Conference in Dornach, where he met many old friends. Then he had planned a holiday in the Black Forest with a Dutch friend, whom (as a diary left behind him revealed) he had originally met on his first visit to Dornach more than thirty years before, and who had introduced him to the work of the Christian Community. Returning from the holiday he was seized by heart trouble, was taken to an hotel in Freiburg, the home of Dr. Doldinger, by his friend, and died peacefully in a few hours. Dr. Doldinger was by his side almost immediately after his death, and conducted the

* 1957.

funeral service, a moving ceremony which was attended by several teachers and old scholars of Michael Hall who for various reasons were in that part of Europe and within call. All unconsciously the German undertakers wrote what was perhaps the epitaph which most befitted him. It is the custom in that part of Germany for the undertakers to write on a card the name, age and occupation of the deceased. For Field they had written with heroic simplicity: Occupation – Englishman.

C. S. Lewis

*A Toast to the Memory of C. S. Lewis
proposed at Magdalen College, July 4th 1975*

When I have heard previous speakers on these occasions, they
have mostly spoken of some aspect of Lewis's work in which
they have taken the greatest delight or from which they have
most benefited. And there is God's plenty to choose from. Far
more than Oliver Goldsmith did Lewis deserve the epitaph
composed by Samuel Johnson: *Nullum fere scribendi genus non
tetigit: nullum tetigit quod non ornavit.** Literary and historical
criticism, verse of many kinds, allegory, history, theology,
Christian ethics and practice, planetary fiction, children's
books – all came from his pen with equal readiness and
forcefulness and in equal abundance. He had a teeming
mind. When his fellow undergraduates were producing one
exquisite lyric (now well forgotten) in a month, he was writing
a young epic; and when he was told that one of its cantos was
not up to standard, he went away and produced another in
the space of a few days.

Like all who read his books – or were privileged to enjoy
his conversation – I learnt very much from him, though
others have made profounder studies in his works and been
more deeply influenced by them. My own great debt to him –
it could not have been greater – was that of an abiding
friendship, which defied all differences of opinion, outlook
and age. I find that many of the experiences which live most
vividly in my memory are those which I shared with him. I
remember one of my early sojourns at the Kilns, when there
had been a heavy fall of snow in the night with no wind. We
went out in the morning into a world transformed.
Everything bore its replica in white. We tried to find words to

---

* There was scarcely any kind of writing he did not touch, and every one
he touched he adorned.

express the beauty – and the silence – of this new world, but ended speechless before it. At the other end of our meetings, on the last occasion when he was well enough to pay a visit to my home in Sussex, we were assailed after sunset by one of those tremendous storms when thunder and lightning were almost instantaneous and the whole house was wrapped in blinding flashes of light. We sat in a darkened room with open windows, overwhelmed by the sheer power of the elements. Jack said afterwards he had rarely been so frightened, and had never so much enjoyed being frightened. An almost equally memorable occasion was when I spent a weekend with him in Magdalen during the war. He had just discovered the works of that incomparable novelist of High Life, Mrs. Amanda Ross. We read one of her books to each other in turn until convulsions overcame the reader, and we ended by – literally – rolling together on the floor in one of those paroxisms of painful laughter which rarely visit one (alas) after one grows up.

He was at his best on walking tours, when his delight in Nature vied with his enjoyment of conversation, in which of course he took a leading part. The day's walk had to be carefully planned so that we reached an inn about one o'clock – he held sandwiches in anathema, as one of his printed letters testifies. There were grand tours with a muster of six or seven; but I remember well two or three walks we took alone. One was down the Wye Valley – then still a pretty remote place. As we came down from the hills to Tintern Abbey he shouted for joy that the hedges were still just as Wordsworth described them:

> "Not hedges
> But little bits of sportive woods run wild."

Whenever I read those lines, I hear Jack declaiming them as we strode down the hill.

In earlier years, when he often stayed with me in London, there were many visits to theatres and picture galleries. I remember especially walking with him to the charming little gallery in Dulwich and his delight in the classical landscapes of Poussin. There was one terrible occasion, of which I was recently reminded on looking through his letters, when – I suppose through dilatoriness – I had failed to secure tickets for *The Ring*. On my confessing my failure, I received a reply in Johnsonian style, of which he was almost as eloquent a master as the great Doctor himself, and which I think may amuse you.

May 7th '34   Magdalen College
Sir,

I have read your pathetical letter with such sentiments as it naturally suggests, and write to inform you that you need expect from me no ungenerous reproach. It would be cruel if it were possible, and impossible if it were attempted, to add to the mortification which you must now be supposed to suffer. Where I cannot console, it is far from my purpose to aggravate; for it is part of the complicated misery of your state that, while I pity your sufferings, I cannot innocently wish them lighter. He would be no friend to your reason or your virtue, who would wish to pass over so great a miscarriage in heartless frivolity or brutal insensibility. . . .

As soon as you can, pray let me know through some respectable acquaintance in what quarter of the globe you intend to sustain that irrevocable exile, and perpetual disgrace to which you have condemned yourself. Do not give in to despair. Learn from this example the fatal consequences of error, and hope in some humbler station and some distant land that you may yet become useful to your species.

Later I received a letter of forgiveness in the same vein, calculated to wither any part of me which the earlier letter had left unscathed.

He was a wonderful guest to have in the house, and always

wrote the most charming 'bread-and-butter' letters to his hostess. He is said to have regretted that he had had so little to do with children, and indeed never felt at home with them. All I can say is that my own children adored him. He entered with complete seriousness into their concerns, swung with them on their swing and went swimming with them, and delighted them by discoursing volubly on some philosophical subject the moment his head appeared after he had dived into the muddy Sussex water. He played with them the noble game of heads, bodies and tails and excelled everyone in his sketches; or, when more literary games succeeded, his contributions (one at least of which has survived) were of course masterly.

All this illustrates the fact that he lived in the present moment. No one was less given to reminiscences – or to repining. I can hear him heartily deprecating all I have ventured to tell you about him this afternoon. He wrote me once that I should not be sorry for him because his illness deprived him of many things he had loved to do, because 'you soon cease to want to do the things you know you can't do'. And his interest was in people, not in institutions. That, I think, is why, when I read his works, I seem to hear him speaking to me. His benefactions, which were very great, were mostly to individuals, not to societies. He had enormous sympathy for the 'little man'. On one occasion, when I was deprecating some modern housing estate, he said: 'But if you could see not the houses, but the souls of the people in them, it might look very different.' Indeed we shall never be true men 'till we have faces'. But I believe he felt that the simple man with his simple virtues might often be nearer that achievement than the sophisticated savant.

I would like to end with a brief anecdote. Some months ago I had to visit the North of England, and I had secured, not a compartment to myself – progress has deprived us of such amenities – but at least reasonable breathing space, when at the last minute a naval petty officer entered with his wife and children, to whom he had plainly been giving a treat in town, perhaps on returning from some voyage. Each child had been given some hideous toy, a doll as big as the child herself, or some monstrous Walt Disney creation, and each was flourishing a Comic of unbelievable vulgarity. The eldest, a girl of about fourteen, had received an elaborate manicure and make-up set – plainly not the first she had used. But she was a friendly child, and when I began to read, she looked up and asked, 'Is that a nice book?' I said it was a very nice book, and in return enquired if she was fond of reading, and what she liked best to read? 'Oh,' she said, 'far the best I like the *Narnia Tales* of C. S. Lewis. I read them again and again.' So we talked about C. S. Lewis, and she was amazed to think she was talking to someone who had actually known him. It happened that I had just received the current excellent Bulletin of the New York Lewis Society, and I had brought it with me to read in the train, so of course I produced it for her to see. She was astounded that people in America knew about Lewis. 'If they know about him there, he must be a great man', she said. (I present the compliment to their country to my American friends.)

All the rest of the journey I was thinking of what Jack had done for that little girl. What a window he had opened from her banal and vulgar surroundings into the world of imagination. Indeed he opened windows for many people into realms hitherto unknown to them. No doubt he would have felt his greatest achievement was to open the windows of Christianity in a way no one else had done in his generation. But I rather think he would have been on another level as delighted by the tribute of the little girl in the train. He has indeed opened windows for us all, or we would not be here. Let us drink to his memory, in gratitude for what each one of us has received from him.

V

Songs and Verses

Composed for Special Occasions

A PROLOGUE

You who saw us yester-year
In a garden green appear,
Pleading from a grassy plot
For a stage that yet was not
(While you scarce could catch a sound)
See how Time turns all things round,
And fitly brings it now to pass
That from a stage we plead – for grass.
O, if our poor play have power
A second time to grace an hour,
Say not that our actors wrong you
To send once more their elves among you,
Think how bounteous are the flowers
In these high Midsummer hours,
You are flowers, and they are bees,
Send them home with rich increase,
So shall we ever strive to please.

SLEEPING BEAUTY

Princess in a castle fair
Spinning thread as fine as hair

Pricks her finger sharp and deep;
Down she falls and sinks to sleep.

With her sinking King and Queen
Fall asleep and fall a-dream.

Cook and scullion, groom and maid,
A hundred year in sleep are laid.

Round them grows a hedge of briar,
Twined with roses red as fire.

Comes a Prince with sharp sword edge,
Hacks a pathway through the hedge.

See, a Princess sleeping lies –
Open with a kiss her eyes!

All awake. O happy day!
A Prince has come. Hurray! Hurray!

FOR A NEW HOUSE

The gate.   Kings in a Gate's strict room
        Have made their judgement place
    And pardon dealt or doom
        And read each passing face;
    Think as you tread these gates
        To enter or to part,
    What end your going waits,
        What bring you in your heart.

The garden. A garden where man found
        And lost his innocent breath,
    God in a garden bound
        And Love led forth to death;
    Think when these flowers profuse
        Are bright with sun or rain,
    Here's Paradise to lose,
        Or Love's fresh rose to gain.

The house.   A room with table spread,
        For light and darkness laid,
    The Word that blessed the bread,
        The whisper that betrayed;
    Think when you gather here
        Your word is peace or strife,
    Your will to bless or sear
        Shall murder, or give life.

GRACES BEFORE and AFTER MEAT

(being free renderings of the German originals by Rudolf Steiner)

BEFORE

Remembering the Sun in the bread
We will not forget
The Spirit's Light of the World
That quickens the hearts of men.

We break this bread together
With hearts aware
Not bread alone, but God's life
And love we share.

The Spirit of the World
Lives in the earth's will
To nourish mankind:
The deeds of men
Reveal to the earth
The Spirit of the World.

No bread without sun,
No sun without God,
No soul without life,
No life without love.

Sun, Earth and Air
Have wrought by God's care
That the plants live and bear;
Praising God for this food
In truth live we would
And bear beauty and good.

AFTER

Through the soul's gratitude of man
The fruits of the earth are renewed
In the deed's light of the Spirit.

May the renewing earth
Be itself renewed in the heart's love of man.

CHILDRENS' BIRTHDAY SONG

Many the stars that stand over the earth,
  And the days as the years go by,
But one star over the place of my birth,
  One hour, when first was I,
Looked for the light where the new child lay,
  Listened and heard the sign,
And the great sun rose on my life's first day,
  And the glory of earth was mine.

Fine things, O Earth, you have shown to me,
  Rare things from you I have heard,
The laughter of light on the splendid sea,
  The song of the covert bird;
And I have dreamed with the dreaming rose
  Whose slumber the butterfly shakes,
And wakened and watched with the silent snows
  When the whole world watches and wakes.

And once and again in the dance of the days
  Leaps out my day and my hour,
And I see above me the one star blaze,
  And its presence I feel like a Power.
And I say to that steadfast star I see,
  'O star, be my light like thine,
The sun in the heavens thy comfort be,
  And the Christ on earth be mine.'

THREE POEMS FOR PRACTICE IN EURYTHMY

I

O FOR AN O

O for a boat to sail the high seas,
O for a go on a flying trapeze,
O for a stone to drop down a well,
O for the tone of a silvery bell,
O for a pony to joggety jog on,
O for some snow for my new toboggan,
O for the glowing of coals on a fire,
O for the lowing of cows in a byre,
O for a hone to give my knife edge,
O for a rose on a briery hedge,
O for a cloak of soft warm down,
O for a coach to take me to town,
O for the smoke of a good log fire,
O for a rope to climb higher and higher,
O for a home on a cliff by the sea,
O to be you, and O, not to be me.

II

NOON MOOD

Loose not the strings of the lute,
   They have their order due,
And even when they are mute
   Should rest in concord true.

Ape not the fickle moon,
   Inconstancy eschew,
Be ever sun at noon,
   No cloud your light subdue.

So would you prove your wing,
   Or when you nothing do,
Be centre you or ring,
   To your own self be true.

III

STAR MOOD

O star of day, awake, unbar
  The marvels of the morn,
The thrilling lark, so near, so far,
  The sparkle on the lawn.

The leaves all eager for the dance,
  The greening larch, the pine,
The garden where the daisy's glance
  Does ever sunward shine.

Then fade, O day, that next we may
  The westering planet mark,
No moon to mar the faintest star,
  All glorious in the dark.

A SONG OF KING ARTHUR'S CASTLE

King Arthur's walls are strong and steep,
 By Western seas they stand,
Three sides sheer down upon the deep,
 And one upon the strand.
And cliff and tower and crag resound
 To Hail or Farewell shout,
As on that adamantine ground
 The knights ride in and out.

White waves on Arthur's castle wall
 And Sun-gold in the spray,
And knights like stars in Arthur's Hall
 And he like Sun of Day.

In Arthur's hall with bread and wine,
 The feasting-board is laid,
And they who at that table dine
 With Spirit strength are stayed,
While music, like the cleansing sea,
 Does so renew their heart,
That who sits down in misery,
 In steadfast joy shall part.

White waves on Arthur's castle wall
 And Sun-gold in the spray,
And knights like stars in Arthur's Hall
 And he like Sun of Day.

The knight that rides from Arthur's court
    Rests not save in the field,
Till fiend or foe be all down fought
    Or sorest quarrel healed,
And wild men see the armour gleam
    As through the wood they range,
And stand and gaze as in a dream,
    And feel a blessing strange.

White waves on Arthur's castle wall
    And Sun-gold in the spray,
And knights like stars in Arthur's Hall
    And he like Sun of Day.

Or when he wrestles, fiend beset,
    At midnight hour malign,
He feels the splendour o'er him yet –
    Arthur's seven-starred sign,
Then round him shines that castle tower,
    And in its might he stands,
And all King Arthur's men with power
    Strike battling in his hands.

White waves on Arthur's castle wall
    And Sun-gold in the spray,
And knights like stars in Arthur's Hall
    And he like Sun of Day.

THE SEASONS

When hollyhocks line cottage walls,
  And lanes are leafy bowers,
When broken-voiced the cuckoo calls,
  And thunder brings the showers,
Can I recall the silent snow
  That hardens under heel,
Or think the frosty stars aglow,
  Can I their clearness feel?

When mists like lakes in valleys lie,
  When birds in bushes freeze,
When gulls on inland furrows cry,
  And cows face down the breeze,
Can musing thick the hedge with leaf,
  Or fire the quivering haze,
Can the desirous heart conceive,
  And bring the sun to blaze?

O thou who eatest still thy bread,
  When frozen creatures pine,
Feel then in every crumb and shred
  The golden sun to shine,
So shalt thou fend the frosty power,
  That brings the rose to thorn,
And in thy thought, pure winter flower,
  The Lily of Christ be born.

KINDLING SONG FOR A ST. JOHN'S FIRE

Now the high midsummer sun
    Burns the dreaming hours away,
Kindles blossoms bright as flames,
    Flashes light from leaf and spray.
Earth and Man, have you no fire
    To greet these Heaven-kindled hours?
Earth has fire, and hearts have fire —
    Light the flame among the flowers.

Light is quivering on the moor,
    Air is hot with honeyed smells,
Golden rivers burn and glide,
    Shining brooks are singing spells.
Earth and Man, have you no fire
    To greet these Heaven-kindled hours?
Earth has fire, and hearts have fire —
    Light the flame among the flowers.

Butterflies, like flowers a-wing,
    Tremble as they drink the light,
Golden pollen fills the sky,
    Downy seeds soar out of sight.
Earth and Man, have you no fire
    To greet these Heaven-kindled hours?
Earth has fire, and hearts have fire —
    Light the flame among the flowers.

When the Traveller Sun goes home,
    And stars come slowly overhead,
Lingering lustres track him round
    Till the flush of dawn is red.
Earth and Man, have you no fire
    To greet these Heaven-kindled hours?
Earth has fire, and hearts have fire —
    Light the flame among the flowers.

Look, the very sea's on fire;
    Trees lift up a flaming crown,
Soon will all their sunburnt leaves
    Fall in glowing embers down.
Earth and Man, have you no fire
    To greet these Heaven-kindled hours?
Earth has fire, and hearts have fire –
    Light the flame among the flowers.

MICHAELMAS SONG

Wind in the trees blows loud for summer's last song,
Threshing the boughs, pelting the leaves along:

Sleepers awake, hark to the word of the wind
Breaking old summer's dull drowsy spell,
Show us the way, go with thy spear before,
Forge us the future, thou Michaël!

Frost on the ground at misty dawning shines bright,
Cracking the clod, lining the twigs with white:

Sleepers awake, hark to the word of the frost
Breaking old summer's dull drowsy spell,
Show us the way, go with thy spear before,
Forge us the future, thou Michaël!

Myriad stars shine in the frosty clear skies,
Outshining all, the meteor earthward flies:

Sleepers awake, hark to the word of the star
Breaking old summer's dull drowsy spell,
Show us the way, go with thy spear before,
Forge us the future, thou Michaël!

With hearts aglow men mark the changing fresh world,
When from the stars Michaël's spear is hurled:

Sleepers awake, hark to the word of the world
Breaking old summer's dull drowsy spell,
Show us the way, go with thy spear before,
Forge us the future, thou Michaël!

WARRIORS

What news of heroes old
  With fiend or man who fought,
Who kept the leagured hold,
  Whose blood the kingdom bought?
What of that warrior host
  Who struck the heavens along
When Satanas dared boast
  Himself the strong?

They walk the earth no less
  Than when man sang their praise,
Their hearts as strong to bless,
  Their Spirit to upraise;
Nor less does Michael show
  His strength, and call them friend,
Who fear not, for they know
  The struggle's end.

O MAN, LIFT UP YOUR VOICE

O man, lift up your voice,
  In you all creatures call,
Then sing to Heaven their joys,
  Who are the word of all,
O man, lift up your voice.

O man, lift up your hand,
  And bring a blessing down,
Beneath the stars you stand,
  Dishonour not your crown.
O man, lift up your hand.

O man, lift up your head,
  For you are made the stair,
Where Heaven's angels tread
  That unto earth repair.
O man lift up your head.

O man, lift up your heart,
  Where God lies sacrificed,
So bear you His own smart,
  So lift you up the Christ.
O man, lift up your heart.

ALLELUIA FOR ALL THINGS

Of all created things, of earth and sky,
Of God and Man, things lowly and things high,
We sing this day with thankful hearts and say,
    Alleluia.

Of Light and Darkness, and the colours seven
Stretching their rainbow bridge from earth to heaven,
We sing this day with thankful hearts and say,
    Alleluia.

Of Sun and Moon, the lamps of Night and Day,
Stars, and the Planets sounding on their way,
We sing this day with thankful hearts and say,
    Alleluia.

Of Times and Seasons, evening and fresh morn,
Of Birth and Death, green blade and golden corn,
We sing this day with thankful hearts and say,
    Alleluia.

Of all that lives and moves, the Winds ablow,
Fire, and old Ocean's never resting flow
We sing this day with thankful hearts and say,
    Alleluia.

Of Earth, and from earth's darkness springing free,
The flowers outspread, the heavenward reaching tree
We sing this day with thankful hearts and say,
    Alleluia.

Of creatures all, the eagle in his flight,
The patient ox, the lion that trusts his might,
We sing this day with thankful hearts and say,
    Alleluia.

Of Man, with hand outstretched for service high,
Courage at heart, truth in his steadfast eye
We sing this day with thankful hearts and say,
    Alleluia.

Of Angels and Archangels, Spirits clear,
Warders of Souls, and Watchers of the Year,
We sing this day with thankful hearts and say,
    Alleluia.

Of God made man, and through man sacrificed,
Of Man through love made God, Adam made Christ,
We sing this day with thankful hearts and say,
    Alleluia.

POEMS, SONGS and VERSES

Index of first lines

All day I sought from street to street, 59
Along the narrow corridor, 29
Darling, do you remember, 23
Earth and Water, Air and Fire, 69
Here in the daytime, open-eyed, 24
How can I pipe my dances, 58
I dreamed I suddenly was one, 56
I hold that Love is king and lord, 55
I took a plank of close-set grain, 78
I waited, when my childhood perished, 36
King Arthur's walls are strong and steep, 308
Kings in a Gate's strict room, 301
Listen, unquiet moth, and know what's said of you, 34
Loose not the strings of the lute, 306
Many the stars that stand over the earth, 304
Midnight, and O the deeper gloom, 26
My soul, there is a river, 52
No bread without sun, 302
No hedge on the road, 76
Nous n'irons plus au bois, no more
O friend! O friend! 31
Now Light is Lord; the high hour of the sun, 68
Now the high midsummer sun, 311
Now, when the wheeling stars, 73
Of all created things, of earth and sky, 316
O for a boat to sail the high seas, 305
O man, lift up your voice, 315
Only between the rock and sky, 66
O star of day, awake, unbar, 307
O Sun of Worlds!, 81
Princess in a castle fair, 300

Pyramids, lady, stood and stand, 32
Remembering the Sun in the bread, 302
Return, O stars. Countless as you, they wait, 51
Sun, Earth and Air, 303
The preacher paused, the people shook, 61
These are the blocks I trod on, 21
The Spirit of the World, 302
The sun sees not the light it throws, 72
The waterfall is clamouring to the stars, 80
They were the nobler days, those days of war, 37
This is the day that dearth has died, 67
Through the soul's gratitude of man, 303
We break this bread together, 302
What elfin thought possessed, 28
What news of heroes old, 314
Whenever the monks went into the Chapter, 74
When has there been a waiting as now we wait?, 60
When hollyhocks line cottage walls, 310
When I straighten my body into my bed at night, 54
Why yes, but though a Hodge, Sir, 25
Wind in the trees blows loud for summer's last song, 313
You passed me, running through the night, 77
You who saw us yester-year, 299

BOOKS AND TRANSLATIONS BY
A. C. HARWOOD

Shakespeare's Prophetic Mind, *Rudolf Steiner Press, London 1964.*

The Way of a Child, *Rudolf Steiner Press, London 1940.*

The Recovery of Man in Childhood, *Hodder and Stoughton, London 1958.*

Eurythmy and the Impulse of Dance (co-author), *Rudolf Steiner Press, London 1974.*

The Meditative Year (rendering into English of Rudolf Steiner's *Calendar of the Soul*), *Rudolf Steiner Press, London 1972.*

Christmas Plays from Oberufer (translation), *Rudolf Steiner Press, London 1944.*